PRAISE FOR SUITCASE CHARLIE

Every detective has a case that haunts him… The sheer cruelty of the case's multiple murders demands coarse language, at which Guzlowski excels… He lets us know that, back in the day, the city of Chicago was an all-around rough town.

— Marilyn Stasio, *The New York Times*

A tough-as-rusty-nails police procedural… Each environment seems spookier than the last in a narrative driven by lyrical anxiety. Little by little, Purcell— treading the blurred line between burnout and breakdown—perceives these sickening new crimes as the fruit of diseased notions and lingering hatreds from earlier decades and even centuries.

— Tom Nolan, *The Wall Street Journal*

John Guzlowski beautifully conjures up the seamy side of the allegedly innocent 1950s with a thrilling serial murder mystery featuring two boozehound detectives… survivors of the mean streets, appealing in their humorous repartee and in their willingness to seek justice, even if insubordination is part of their means to that end… The plot moves sure-footedly to a powerful and plausible conclusion… The novel's greatest attractions are the characterizations of the partners and the stunning evocation of time and place in a great American city. In important ways, Chicago is the main character, and Guzlowski gives it muscle, pulse and breath.

— Philip K. Jason, *Jewish Book Council*

The author grew up in Chicago during the time of the novel, and it shows in his details of places, people, and the prejudices of the era… Whether it's the cops talking with each other or neighbors and crooks casually chatting, the talk always rings true… This vivid re-creation of a time and place may not be enough to make Chicago your kind of town.

— *Kirkus Reviews*

SUITCASE
CHARLIE

John Guzlowski

Kasva Press

Make its bowls, ladles, jars and pitchers with which to offer libations; make them of pure gold.

וְעָשִׂיתָ
קְּעָרֹתָיו
וְכַפֹּתָיו
וּקְשׂוֹתָיו
וּמְנַקִּיֹּתָיו
אֲשֶׁר יֻסַּךְ
בָּהֵן זָהָב
טָהוֹר תַּעֲשֶׂה
אֹתָם

St. Paul / Alfei Menashe

Kasva Press LLC
Alfei Menashe, Israel
St. Paul, Minnesota

www.kasvapress.com
info@kasvapress.com

Suitcase Charlie

ISBN:
978-1-948403-04-7   Trade Paperback
978-1-948403-05-4   Ebook

M 9 8 7 6 5 4 3 2 1

SUITCASE CHARLIE

To my mom and dad,
who first introduced me to Humboldt Park.

PROLOGUE

October 18, 1955 — Associated Press Wire

The bodies of three boys were found nude and dumped in a ditch near Chicago today at 12:15 p.m.

They were Robert Peterson, 14, John Schuessler, 13, and brother Anton Schuessler, 11.

They had been beaten and their eyes taped shut.

The boys were last seen walking home from a downtown movie theater where they had gone to see "The African Lion."

CHAPTER I

THERE WASN'T ANY point in hurrying. By the time Hank Purcell and his partner Marvin Bondarowicz got there that night, they couldn't even get close.

For a block in every direction, it was like a midnight cop convention. The new black-and-white squad cars, with their red lights twirling and lighting up the darkness, were scattered along all the streets leading to the intersection, and a mob of detectives and uniform cops were there, some standing around sweating in the heat, others swarming and going nowhere.

Hank couldn't imagine what the beef was, why they'd need so many cops. But he had to park the car, so he drove down Rockwell toward Division and finally double-parked in an alley a couple blocks south of where the action was. Then he and Marvin started hoofing it back.

When they finally got to the intersection, it was cordoned off.

Hank pulled his handkerchief out of his pocket, wiped his face, and looked around. Yellow police barricades kept the folks who were still awake out of the intersection and on the sidewalks. It was quite a crowd. At the White Eagle Tap, the corner Polack bar, the drunks and third-shift drinkers stood in the doorway watching the commotion; some had beer bottles in their hands. Kids were sitting on the barricades, craning their necks and bopping up and down to see what was up. The windows in the apartment buildings fronting three of the corners had a few lookers in them, old guys watching and smoking, young girls and women in bathrobes and curlers.

Rubberneckers. Lookie-loos.

Hank wasn't surprised. He'd seen crowds like this before. At accidents and fires, shootings even. What surprised Hank was that there wasn't a lot of talking or shouting here. Even when they were pulling bodies out of flipped taxis and burning buses, you could hear some kind of yakking, shouting, crying, moaning even. But there wasn't anything like that here. All Hank could hear was a low buzz, the kind of human hum he remembered hearing at the ball field when the Cubs were losing, or maybe at a church when the priest was trying to talk the congregation into donating more money so their souls wouldn't scorch so long in hell. It was that kind of buzz.

Hank wiped the sweat off his neck with his handkerchief and tried to figure out what was going on. Some cops were coming in; some were going out. A darkened ambulance with its back doors swung wide open stood off about twenty feet down Evergreen Street. Three medics stood with their backs to him, but there was enough light from a streetlamp so Hank could see they were smoking. Their heads were together; they were probably talking too.

At the northwest corner where the nuns' convent stood, Hank saw a half a dozen cops, officers and detectives mostly. They were clustered around something. He spotted his boss, Lieutenant Frank O'Herlihy, on the outskirts of the bunch and poked Marvin's shoulder.

"Come on." Hank started across the street, and Marvin followed.

Captain Feltt from the 5th Division, Shakespeare Station, was talking. Hank saw him jerking his head and yammering. The rest of the brass were listening. Feltt was worked up, agitated like he'd just got demoted or shifted over to one of the colored police precincts down on the South Side of Chicago, in the Bronzeville section. Hank eased next to him and listened.

Feltt was blabbering the stuff cops always blabber, "Jesus Christ, we'll get the son-of-a-bitch bastard." Then Captain Feltt stopped jerking his head and looked down at the sidewalk.

Hank followed his eyes. A brown suitcase lay open on the sidewalk at the Captain's feet. There was something in it, but Hank couldn't tell what it was. The shadows of the detectives and the uniform cops clustered around made it difficult for him to figure it out. He wanted to ask but didn't. Instead, he leaned a little closer and inched his head forward.

Then he wished he hadn't.

Hank spun around and threw up into the gutter. The beer he had with Marvin in the alley a while ago was the first to go. Flat and raw, it came up hard. The acid at the bottom of his stomach poured up next, quick as a flush toilet, all hot and burning and twisting his stomach. It was doing what it wanted to do. It churned and brought up just about everything Hank had left in him that wasn't tied to his insides. Bent over, his hands on his knees, he started coughing and tried to spit the acid out of his mouth and throat.

Marvin was next to him then, holding Hank by his shoulders, steadying him, as his lungs kept hacking and his head kept jerking.

Marvin whispered, "What the hell, Hank, what the hell?"

Hank didn't say anything, couldn't say anything. He tried to clear his throat, and he couldn't do that either. He threw up some more of whatever was left in his guts. Finally, he stood up a little straighter and used his sweat-damp handkerchief to wipe the vomit from his mouth and hands.

"There's a dead kid in the suitcase," Hank said.

"A dead kid? You're crazy, man," Marvin said as he turned around slowly.

Hank followed him back to the suitcase. Some of the cops had drifted away while he was puking. Others had come up to take their place. Everybody had to take a good solid look. Get an eyeful. Like there was something here that nobody had ever seen before, some kind of evil that was one-of-a-kind, fresh, and original down to its buttons.

The suitcase was light brown, used but not old, and it wasn't very large, about two feet by three feet. Big enough to hold a child.

And now Hank could see what he couldn't see before. The kid in it was a boy, not a girl. Hank could tell because the kid was naked: not a stitch of clothes on, and his body was twisted. Arms, feet, shoulders, hands — all twisted up like clean rags. The bones had been broken or chopped up before the body had been shoved into the suitcase. Hank could see that the left foot was pressed against the chin. The head was turned face up, and the right shoulder was placed so that it pointed away from the head.

Hank looked at the boy's face now. His eyes were staring straight up at him. The mouth hung open in a funny way. Before he stuck the boy in the suitcase, the killer must have broken his jaw. Broken his jaw and drained the blood out of the poor kid. The child was yellow — his face, his feet, his hands, all yellow, the color you get when there's no blood to keep you alive and pink.

The kid looked like a baby bird that had fallen from a nest in a high tree, a baby bird without feathers.

Hank couldn't turn away.

"Jesus," Marvin said as he stared down at the dead child.

Captain Feltt looked at him. "Yeah, Jesus Christ. You gonna puke too, like your pussy friend here?"

Marvin couldn't say anything except, "Jesus Christ."

Hank stared some more at the kid in the suitcase and shook his head. He wanted to know why all of the cops were standing around staring at the kid. What kind of sense did that make? They should be out tracking down the killer, pounding him when they found him. Smashing bricks against his head, shoving iron pipes up his ass. He looked at Lieutenant O'Herlihy, his boss. "What do you want us to do?"

O'Herlihy looked at him and said, "Fuck," and then he didn't say anything more for a long time.

Hank knew the Lieutenant. He was a good man, clean like a boy scout, a church-loving Roman Catholic. He was like the old broads at St. Fidelis up the street who sat in the back pews and mumbled over their rosary beads, a guy who took any kind of looseness as an insult before God, his personal Father. O'Herlihy didn't appreciate cursing.

So his "fuck" hung in the air between the three men and echoed like a woman's scream in the dark, repeating itself over and over in pain.

Then the Lieutenant shook his head and said, "You know the neighborhood here, Hank. Start talking to people. See if they saw anything tonight. It was hot, so there were lots of people out. See if anybody saw a guy carrying this suitcase."

Hank nodded.

"And when you find him, I want you to hurt him."

Hank nodded again.

"We'll hurt him."

CHAPTER 2

HANK PURCELL AND Marvin Bondarowicz did exactly what Lieutenant O'Herlihy said.

Like the beat cops and the other suit-coat dicks, they started talking to people, canvassing. The Lieutenant told them to cover the north side of the block between the corner where the suitcase was found and Humboldt Park.

Hank knew the block. Tree-lined with poplars and maples, and a dozen or so buildings, mostly single-family homes with a handful of apartment houses thrown in. There was a Catholic nun's convent at the near end of the street and a synagogue at the far end, butting up against California Avenue and the park on its west side.

The two detectives started at the convent. It was the nearest place, a three-story, double-lot red brick apartment building converted decades ago when the Sisters of St. Joseph first came to St. Fidelis Parish back in the 1920s.

Standing at the front door, Hank was about to ring the doorbell when Marvin asked, "You feeling okay?"

"Yeah, I'm okay."

"You didn't look okay when you were puking."

"Yeah," Hank said, "but I'm not puking now."

"I guess you're right. You're not puking. But if you decide to, let me know in advance so I can get out of your way."

"For a little man, Marvin, you sure aren't funny."

"Much obliged and the same to you," Marvin said and smiled.

Hank rang the doorbell. He knew what Marvin and the other guys were thinking: He was a wimp, a weak sister. They'd be talking about his vomiting for weeks, months. He'd been a cop for almost ten years, and a front-line infantryman before that for more than a year during World War II, and here he was puking like a grammar-school boy. He shook his head and looked through the door's window.

He could see the lights were on in two of the rooms on the first floor. He was sure the nuns were up. A hundred cops coming and going, crowds on three of the four corners, a dead kid in a suitcase on the fourth one — it was enough to keep you awake for a long time. Not to mention the heat that still pressed down on the neighborhood like a burning thumb.

Hank waited for a minute and then pressed the bell again. Looking up at the first-floor windows, he couldn't see anybody moving around. The glass was covered with thick window shades and thicker dark blue curtains behind them. Hank wasn't surprised. The nuns were women who spent their days in long black habits, the kind of clothes that hid everything but their faces and hands. Everything else about them was a secret, reserved strictly for their bridegroom Jesus. Nuns weren't the kind who would be living with a view of the street, and they certainly weren't the kind who would be giving you a free peek of what was going on in their lives. The only thing Hank could see through the glass panes on the door was the stairs on the other side of the door, and he had to press his face against the glass to see that.

Marvin turned to Hank. "Say, you ever interview a nun?"

Hank nodded. "Yeah, last December, about a burglary at Our Lady of Angels. Tough broads. Eyes like razors."

"Sure, it's the loneliness that makes them mean. They need a man to kick around. It'd work off their edge."

Hank wondered about his partner. He was always ready with a wisecrack no matter what the situation. Where'd that come from? The way he was brought up? The father who slapped him up and down the block? Hank didn't know. He looked again to see if one of the nuns was going to answer the door.

He was about to ring a third time when Marvin said, "Hey, Hank, here, look, she's coming down the stairs. You better be a good boy, or she'll rap your knuckles and twist your ear."

Hank ignored him and waited for the door to open.

Through the glass, he could see the hem of a black tunic brushing the stairs as the Sister made her way down. Then he could see her hands and face. She was short and plump, and older, maybe fifty, maybe sixty. It was hard to tell with nuns, but what he could tell was that there was no rush in her. She had plenty of time. She took the steps slowly, carefully. He wondered if maybe the nuns didn't know about the dead boy.

Hank expected her to open the door when she got to the bottom of the stairs, but she didn't. Instead, she flicked on a light above the door and looked at him and Marvin.

Without any expression on her face, she spoke through the glass of the closed door. "Yes, can I help you gentlemen?"

"Sorry to disturb you, Sister," Hank said. "We're with the Chicago Police Department. There's been some trouble on the corner here, and we're asking questions in the neighborhood." He reached into his breast pocket and pulled out his wallet. He showed her his shield through the glass.

She unlocked the door, but at first she didn't pull it open. He could see her reach up, probably for some kind of chain, and pull a bolt down. There was another bolt at floor level. She bent down for a long moment and worked that. Hank figured she was having trouble with the thing. Maybe they didn't use this entrance a lot, and the bolt was frozen, rusted in place. Maybe they never opened their doors to anybody. He turned to Marvin, and Marvin gave him a look, one with a lot of eyebrows in it.

The door slowly pulled open.

Hank took his fedora off, and Marvin touched the brim of his and tipped it. The Sister was shorter than Hank figured when he'd seen her coming down the stairs. Maybe she was five feet tall, not an inch more.

"I'm Detective Purcell, Sister," he said. "This is my partner, Detective Bondarowicz. We'd like to ask you some questions."

She didn't tell them what her name was, and she didn't ask him what kind of trouble there was, and she didn't faint dead away like some old doll in the movies. All she said was "Of course," and then she turned around and started slowly climbing back up the stairs. Marvin pulled the door shut behind them, and they followed her.

When she reached the first-floor landing, she stopped. It was a good-sized space, a sort of greeting area, a foyer, the nuns might call it. There was a wooden cross with a figure of Jesus carved out of lead on the wall and a couple of pictures of saints looking at the ceiling. One of the saints was praying and her body was full of arrows. She was wearing a halo.

Hank looked around. He figured this must be where the nuns brought their guests. An old brown sofa with doilies on its arms and three wooden chairs fleshed out the room. The chairs looked like they weren't built for comfort, just for sitting.

The Sister sat down in one of them and nodded for them to find some for themselves.

Hank put his hat on a chair next to him, and then he turned to the nun. "Sister, we're wondering if you or the other Sisters saw anything suspicious tonight. Anybody prowling around the corner late this evening?"

She didn't pause at all. Sitting straight with her hands in her lap and the toes of her shoes barely touching the floor, she said, "Our days and nights are regulated. After dinner, we retire to our rooms and prepare for the next day's school lessons. As I'm sure you know, we teach not far from here, at St. Fidelis School just up the street. At ten every night, we gather together for our evening rosary, to call for God's judgment against Communism. At eleven, we withdraw to our rooms and prepare for sleep. Tonight was like any night, all quite normal. We Sisters don't spend much time looking out the windows, concerning ourselves with the neighborhood. I don't think anyone noticed anything out of the ordinary until the first police car arrived at the corner here. That was about midnight. It was the police siren that drew our attention."

Marvin cleared his throat and looked up from his notepad, "I noticed that your windows are all shut tight. It's been mighty hot these last two days. Do you keep your windows closed and the shades pulled even when there's this kind of heat?"

"Yes, of course. We try not to think about the heat."

"So you wouldn't have seen or heard much of anything from the corner?"

"No, nothing, until the sirens, as I said." She had small, plump hands, and Hank watched them. They were motionless in her lap. They looked like medium-sized potatoes, red ones. Her knuckles, pinched in, looked like potato eyes. She didn't seem nervous or frightened, not even worried. She was a woman used to telling the whole truth, a woman who never gave you half of it. She could talk to school kids and cops, priests — and presidents too, probably.

"Sister, what grade do you teach?" Hank asked.

She didn't speak for a moment, and then she said, "Why do you ask?"

"No reason, just curious."

"Second grade."

"How old are the kids you get in second?"

She looked at Hank. There was a question in her eyes again. Hank could see it. She wanted to know why he was asking about her teaching, her students.

"Just asking, Sister, nothing else." He said it, and he knew she knew he was lying. He was thinking of the boy in the suitcase, how young he was.

"The children range from six to eight. It depends sometimes on how much or how little education the child has had before coming to us. We have a lot of immigrants, Poles mostly now since the war. Some of them come not knowing a letter of the alphabet, and some can read Dante's *Inferno*."

"Thanks, Sister," Hank said, standing up. "We won't bother you or the other Sisters any more tonight, but if any of you remember seeing anything, we'd appreciate it if you'd let us know. Even if it seems unimportant."

She stood up and followed them down the stairs.

"I'm sorry, Sister," Marvin said as he turned toward her at the bottom of the stairs. "But I didn't get your name. We'll need it for the report."

"Of course," she said, "I'm Sister Mary Philomena, the Sisters of St. Joseph."

CHAPTER 3

STANDING OUTSIDE THE convent, Marvin pulled out his memo pad and scribbled down the Sister's name, putting a check next to it. "Well, that wasn't much help," he said. "She didn't even ask us what happened on the corner."

"Yeah," Hank said, and reached for the Chesterfields in his breast pocket. He pulled out a cigarette and lit it with his IMCO.

Marvin grabbed the lighter before Hank could drop it in his pocket.

"What are you doing?" Hank asked.

"You're still dragging around this Nazi piece of shit lighter? Wasn't there some kind of story you used to tell about it and a Kraut field marshal on the last day of the war?"

"No, it was a Russian corporal, a foxy blonde. I traded her a busted PX watch for it. Now give it back."

"Yeah, now I remember," Marvin said, flipping the lid of the lighter. "In Magdeburg. It was the day the war ended. You were wearing green. She was wearing a brown quilted horse-blanket uniform and hand-made hobnailed boots. Ahh, such a beauty she was...."

"Cool it, Marv."

"I bet you got the best of that deal," Marvin said, grinning, as he tossed the lighter back to Hank. "Another victory for the good guys."

"Thanks, man," Hank said, shaking his head. "So that nun, she's a piece of work. Straight out of the book. She didn't give up much."

"Yeah, the Lieutenant would have been pissed if we hadn't even got her name. Philomena? What kind of name is that? I mean, I'm a Jew and I never had much to do with nuns, but 'Philomena' is one for the books. A weird name. I've known some crazy nuns, but they were called, like, Sister Mary Francis or Sister Mary Blow-It-Out-Your-Ear."

Hank smiled at his partner and took a shallow drag on his cigarette. "Sister Mary Philomena? I remember hearing in church once about a St. Philomena. They found her in Italy, in Naples, maybe Venice, dug her out of a grave about 150 years ago. This nun is probably named after her. The Philomena they dug up, she was kind of a mystery. All they knew was that she was a kid, and a virgin. Somebody murdered her."

"Yeah, some things don't change," Marvin said. "Give me a drag off that thing."

Hank passed the cigarette over. "Those cops back then, they never found out who killed her."

"You sure she wasn't murdered here in Chicago?" Marvin laughed.

The Next Day: Thursday, May 31

CHAPTER 4

IT WAS CLOSE to 4:30 in the morning when Hank got to the last house, the one just before the synagogue. Over the treetops toward the east, he could see the night starting to ease up a little. He could almost make out a blush of grayness thinning out the darkness. At the far corner, by the convent where he and Marvin started the canvass, there were still three squad cars sitting in the middle of the intersection, blocking traffic. The squad cars' cherry-red lights circled round and round in a jerky sweep.

He noticed that the ambulance guys were gone. They had waited a long time for the science-fiction boys with their microscopes and paint analyzers and vacuum-tube calculators to go over the dead boy and the sidewalk around the suitcase.

Hank figured that the kid and the suitcase were probably at the labs downtown by now, where some Mr. Wizard was taking the kid further apart, breaking him up into even smaller puzzle pieces so that he could figure out for certain that he was dead and for how long. As if that kind of information would do the kid any good. As if that kind of information would even do the cops any good.

Hank had had enough. He was tired.

After the convent, he and Marvin split up the thirteen houses and apartment buildings on their side of the block, evens and odds. He had finished his six, and he hadn't found out anything, just rediscovered the truth he had already come across a thousand times — the simple truth that death frightens people, makes them jumpy, and terrible death makes them even jumpier. In the last four hours, he had seen too many people who didn't want to know any more than they already knew about what happened to the poor kid. They just wanted to cross themselves and say a prayer and hide out until the cops found the guy who did the chopping, the dirty work, or until the guy drifted off to some other neighborhood, maybe south of Humboldt Park, maybe north. It didn't matter.

It was like this last October when the cops tried to track down the guy who tortured and murdered Robert Peterson and the Schuessler brothers. Every cop in the city tried to talk to anybody who might know something, and all anybody found out was that nobody knew anything and everybody was afraid. And that was it. They never found the guy who killed those boys, and probably never would.

Tonight, Hank had talked and listened to more than a dozen people, and he'd had enough of both. He wanted to go home, kiss his wife Hazel and his daughter Margaret goodnight, and nod off for a couple days.

But he knew he couldn't because he wasn't done here yet. He lit a cigarette and waited for Marvin to finish his six odd houses.

They still had two more buildings to check, the thirteenth one on the block, a two-story brick with — he hoped — no more than a couple of apartments. It stood just before the last building, the synagogue on the corner. Hank took in a slow, long draw on his cigarette, and when he couldn't hold in the warm, gray smoke any longer, he let it drift out even slower. Then, looking at the house next door, he saw Marvin push open the front door and walk down the cement stairs. He wasn't skipping.

"Get anything?" Hank asked.

Marvin got to the bottom of the steps and grinned. "Nothing some Alka-Seltzer tablets and a double shot of my baby's sweet love can't cure."

"Yeah, that's the truth. Let's finish this dump, and then take a quick look at the synagogue," Hank said as he took a final drag. It didn't taste like anything.

He dropped his cigarette on the sidewalk and ground it out. He knew what his daughter Margaret would say. She'd call him a bad boy and shake her finger at him. She was right. He felt like shit. He'd promised her he would quit.

"Come on, Hank," Marvin said, "let's get this over with," and Hank followed him up the wooden stairs and onto the wide front porch of the thirteenth house.

Marvin pressed his thumb on the bell, but they didn't hear any ringing. The thing was probably busted, so he knocked on the door, and they waited. The apartment on the second floor was dark, and Hank looked in the picture window of the first-floor apartment.

There was a small sign in the front window that read "English Tutor" in block letters. Behind the window, Hank saw that the kitchen light at the back of the apartment was on. It was a low-watt bulb, maybe a twenty-five, and it didn't give off much light, nothing but a dusty yellow haze so that you had enough light to open up a can, but not enough to read the label. With that kind of light, a guy couldn't tell whether he was eating Heinz Pork and Beans or Campbell's Vegetarian Vegetable.

Then Hank saw something at the back of the apartment. A shape moved slowly beneath the hazy light. Man or woman, Hank couldn't tell. It moved into the backlit darkness of the front room, and a moment later Hank heard someone trying to undo a latch, fumbling with the key. The person was having a hell of a time. He first tried for the latch, and then he tried for the lock. Hank wondered why the dope didn't just flick on some light.

Marvin did better than wonder.

"Hey," he shouted through the glass, "we're the police. Turn on the light and open up, for Christ's sake."

That did it. After another quick moment of scratching and fumbling, the light behind the door finally came on, and then the latch was thrown and the door unlocked.

The guy who opened the door looked like some kind of gnome. Under the weak hallway light, he was bearded and old, probably at least sixty-five, maybe as much as seventy. He carried his shoulders hunched together and pushed forward, curving his back.

A gnome or a troll, Hank thought, maybe an elf. Whatever the hell that was.

But one thing Hank was certain about was that the elf looked like he was afraid, afraid that the police officers would slap him or kick him, spit at him or curse him. He stood that way for about a minute, not saying anything, his face twitching in the weak, yellow light. It scared Hank. In almost ten years as a cop, Hank hadn't seen this kind of fear often.

"Yes?" the gnome asked in a syrupy, sing-songy voice.

"I'm Detective Purcell," Hank said, "and this here's my partner, Detective Bondarowicz. We're with the Chicago Police."

"My name is Mr. Fisch — Samuel Fisch. How can I help you?"

"We're canvassing the street," Marvin said, "looking to see if you heard anything or saw anything that might help us with a crime committed earlier this evening."

"Please, officers, I don't mean to be disrespectful, but I would like to see your badges. This neighborhood isn't what it used to be in the old days before the war. It's better to be safe than sorry."

The old guy was a mess — Hank could see that. He was frightened, and his eyes were blinking and his cheeks were twitching as he asked to see their badges. Hank was surprised he had the courage to do that. Marvin gave Hank a look and then took his wallet out, flipped it open and flipped it closed quickly. Then Marvin asked, "Is that good enough?"

The old man jerked back. Hank thought he seemed startled. In the deep shadows of the doorway, Mr. Fisch looked for a second like he was going to say something to Marvin, give him an argument maybe, but then he seemed to think better of it. "Yes, thank you, officer, that's fine," he said.

Hank was tired of dragging his badge out, but he did it anyway. He extended the badge toward the gnome, and the gnome looked down at it carefully. He brought his head down so that his right eye was almost on top of it.

"My eyesight is not so good anymore. But the badge, it's not like the Star of David," he said lifting his head.

Hank pulled back a little. "What do you mean?"

"The Star of David. It has six points."

"No sir, our police badge is a five-pointed star. Not a six."

"Sometimes I go to the motion pictures, and I see westerns, cowboy-and-Indian movies. The sheriffs have badges like David's Star, the Shield of David. I wonder about that. Why cowboy policemen in America should carry the Star of David, maybe you can tell me, officer?"

"I wouldn't know, sir. Can me and my partner come in and ask you a few questions? You'd be helping us out."

"Yes, certainly, of course," the old man muttered and led them into the front room. "Please, sit down."

There wasn't much furniture in the room. A burgundy-colored couch sat beneath the wide picture window, a light coffee-table stood before it. Three wooden-back chairs with armrests sat in a semi-circle across from it.

Hank took his hat off and sat down at the end of the couch near the door; Marvin parked himself across from his partner on one of the wooden chairs. He didn't take his hat off. Hank reached for the table lamp near him and switched it on without asking the old man's permission. The lamp washed the room in a shallow yellow light.

The old man moved some books out of the way and took a seat on the other end of the couch. "Thank you for turning the light on," he said. "I spend so much time here by myself that I forget sometimes that the lights are off."

Hank turned his hat in his hands and looked at Mr. Fisch. He seemed less nervous here in the front room, sitting down. His face wasn't twitching anymore, and his eyelids weren't fluttering either.

"Have you heard about what happened earlier down on the corner by the convent?" Hank asked.

Mr. Fisch didn't say anything for a moment.

Then he coughed and nodded. "Yes, my neighbor upstairs, Mr. Bujak, he told me when he came home from work. He works near Milwaukee Avenue and Damen, at the spring and coil factory there."

Marvin took that as his cue. He pulled his blue memo pad out of his breast pocket and started scribbling. He looked at Hank and nodded.

"What time was that?" Hank asked the old man.

"I can't be sure, but I think it was late. I couldn't sleep. It was so hot. Maybe it was about 12:30, maybe earlier."

"What did Mr. Bujak tell you?"

"It was terrible news. He said a boy was found on the corner, dead, chopped up, in a suitcase."

"Did you hear or see anything out of the ordinary before Mr. Bujak talked to you?"

"No, I don't think so," Mr. Fisch said and rubbed his upper lip. "Yes, it was a noisy night, the children were screaming so loud, but every night's like that. And tonight it was exceptionally hot. May, and already so hot. What will it be like in August? I think truly the world is getting hotter. I couldn't breathe, and I had a headache, a migraine. I had to sit with a cold compress on my forehead, and the children kept screaming. It made my heart race too. I forced myself up and opened the door and asked them to be quiet. I did. So many times. I was trying to read tonight, Marcel Proust's *Swann's Way*, but the boys kept running past my house to the corner on California, across from the park, by my synagogue. They were running and screaming, like Indians. I asked them. I said, 'Boys, boys, please be quiet, it's so hot and I have to read my book.' But they just ignored me and kept running and shouting. Even the girls. So loud. They didn't care that I was reading Marcel Proust."

Hank listened to Mr. Fisch's voice. Coming out of the shadows at the end of the couch, his jittery sing-songy cadences were soothing. Hank began feeling how tired he was. Nothing could keep him awake. He felt his eyelids growing heavier, his breathing getting slower. Soon he would be asking the old guy to move over so he could take a nap on the couch.

He remembered it was like this in the war sometimes. He had

been in the infantry in the Ardennes, and the guys in his platoon would be shaking with fear, waiting for the Krauts to bust through the ring of birch trees, and he would be nodding off. His pals thought he had balls of steel, but that wasn't it at all. It was just that sometimes a bad thing was too bad, and your body took over and started turning off all the switches that kept you awake, alert and primed.

And what was the bad thing here? This old Jew guy and his fear? He was sure giving off the funk of some kind of fear. Hank could feel it, the way they say one twin can feel what the other one's feeling even if they're separated by oceans. So what was Mr. Fisch afraid of? Kids? Cops? The bad thing he did? The sure knowledge that somebody would find out and fry his wrinkly old ass?

Hank forced his eyes open and tried to pull himself back into the room, into the investigation. "What time was that?" he said.

Mr. Fisch seemed confused by the question, and Hank wondered how long he had been drifting and nodding. He wondered if his question about the time was the right question. Had he asked Fisch something after that? Had Marvin asked a question?

Then Fisch ran a handkerchief across his forehead and answered the question, "The running and screaming? Oh, all evening, officer. It started right after dinner, and it kept up until almost ten o'clock. I don't understand why their parents don't call them in sooner. Maybe to do their homework, or wash up, or do chores. Don't children do chores anymore?"

"I'm sure they do, Mr. Fisch," Hank said, "But you don't think there was anything unusual about any of this?"

"Oh no, they're always like this. Screaming and running. Sometimes the children, the bold ones, sneak up to my front door and knock and knock and knock. They're terrible. Always bothering a person. I've told them I would report them to the police at Shakespeare Station, near the El train, but it does no good. True hooligans."

Marvin looked up from his memo pad. "Hooligans?" he asked.

"Oh yes, officer, definitely. They have no self-control, no *disciplina*. What the men and women of my generation called 'strength of mind'. These children do not have it. They have nothing to keep them from giving in to their urges. It was like this in Germany before the war, too. With the Nazis. I was a tutor in France — in Strasbourg — then, so near the German-French border. I was tutoring English there just as I do now. But I saw what was going on in Germany. The urges there! I saw it all. I did. Yes, the urges."

Hank felt himself drifting away again. His body was turning itself off. He looked at the walls. There were framed pictures on the walls, paintings, but the light was so dim he couldn't really make them out, couldn't tell if the white blotch in the frame was a cow or a cloud, so he turned again to Mr. Fisch. "What kind of urges did you see, Mr. Fisch?"

"The children there were like the children here. Always running and shouting. Many times, they would run up to me and put their faces so close to mine, screaming. They knew I walked slowly and that I couldn't catch them, so they would run up to me and scream all kinds of bad things. Words that I can't repeat, even to you gentlemen. The boys would rush up to me with their fists pumping and push their faces at me, so I had to stop and pull back, and then they would shout these terrible things, things about the Jews. This was in Strasbourg, before the war, when I was a tutor."

Hank reached for his hat on the side table and began slowly running his thumb back and forth over the brim. "What did you do when the kids acted like that, Mr. Fisch?"

"What did I do? I did the same then that I do now. I said, 'Boys, please, you should know that you need to behave.' But they wouldn't. They would laugh and push their faces into mine."

"What then? What did you do?"

Mr. Fisch didn't say anything. The fast, frantic talk that seemed to come so easily to him, spill out of him like applesauce spilling out of a jar, suddenly stopped. He sat bent forward at his end of the burgundy couch, looking at his shoes. Hank couldn't see his face, but he could see the shoes. Even in the quarter light of this dark living room, he could tell the brown shoes were heavily polished. These old guys, Hank thought, could be in rags and living in a cardboard box, but they loved their shoe polish.

Mr. Fisch finally looked at Hank's face and asked, "What could I do? I was a Jew, a tutor of English and French, a small man with small hands. I did what I did. I let the boys frighten me. I let them push their dirty faces into mine. Sometimes that's enough for them. The hooligans want to see some fear. Your fear is the coin that will buy your passage — sometimes."

Hank could hear Marvin scribbling something with his fountain pen. Then he heard some kind of sound coming from Marvin on top of the pen-scratching. It was a grunt or a snicker. Mr. Fisch heard it, too, and looked across the room at the other detective. "Why this sound? Why do you make it?"

Marvin ignored him. Kept his head bent as he scribbled.

Hank looked at Marvin and shook his head. "Don't mind Detective Bondarowicz, Mr. Fisch. He suffers from digestive gas, and his hearing isn't so good, a war injury."

The old man's left cheek twitched several times, and he pulled a long white handkerchief out of his pants pocket. He patted the sweat off his forehead and chin. "I don't expect the children running in the street to be respectful, but a police officer should show a little respect."

"You're right, Mr. Fisch," Hank said. "Let me ask you one more question. Can you just give me a quick rundown of what you did yesterday?"

"Certainly. Yes, I can do that. Yesterday was like any other day. I had breakfast and read in the morning. After lunch, I walked around the block twice, and then I came back to do my tutoring. I usually do that until 7:30, but last night my last session ended later. Then I had dinner."

"Tutoring? Yeah, we saw the sign in the window. Tell us about it."

"Yes, I tutor children and adults in English and other languages. These are immigrants here around Humboldt Park, and many of them need help with English."

"Adults?"

"Yes, as I said, adults too. They hope to learn English so they can become citizens or get better jobs. There are immigrants and refugees here who in the old country were doctors and professors. Here some of them work in factories, others do other things, but they all want to do better in their new country. Just yesterday, I tutored a professor. He was my last one. Professor Zcink, a Hungarian. He came later than usual, about 8:30. He had had car trouble."

"A professor? And what time did he leave?"

"Oh, maybe around ten o'clock. It was a long session. He wanted my help translating some papers he's researching."

"Thanks, Mr. Fisch," Hank said as he stood up. "Would you mind if I took a look around your apartment while Officer Bondarowicz asks you a few more questions?"

"No, sir, not at all. I have nothing to hide."

"Thanks, just routine."

Hank left the front room and stepped into the hallway. He needed to get up and walk around, shake his body awake. He knew where the hallway led. He had been in this kind of flat a thousand times, lived in one just like it when he was a kid.

The detective looked into the bathroom on the right and switched the light on. The small room was clean. Nothing on the floor. No crap in the toilet. No piss either. Fresh pastel yellow towels in the towel rack. The bathtub scrubbed. No ring around it. No blood stains either. This guy might be a screwy old gent, shaking with his fear of kids who scream and run too much, but he was a clean screwy old gent.

Was he the killer? Hank couldn't tell. He was no Dunninger the Mentalist, deep-probing the minds of his victims until every sin and dark pleasure was laid out on the table plain as tomato soup.

He walked a few more steps down the corridor and looked at the bedroom on the left. This must be the old guy's study. A window opposite the door opened onto the back of the synagogue that stood on the corner. To the right of the window, a desk without drawers stood facing a wall. There were bookcases along two of the other walls. Near the bookcases, there was a handful of medium-sized cardboard boxes, and he walked up to them.

He could hear Marvin in the other room. He was asking Mr. Fisch about how long he had been living in this neighborhood. Marvin was a good guy for this kind of work. He could ask the old man a million useless questions while Hank nosed around.

He opened one of the boxes and found a set of old encyclopedias. They were *Britannicas*. He pulled out one of the volumes and thumbed it open. It was the 1910 edition. He remembered he once heard a book dealer on Clark Street swear that the 1910 was the best edition there ever was, and everything you ever needed to know was in it. That guy was all Frenchy and highfalutin, with a lot of bughouse notions.

But was he right? Was everything you needed to know in this 1910 encyclopedia?

Hank didn't think so. The stuff he had seen during the war sure as hell wasn't in this encyclopedia. That stuff was brand new and up-to-date. Nazi butchers and super-weapons and concentration camps, and that was just the headlines. And under those headlines? People in those camps eating dirt and cow shit to stay alive, children shot in the head and left in the mud beside the road, their mothers and fathers dying in furnaces big enough to power the Titanic.

He had seen those ovens in Buchenwald, and he had seen plenty of the other stuff that wasn't in the 1910 *Britannica* while he walked across Europe with the other G.I.'s. The German mayor he shot in the face wasn't in this 1910 *Britannica*. Nor was his wife. Nor his kids — his son in the leather shorts and his daughter in the blue apron with little white flowers. And the fucking Atomic Bomb wasn't there either. This 1910 *Britannica* was begging for the A-bomb, pleading for it on its hands and knees. For two of them, in fact, the one that fried Nagasaki and the one that fried Hiroshima and all those skinny starving Nips with their buck teeth and coke-bottle glasses, just like in the funny pages. He remembered Captain America screaming, "Die, you dirty rats, die! Rat-tatta-tat-ta!"

Hank put the dark brown volume back in the box he found it in and walked into the kitchen. He was shaking, and he had to stop.

The kitchen was like the bathroom and the study and the front room. Clean as hospital sheets.

No pots or plates out. No mouse traps along the baseboards. No stacks of old newspapers moldering into fertilizer and rat fodder. But the old guy did have some things. He had a two-burner hot plate and an icebox. Yeah, an icebox. Hank saw fewer and fewer of them every week. Soon everybody in the country would be keeping their ground beef and Budweisers cool in a brand-new General Electric refrigerator or a Frigidaire like the one he had at home.

Fuck 1910. Welcome to the future. Progress is our most important product. Wasn't that what the GE commercials were always squawking about? Progress? Bigger and better? Better things for better living through chemistry and automation? The future? He hoped there wouldn't be any more kids hacked up and stuffed into suitcases in the future. He wanted the future clean and crime-resistant. He wanted a lot of things.

He looked at his hands, turned them slowly so he could see his palms and the backs of his hands. They weren't shaking much.

Hank pulled open the door of the icebox with his right hand. There wasn't much in it. Just the stuff old guys try to keep on ice, to keep from going bad: an opened can of Milnot Milk, a plate of fried fish covered with wax paper, a couple of apples. Maybe red delicious ones. There was also something wrapped in paper from Joe Pierce's Deli down on Division Street. Cold cuts, probably. Hard salami, hopefully.

The detective lifted the paper off the cold cuts. He was right. It was Genoa salami. The kind he liked. His fingers peeled a slice off the top, and he stuck it in his mouth and chewed. The salami tasted just the way he liked it, peppery and dry, with plenty of garlic. He looked around the icebox for some mustard, but there wasn't any.

There weren't any kid's knuckles or shoulder bones either. No baby boy's liver or little girl's heart wrapped in soggy wax paper. No layers of human skin on a plate. No Mason jars filled to overflowing with dark red blood.

...Or maybe just one jar.

On the top rack, way in the back behind the dish of fried fish, Hank spotted a Mason jar, quart-sized, filled with some kind of dark red liquid. He bent toward it to get a better look. The liquid was a funny kind of red. Sort of burgundy colored, like the sofa in the front room. There was no light in the icebox, and the dim kitchen light cast more shadows than light, but he was certain it was red. Maybe it was plum-red. Like blood.

Hank tapped his fingernail against the glass. He was hoping to stir something, a noodle or a blood clot or two, but nothing moved inside the jar, and he stood up.

"Say, Mr. Fisch," Hank called back to the front room as he closed the door of the icebox, "Could you come down here to the kitchen for a minute?"

He heard the old guy get up and shuffle past Marvin.

"Yes, I'm coming, officer. Yes, here I am. Is something wrong?"

Hank didn't say anything. He heard Marvin get up too and follow Mr. Fisch. The old guy was a slow walker, so it took them a moment or two before they were both standing in the clean kitchen.

"Now, I'm not saying anything," Hank said, "but I do have a question."

"Yes, officer?" Mr. Fisch said in a wobbly voice as he stood next to the Formica-topped kitchen table, his right hand holding onto it for support.

Hank opened the door of the icebox and pointed toward the back of it. "See that Mason jar back there, Mr. Fisch, next to the Milnot?"

"Yes, certainly, yes, I do."

"Would you mind telling me what's in it?"

The old guy walked over to the icebox, bent down, and pushed his head into it.

"Yes, I know exactly what it is," he said. Then he grabbed the jar with his right hand and slid it out along the wire rack. "It's soup. Mrs. Olejniczak made it for me. It's *czarnina*. It's not kosher, but I am sorry to admit I have a weakness for it, and I wouldn't want to insult Mrs. Olejniczak in any case." He placed the jar on the table and stepped back. "Why are you interested?"

Hank didn't answer. They needed some light. He looked around and noticed that there was a bulb in a socket on the wall above the sink, and he asked Marvin to turn it on.

"That's better. Let's take a look."

Hank picked up the jar then and shook it gently. He couldn't see anything but the dark liquid. He made sure the lid was on tight, and then he turned the jar upside down. Nothing. He put it back on the table and unscrewed the metal cap. Then he bent forward toward the jar's open mouth and sniffed.

"Jesus," he said and jerked his head back quickly.

There was something sweet about it, but the sweetness was old, rancid, like the sweetness of unpicked apples rotting on a tree. There was a sharpness to it too, dirty and metallic with an acidic edge to it. Hank shook his head, and Marvin took a whiff.

"Whew, it smells like a butthole," he said, and pulled back toward the wall, away from the jar. "What the hell kind of soup is this?"

"Gentleman, please," Mr. Fisch pleaded in a high whine. "It's *czarnina*. Duck's-blood soup."

"I've heard of it before, but never smelled it," Hank said as he looked closer at the liquid. "It's not clotting. If it's blood, how come it's not clotting?"

"The vinegar Mrs. Olejniczak uses keeps it from clotting. Sometimes she uses too much, and it smells acidic, just like this."

Marvin stepped toward the table again. "My mom was from the old country, Poland. She tried to make this stuff once, and my old man told her he would divorce her if she ever made it again. He said he hated the smell of it, and now I know what the hell he was talking about. Screw that lid back on, Hank. Tight. That soup is making my eyes boil and my stomach churn."

Hank twisted the lid back on and handed the glass jar to Marvin. "I think we're done here, Mr. Fisch. If you see anything suspicious or unusual, call the officers at the Shakespeare Station."

"Certainly, officer, yes," Mr. Fisch said, "But are you taking my soup?"

Marvin looked at the jar in his hands and nodded. "I think we have to, Mr. Fisch. I apologize for any inconvenience, but we need to check this soup out."

"Will I get it back?"

"Not likely."

CHAPTER 5

AFTER LEAVING Mr. Fisch's apartment, the two detectives tried the flat upstairs where he said Mr. Bujak lived.

Marvin pounded on the door for a solid minute, but it didn't rouse anybody. Not a peep. Finally, he made a note of this in his memo pad and followed Hank down the stairs to the sidewalk.

They stood there looking at the synagogue next door for a long time. It was a big old building, red brick like many of the apartment buildings on the street, and three solid stories high, wide enough to fill the double-wide corner lot. Maybe once it was a school, or an auditorium. Hank didn't know. There were a lot of these old buildings scattered around the perimeter of the park.

Hank checked his wristwatch.

"You wanna know what time it is?" he asked Marvin.

"Not if it's going to hurt."

"Okay, I won't tell you. But you tell me, what're you going to do with that blood soup?"

"This shit?" he said as he shook the jar. Then he lifted it up to the light from a street lamp. "I'm going to stick this in the trunk of the squad car and leave it there for the next guy."

"Jesus," Hank said, walking toward the door of the synagogue. "Why'd you take it? You knew it was just soup."

"I hate those old Jewish guys with their whiny voices going on about the little boys making too much noise and how they need a little *disciplina*. My dad was that kind of Jew. I heard that stuff from him and his Jew friends from the moment I got off my knees and stopped crawling."

"You know, Marvin, for a Jew, you sometimes sound like an anti-Semite."

"Yeah, and you sometimes sound like an asshole, but I don't hold it against you."

Hank smiled and said, "Thanks for the consideration. So let me get back to where I started — the soup. How come you took Mr. Fisch's soup?"

Marvin didn't hesitate. "Better that than slugging him with a sock full of nickels."

"I guess," Hank said as the two turned the corner onto California Avenue.

At the entrance to the synagogue, Hank and Marvin met a uniform cop they knew, Billy Gajewski, a tall guy. He was smoking a cigarette, his 8-point patrolman's cap pushed back on his head.

"Hi, Purcell. Hey, Bondarowicz. You guys took your own sweet time getting here. Lieutenant O'Herlihy said you were supposed to be here helping us with searching the synagogue. We needed the help. This is some huge dump."

"Yeah, we've been delayed," Hank said. "We were cooking soup and had to wait for the stuff to cool."

"That's for sure," Marvin added, "but we saved you some." Holding the glass Mason jar in the palm of his hand, he extended it to Patrolman Gajewski. "This is for you, Sugar. Every Bohunk's favorite. *Czarnina!*"

Gajewski flicked his cigarette into the street and put up both of his hands, palms out, to ward off the soup. "Jesus! No thanks, Bondo, I hate that Polack stuff. Keep it for your granny."

Hank stepped forward. "So what's the scoop here, Chief?"

Gajewski pulled his cap forward. "They're done with the synagogue. They spent a couple hours here and didn't find doodly-squat. O'Herlihy's calling all you detectives and the press together at eleven this morning, at Homicide, downtown. He said for me to tell any of you square holes who come around, 'Be there. Period.' And I think he wants to talk to you two at his office there before the big meeting."

"Appreciate the news bulletin," Marvin said. "We better get moving, Hank. Now, where did we leave the squad car?"

Hank shook his head and shrugged.

"I think it was just off Potomac," Marvin said, and started walking.

Hank didn't follow. He stood on the corner and looked around, admiring the scenery.

The sun was coming up in the east, over the lake. He couldn't see it yet, but he knew it was there. Hank could feel it, even in the near darkness in front of the synagogue. He knew in another ten minutes everything would be clear, visible in the morning light.

He lit a Chesterfield and looked across California Avenue.

Humboldt Park was still dark. A wall of tall bushes and taller trees hung over the sidewalk that bordered the east side of the park. Hank couldn't see anything at all beyond that vegetation except more bushes and more trees. And more darkness.

For a moment, he remembered the war, those last five months, first in the Ardennes, then in the Hartz Mountains. It was dark at noon in those forests, darker at midnight. He remembered pressing for warmth against the wall of his foxhole, a camouflage of thin branches above his head, his eyes searching the darkness and seeing nothing, his ears hearing only the blood ticking in his veins, the wind rubbing through the dark trees he couldn't see. He was always afraid back then, shaking in the dark.

Humboldt Park was that kind of dark place at night.

He knew it was the kind of darkness that a killer could be hiding in. There was enough room for an army of killers. The park was more than two hundred acres, with hills and brambles, lagoons and islands. There were primitive, undeveloped sections in the southwest quarter of the park where a guy could set up a hut and nobody would know.

Silent. Dark. Isolated. Lonely. Hushed. Out of the way. Spooky.

A man out there would be alone in the dark, even when he was with a buddy drinking beers or with a girl doing stuff that the priests warned him against. He'd still be alone with his fears and desires in the darkness of trees and bushes. And alone with his urges, like Mr. Fisch said. Urges....

At night, Humboldt Park was a place where if you knocked, you prayed nobody would answer.

CHAPTER 6

HANK DROPPED MARVIN off at his flat near Belmont and Milwaukee and kept driving west on Belmont. He was going home to the bungalow he shared with his wife Hazel and their kid Margaret.

It was almost seven in the morning, and the sky was stone gray. After yesterday's heat, he figured today would be cloudy, cool, and probably wet. He felt good about that, but he was tired.

He didn't want to think about the canvassing they did after they saw the kid in the suitcase. It was stupid. Lieutenant O'Herlihy told them to get the killer, and he and Marvin wanted to, but they hadn't done much of anything. You can't find a killer the way you find a hole in your pants leg or a wad of chewing gum on the bottom of your shoe. You can't say, "Oh, here it is, Lieutenant. I was stepping on it all the time." That's the kind of bullshit Hank used to see in those old Charlie Chan films he watched at the Logan Square Theater when he was a kid. Even that TV show *Dragnet*, the one that pretended to be telling it on the level, was just Hollywood bullshit 99.9% of the time.

Hank and his partner had poked around the buildings on their side of the block like the other detectives and cops canvassed the block across from them. They all poked and poked. It was just some kind of game, and he'd bet that nobody found anything that would bring them any closer to the bastard who killed that boy and layered his chopped bones in a suitcase.

Now he was driving home for a pit stop, some food and a shower, driving past the bungalows where people were probably just getting up to read their copies of the *Chicago Tribune* or listen to the news on the radio. Just waking up to a dead boy drained of blood, axed into pieces and stuffed into a brown suitcase.

Hank's brick bungalow on School Street looked like every one of these bungalows he was driving past: the same height, the same sandy-yellow brick, the same kind of front porch with its metal railings, and the same spit of lawn in front. The only thing different, probably, was that he had brand-new metal awnings, and they were forest green. Most of his neighbors didn't bother with awnings. They didn't get the point.

He did. He liked a little shade.

Marvin was always complaining that Hank lived in a little-bitty house that looked just like everybody else's. But Hank didn't mind that his house looked like about fifty thousand other houses in Chicago. In fact, he liked it — liked it the way he liked shade in the summer.

The bungalows were clean and neat and new, and his neighbors took good care of their homes just like he took care of his.

It was nice.

He spent the working day, every day, scratching his way through old shit, dirty shit, shit that wouldn't make sense even if you were Albert Einstein and had a microscope as big as a bazooka. So Hank liked to come home to where things were clean and new, and you didn't have to worry that some jerk was going to throw a brick through your picture window or scrawl some kind of "fuck you jimmy" on the front of your bungalow in tar or black paint. No kids screaming and kicking at your door like the way the old Jew Mr. Fisch told it. Hank agreed with Mr. Fisch on that point: they both gave the nod to a little of that old-fashioned *disciplina*.

Hank liked his bungalow. It was spic and span, and he could push back the memories of drunks pissing on tires and killers hacking up kids and shoving them into suitcases. Or at least he could try to push them back, ignore them for a couple of days or hours. Sometimes it worked, sometimes it didn't.

He figured this was one of the times it wouldn't.

Hank parked his Ford in front of his house and walked up the stairs to the door. It was a little after seven in the morning, and he figured Hazel would be getting Margaret ready for school. He wished he had waited until they were both gone. He didn't like them to see him coming off the job, especially after a night like last night. The little yellow boy in the suitcase hung around his neck. He didn't want his wife and daughter to see him until he had a chance to push back some of what he saw and felt, but he couldn't help it. He was dead, needed some sleep.

As he pulled the house key out of his pocket and was about to unlock the front door, it swung back. Hazel stood there.

Hank could see she was ready for work, with her light-blue dress, her white sweater and her pearls. He was dopey, and she surprised him. He hadn't thought about what he would say to her about what he had seen. All he knew was he'd rather not tell her about the kid in the suitcase who looked like a featherless baby bird. He didn't want to bring the dead boy into the house with him. But it finally didn't matter what he wanted or didn't want.

"I heard about it on the radio," Hazel said. "It's all WGN is talking about."

He stared into her dark-gray eyes, and he could see she wanted to talk about it, ease him into the house, make it okay for him to take an easy breath and think about something other than the kid's body chopped up and pressed into a suitcase. It was what she was good at, and it was one of the things he liked about her, loved about her. He knew it was a stupid thought, but a lot of times he felt she was like this bungalow, something that pushed back all the shit work that rolled toward him every day. A good-luck piece, a statute of Saint Theresa that always answered his prayers.

He wanted to kiss her and hold her and sink down into her strength, but he knew he couldn't. He couldn't kiss her. He couldn't touch her or be close to her. The kid's death was garbage, and it hung on him and made him dirty.

He stepped past her into the living room.

"Hank," she said standing at the door, her voice pleading.

She was talking to his back.

"Where's Margaret?" he asked, walking to the kitchen in the back.

"I took her next door. Mary's going to drive her to school with her kids."

"Good idea."

"You want me to make you some eggs and ham?"

He couldn't answer her. Instead, he walked over to the refrigerator and took out a quart bottle of milk. Peeling its paper lid back, he walked to a white kitchen cabinet and took out a box of Cheerios. He set the milk and the cereal down on the table in the corner of the kitchen and got a bowl out of the cabinet and reached for a spoon.

He knew she was watching him, waiting for him to sit down. He did, and she crossed over to the stove and poured herself a cup of coffee from the Pyrex percolator. Then she came over to the table and looked at her wristwatch. "I've got some time before I have to catch the bus to work."

He nodded, and she drew one of the chairs out from under the table and sat down. He took two soup spoons of sugar from the sugar bowl on the table and sprinkled them over his cereal; then he put his spoon into his cereal bowl and watched it fill slowly with milk and Cheerios.

He looked at Hazel across the table from him. She held her coffee cup in both hands and sipped the hot black liquid. She was staring at him over the rim.

He looked back at his cereal and said, "I'm tired."

"I know."

"What did they say on the radio about what happened?"

"They weren't giving out much. You know how that goes. They have one thing to report, and they keep repeating it over and over, forwards and backwards. Trying to make it sound like they got something more than what they've got."

"Yeah," Hank said and stood up. He poured himself a cup of black coffee and carried the pot over to Hazel and topped off her cup.

"I would have gotten the coffee for you."

"I know," he said. "That's okay. You're going to be doing for people all day long. I can get myself some coffee." He put the pot back over the low gas flame on the stove and sat back down.

"That kid," he said, and paused.

He could see it in her eyes: she wanted him to continue. But he didn't say anything. He just looked at her, and it seemed to him that they were both waiting to see what would come out of his mouth.

Finally, he took a spoon of the sweetened milk out of his bowl and poured it slowly into his coffee. He had never done that before.

He had always taken his coffee black and without sugar, and now he was pouring sweetened milk into his coffee. He chuckled and shook his head.

"Just like a kid," he said to Hazel, and he knew she understood. "I threw up when I saw the boy in that suitcase. It was funny. I saw some terrible things when I was in the infantry during the war. Terrible things: guys getting shot, bombs falling, people doing crazy things all around, you're bound to see terrible things, and I saw my share, but I never threw up. I don't get it."

"Maybe it was the heat," Hazel said. "It was hot in the city last night. Around 80, even at midnight. Maybe that's what made you do it."

"No, I don't think so. Besides, it's not the puking that has me rattled. It's that poor kid. What he must have gone through," Hank said that, and then he stopped talking again. He patted down his shirt pocket looking for smokes, but there weren't any.

Hazel stood up and opened one of the drawers and got out a pack of her Lucky Strikes and an ashtray. "You want one of mine?"

"Hmm," he said, and tapped a cigarette out of her pack and paused. He remembered his promise to Margaret; then he lit the Lucky with his IMCO. Hazel took one too, and they sat in the kitchen for a couple of minutes smoking and not talking.

"You know what gets me?" he asked. "It's that I thought all of that bad shit would just disappear when the war ended. And it didn't. It's still here. That's what hit me when I saw that kid."

"Hank," Hazel said, "I can't stay here with you today."

He took a short drag on his cigarette, tapped the ash off, and crushed the cigarette out in the blue glass ashtray. "That's okay. Don't worry. I'll be okay."

"I can't stay, really. I've got the shipping bills coming in from that thread company on Diversey and Central Park, and Lucy's been out for the last two days."

"Really, it's okay. I've got to get back for a meeting O'Herlihy called. A shave and a change of clothes, and then I'm picking Marvin up and back to work."

Hazel smiled. "How about taking a shower and brushing your teeth too?"

Hank returned a part of her smile. She was a funny woman. He liked that.

"Yeah, the teeth, especially after all that puking. I'm sorry I'll be gone when Margaret gets back from school this afternoon. I can't help it. You tell her I'll see her tonight."

As they sat across from each other in the bungalow's kitchen, Hazel put her cigarette in the ashtray and placed her hands over his. "I'll tell her."

He looked at her hard. He wanted to kiss her, wanted to tell her she was what he needed most today, but he didn't. Couldn't.

Instead, he said what he could, "Thanks. You know what they say. It's the first couple of days. That's when most crimes get solved, if they get solved at all."

"Yeah, I know. You got to get back."

CHAPTER 7

LIEUTENANT O'HERLIHY'S OFFICE was open, but he wasn't there.

Hank stopped in the doorway and checked his watch. It was a little after ten, and the Lieutenant had said he wanted to see them before the eleven o'clock meeting.

"Where the hell is he?" Hank said.

"Don't be so grumpy, Hank," Marvin said, pushing past him and grabbing one of the two chairs in front of O'Herlihy's desk. "Have a seat and don't worry about it. O'Herlihy will show up sooner or later. We might as well get comfortable."

Hank didn't smile or nod, didn't even shrug. He just sat down. He was tired. He'd thought the shower would wake him up, get his blood moving, but it hadn't. It hadn't erased the memory of what he saw in the suitcase, either. That was still as fresh as ever. It was an image that would never get tired, slow down, fade away.

He reached for the pack of cigarettes in the left inside pocket of his sport coat, and then he remembered he had stopped smoking.

"You look like a man who needs a smoke, Purcell," Lieutenant O'Herlihy said as he stepped into the office. "Want one of mine?"

Hank looked up. "No thanks, Lieutenant. I promised my kid."

"Right, I remember you saying. So what do you got so far?" the Lieutenant asked as he sat down behind his desk.

44

"Nothing," Marvin answered. "We canvassed our side of the block and found nothing — double nothing. We checked out maybe fifteen buildings."

"Yeah, we spoke to eighty-four people," Hank added, "and left cards at the doors of twenty others who weren't in, asking them to give us a call. We checked up on those people with their neighbors to see if there was anything suspicious we ought to be checking into. Nothing."

"Nothing," O'Herlihy repeated and brushed his thumb across his thin mustache. "We need something. Does anybody look good for surveillance or a follow-up."

"I don't think so."

"What about the old Jew guy, Mr. Fisch?" Marvin threw in. "Something about him seemed off. A little fishy."

"Is that supposed to be a joke, Bondarowicz?"

Marvin smiled. "Yes, Lieutenant."

"You're a moron," O'Herlihy said, and turned to Hank. "Tell me about Mr. Fisch, Purcell."

"He's around sixty-five, maybe a little older, short, an English tutor. He was in Germany before the war. He seemed kind of nervous, like Marvin says."

"Nervous?" his partner prompted. "He was like Peter Lorre in that old Kraut film, *M*, the one about the guy killing little girls. Remember, he was all sweaty and stuttering."

"Come on, Marvin. Yeah, he seemed nervous, jazzed up about the neighborhood kids not showing him respect, but there was nothing that made it look like he was involved."

O'Herlihy leaned forward. "He complained about the kids?"

"I don't see it. He just seemed like an old Jewish guy pumped up because of the Nazis and kids making noise when he's trying to read. There wasn't enough for a second look."

The Lieutenant turned to Marvin. "What about you?"

Marvin took his hat off and looked at the brim. Then he shrugged.

"Anyway, Purcell, keep an eye on Mr. Fisch. Maybe it's nerves and maybe it's something else."

"Sure, but it doesn't sound like we have anything yet, Lieutenant," Hank said.

"That's right. None of the other teams working the streets around the crime scene had anything either. In fact, your nervous Jew looks pretty good at this point, since everybody else looks bad."

"Is there anything connecting this murder to the Peterson-Schuessler killings last year?"

"Just two things, but we're not pinning anything on them. This boy was naked like those three boys were, and they were all boys."

"That's it?"

"That's it."

"The boys last year were beaten, beaten bad. Was this kid beaten?" Hank asked.

"Not a lick, and this boy was younger, and he didn't have any tape over his eyes either."

"Yeah, I saw that pretty plain," Hank said, looking steady at the Lieutenant's eyes.

Marvin leaned forward. "How about the other teams working the neighborhood?"

"You're not listening, Bondarowicz. If they had something, I'd be telling you about it. Like I said, Mr. Fisch is looking pretty good. Check up on him in a couple of days. See if he's still nervous. Besides that, you know what to do. Check up on your usual informants.

Maybe somebody saw something, knows something."

"Lieutenant?"

"Yeah, Purcell."

"What are you going to say in front of the reporters?"

"I guess we'll both find out when I open my mouth."

Chapter 8

DRIVING WEST ON Division toward Humboldt Park, Hank didn't have much to say to Marvin. They were heading to the tavern across the street from where the dead boy had been found yesterday, the White Eagle. It was almost 5 o'clock in the afternoon, and it was cool, a spring day rather than the summer day promised by yesterday's heat, and he and his partner were driving into the golden, dreaming sun.

Lieutenant O'Herlihy's meeting had been what Hank figured it would be, a waste of time. The room had been full of brass and detectives. They were pressed against the walls and taking up most of the floor space, listening as hard as they could to O'Herlihy spin out the knowns and the unknowns of the case, but the real audience wasn't the cops in the room. It was the press boys in the front seats and the people they wrote for, the guys and gals who found out about what was going on by reading what the word-slingers and cub reporters, the Jimmy Olsens and Lois Lanes, had to say.

Hank turned to Marvin. He was pressed back in his seat, his eyes closed and his mouth open wide. He looked like he was asleep.

"You're looking at me," Marvin said, opening his eyes. "I'm a cop. I can feel it."

"What are you thinking?"

"The same thing you are. The stupid meeting. O'Herlihy droning on about our strategy. The brass behind him nodding, the detectives trying to look like they're raring to get out and nab the bastard. It was all bullshit."

"Yeah, you don't need a Ouija board to tell you we don't know shit from Shinola when it comes down to who did it and why. The Lieutenant dragging out those photos of the suitcase and the kid... I mean, it was like he figured that all those photographs held some kind of clue. Like, if enough eyes looked at them, they would be telling us something that would let us pin the murder on somebody. But all that was bullshit for the newsboys so people would think we were on the job."

"Yeah," Marvin said, and closed his eyes again.

Hank kept driving, working through the late afternoon's heavy traffic. The meeting had ended four hours ago, and he was sure no killer had been captured and made to pay yet. Hank, Marvin, and the other cops in the crowded room were sent out like good soldiers into the streets of Chicago with all their squealing and racing cabs and buses and Buicks and Fords to find the clue that would bring in the suitcase killer. Just like in the comic books and TV shows.

Would anybody find the clue, the one that would nail this case shut?

Hank hoped so, but he didn't think it would happen soon. Definitely not today, and probably not tomorrow either.

"You know," Marvin said, "every day somebody in Chicago gets shot or stabbed or drowned or hanged or beaten or burned to death, and we show up at the scene of the crime. And what do we do? We worry the clues and facts out of the linoleum and the fibers on the bed, and we figure out some things and don't figure out some others."

"Yeah, but what almost never happens is that we find out who did the killing."

Marvin stretched his neck back again and said, "You've got that, pops. We'll find the killer if he's standing there with the bloody club in his hand and there's brains and guts dripping down the front of his shirt. Then we got no problem solving the crime."

Marvin didn't say anything for a while after that, and Hank kept driving.

He thought about what it was like when the cops did find the killer standing over his dead victim. That's when the cops acted like junior G-Men, busting their little buttons with pride and bestowing sunny smiles on all and sundry; but Hank knew that when a body showed up in a suitcase on a dark corner in some Polack neighborhood on the near northwest side and it was cut to pieces and there wasn't a man with a hacksaw in his hands standing over it and mumbling, "I'm the guy who did this," there wasn't much chance the killer would be found today or tomorrow or the next day. Chicago was a city of hundred-year-old cemeteries packed full of John Does and Jane Does still waiting for justice and the sweet sword of God's almighty retribution. Yeah, the sweet, swift sword.

Passing Western Avenue, Marvin lit a cigarette and drew in a thin drag of smoke and heat. "You want one, Hank?"

"Yeah, but I'll pass. I promised."

"Right, yeah, your kid. I remember," Marvin said, and took another puff. "I've been thinking about the boy who was killed. According to O'Herlihy nobody's come up to claim him. That's strange, man. This kid's picture's plastered all over the city, in all the papers, and on TV, and nobody's come out and said, 'Hey, that's my son, that's my Billy or Johnny.' I don't get it."

"That makes two of us."

"It's nuts. Where the hell are his parents? You'd think some teacher would show up, or some kid. I mean, how many people does the average seven- or eight-year-old come in contact with on a day-to-day basis? Twenty? Thirty?"

"Give me a drag," Hank said, and took the cigarette from Marvin. "Somebody will show up, some teacher or the kid's pal. It's still early."

"Early? You think so?"

CHAPTER 9

HANK PARKED UP alongside the hydrant outside the White Eagle Tap and stepped out of the black Ford. He and Marvin were doing what Lieutenant O'Herlihy wanted them to do, checking in with their usual informants. That's why they were starting their search for the killer by hitting the White Eagle. The bartender, Stashu Dombrowksi, was a good Joe with a lot of contacts. Besides, the White Eagle was the bar across from where the suitcase was found.

Pushing the brim of his hat back, Hank looked across the intersection. The yellow sawhorses the police had set up the night before were still there. A patrolman in a short-sleeved white shirt leaned up against one of them, talking to a bunch of kids. He seemed comfortable yakking with them, like he was enjoying being the big shot.

The kids were talking loud and pointing at stuff: the cop, the spot where the suitcase had sat, the convent just up the street.

Hank knew what they were talking about, but he wondered what they had made of the killing. They probably had more information, better information, than he had. They seemed happy and excited too. It was like they suddenly found themselves transformed from boring snot-drippers into young heroes in a Technicolor movie starring Roy Rogers. The cop, the suitcase that was no longer there, the murder of the boy — all of that was juicing them up, giving them the stuff that made them ten feet tall and tougher than John Wayne.

Hank wasn't surprised. He had seen the way death, violent death, transformed people. If it wasn't you who was ending up splattered and dead on the sidewalk, it was like winning your three favorite numbers or liking the nag that was going to win the derby at 50 to 1.

Hank suddenly heard one of the kids, a fat, short kid in a black Nazi helmet, shouting something. It sounded like a name. He hadn't heard it clearly, so he listened tighter, closer. The kid was screaming, "Suitcase Charlie did it. Suitcase Charlie! Yeah!"

Fat Boy shouted that again and again, and he spun around a couple of times. Then he pretended to be an old, humped-back man, some Quasimodo, carrying two imaginary suitcases, one in each hand, waddling to the left and right under the weight of the imaginary bodies they carried.

Hank turned to Marvin and pointed to the kid. "Hmm. Suitcase Charlie? Where the hell do you think he got that?"

"I don't know. Maybe you should ask the patrolman, Detective."

"Yeah." Hank said as he started across Washtenaw and walked over to the cop leaning against the sawhorse, talking to the kids, his little pals.

"Say, Bud," Hank said to him, "I'm Detective Purcell and this is my partner. I heard the kid in the Kraut helmet call our man 'Suitcase Charlie.' Where'd he get that?"

"I guess it's what the kids are calling him," the patrolman smiled, and then he shrugged. "I guess I didn't ask."

Hank looked at him and said, "Yeah, I guess."

The young cop turned to the boys, who were laughing and jiving all around him. "Hey, hey, simmer down, you guys. Listen. The detective here, he wants to know, how come you kids are calling this guy Suitcase Charlie? How do you figure that's his name?"

Rolling from side to side, the fat kid in the helmet pushed back two of his friends and waddled up to the cop, chanting, "Suitcase Charlie eats your liver, heart and brains, Suitcase Charlie pours your gizzards down the drain."

"Take it easy, kid, listen, these here are detectives, investigating the crime. They got a question for you."

Fat Boy made like he was going to lurch away; he shouted that the cops were arresting him for the murder, that he hadn't done it, and that he wanted his mamma so bad. Marvin grabbed his shoulder tight with his right hand and jerked him toward the curb, away from the crowd of boys.

"Listen, kid, stop fooling around," Marvin said to him. "You can help our investigation. Just tell us where you heard that about his name. Suitcase Charlie."

Fat Boy made to pull away one more time and then stopped dead. Marvin had a lock on him. He wasn't going anywhere.

"Come on, kid, help us out here," Hank said. "What's up with the name?"

The fat boy grinned at his friends and then suddenly stopped. He pulled himself up tall and looked serious. He took off the helmet and put it down, upside down, on the narrow strip of grass that ran along the curb. The boy's black hair was wet and matted, and he seemed relieved to have the helmet off his head.

"I heard it at school today," he said, brushing the wet hair out of his eyes. "One of the kids in my class said it. 'Suitcase Charlie', he said, and then the other boys started calling him that too."

"Do you remember the kid's name? The one who started it?" Marvin asked.

"Yeah, sure I do. It was Stanley Czarnik. A fourth-grader, like me, at St. Fidelis."

"Thanks, kid, you've been a big help."

"Do I get a reward?"

Marvin smiled and picked up the kid's helmet from the sidewalk. "Yeah, the reward, sure. If we catch him, and if his name is really Charlie, and if you stop wearing this stinking Kraut helmet, you'll get a reward." He walked over to the patrolman and gave him the helmet. "Keep this as evidence, Barney."

"Sure thing, Chief. 'Til hell freezes over and the pipes don't burst," the patrolman said.

Marvin nodded. "You got that right, Barney."

Crossing the street to the White Eagle Tap, Hank and Marvin could hear the boy whining about how he wanted his helmet. Wanted it bad because it was his, and his dad brought it home from the war for him.

CHAPTER 10

HANK TRAILED MARVIN into the big dark main room of the White Eagle. Hank knew the place. He'd been here before. Morning, noon, and night, he'd been here. It was a neighborhood bar, and the neighborhood was mainly Polacks, and Polacks, Hank figured, liked to drink in the dark. Even with the afternoon sun still strong outside, this place had its own special gloom.

The only real light came from a couple of lit-up beer signs nailed to the wall behind the bar. In one of them, Hank's favorite, a fat-ass bear with a fishing pole and a big smile was fishing for trout in a rich blue mountain steam, and he'd just caught a big one. He was yanking on his string as happy as Adam on the day he was born.

Hank looked down the row of guys at the bar and wondered how much any of them knew about fishing or bears. Probably nothing. The guys were drinking and yakking some. He could hear a mix of Polish and English coming from them, but mostly Polish.

"Hi, guys," Stashu the bartender said to the detectives in his almost-English. "Stopping in for a short one after work, a *mala kropnic?*"

"Not today, Stashu, no *dropnik* for us. Just business," Hank answered as he and Marvin walked to the empty stools at the end of the bar. Stashu followed them down.

"How about some ginger ale, then? You guys look like it's been a long tough day." Stashu put his left hand under the counter and came up with a couple of tall glasses. He stuck one under a drinks spigot and pulled it down with his right hand.

Hank watched the hand the way he always did. It was carved out of hard black rubber and looked like a frozen claw, like the letter "C". Stashu got it when he lost the real one in the war, shoving a grenade into the treads of a Nazi tank during the Warsaw Uprising. The new hand wasn't perfect, Stashu liked to say, but it wasn't bad. He couldn't jerk off with it, but he could jerk a spigot. He'd say that and laugh. For a one-handed guy, he had a terrific sense of humor.

With his good left hand he placed the tall glasses sparkling with icy ginger ale on beer coasters in front of Hank and Marvin.

"So, it's business," Stashu asked. "What kind business? The kid the *polizia* found last night?"

Marvin picked up the ginger ale and took a short drink. He ran the tip of his tongue over his lower lip and put the glass down on the counter, and then he pushed it toward Stashu. "Yeah, the kid. Could you squeeze a little Canadian Club into this ginger ale? It's got a funny taste."

"Sure, Detective, I was just waiting for you to ask."

"Yeah, but don't squeeze too much in now." Marvin smiled. "I'm on duty."

"Of course," Stashu said, reaching for a bottle under the counter.

Hank turned to look at the guys down the bar. He figured they had all been talking about the murder before he and Marvin had gotten there. Now, they were pretending to be talking but probably they were just listening, listening and waiting to hear what Stashu and the detectives had to say.

"Let's go to a table," Stashu said. "Too many ears here." He stood up and walked over to the wooden tables on the left side of the room. Hank and Marvin followed, carrying their drinks.

Stashu sat down with his back to the wall and his face turned to the bar and the guys drinking there. "Wally, you work the bar for me," he shouted to a short guy standing at the bar drinking. "I'm talking to my friends."

Hank took out his memo pad and started to write. Stashu shook his head and waved the pad away with his black hard-rubber hand. "I'm talking, but no writing."

Hank said, "Sure. So what do you know, Stash?"

"I'll tell you the same thing I told the other police last night. I don't know much, but I told them I know you're not going to find anything by talking to guys like me in bars, or women who just got home from the third shift down at the factory, or the holy Sisters in their convent. Something like this, chopping a kid up, takes a special kind of person. An evil person, sure, but somebody that has a lot of time on his hands, probably a guy who doesn't spend a lot of time working like you and me and the guys here at the bar. It's not a working man who done this. You know what else?"

Hank looked at him and shrugged, took a sip of the ginger ale. It was getting warm, and its fizz was gone. "What?"

"The call that brought the first cops came from the White Eagle, right here. Did they tell you that?"

"Yeah, I heard it from the Lieutenant."

"Did they tell you that a Polack, a D.P. fresh off the boat, coming home from work, brought the news?"

Hank nodded. "Yeah, they told us he was a recent immigrant, a refugee."

Stashu took out a white cloth and wiped the table between him and Hank and Marvin and said, "Yeah, the Polack ran in. He was crazy, screaming, pleading to God, *"Boze Moje, Boze Moje,"* and beating his chest with the flat of his knuckles. Like in the old country. A real peasant, a *goral.* He was the guy found the suitcase, and what did this Polack figure? He figured what the hell, here in America you can find good suitcases on the sidewalk, maybe no gold in the street, but sure they got suitcases. So he opens it up, and he almost has a heart attack right there, a stroke. If he knew any English, he forgot it when he saw that kid."

"They got the D.P. in one of the holding cells at Wood Street Station, in the basement."

"You think he's gonna come out looking good?" Stashu took his rubber hand off the table with his good left hand and put it in his lap. He looked at the glasses in front of the detectives. "Say, you fellows want some more ginger ale?"

"We're fine," Hank said, and reached in his pants pocket for his lighter. He liked to have something in his hand. Something he could feel, press his fingers against, hard. "Don't worry. The DP will be fine. They won't rough him up too much."

Stashu looked at Hank and then at Marvin. Hank knew what the bartender was thinking. He was a guy who had seen the way the Gestapo worked. He knew the kind of business cops were in. Hank knew he was lying to Stashu when he said the boys at Wood Street Station wouldn't rough up the Polack. Stashu knew it too.

Marvin finished his ginger ale and Canadian Club and put the glass on the table. "So what do we have here? You got anything for us that we don't already know?"

"The D.P.'s named Janusz Lorys," the bartender said. "He doesn't talk much English besides what he knows from work, and he doesn't know anything about the boy who got killed."

"We'll see what we can do," Hank said, and he and Marvin stood up to leave.

Still sitting at the table, Stashu smiled and spread his arms out wide. "You boys do a good job. I know. You catch this *gnoic*, this piece of shit. And you want to work somebody over with a rubber hose? You take a look at Joe Rosetti, Joey Roses. He's the Polack who knows everything that's going on around here. He runs with the colored gangs too sometimes. Maybe he knows something through them."

"Rosetti's a Polack?" Marvin said. "I always figured with that name he had to be Italian."

"Maybe a little Italian on his father's side," Stashu grinned, "but not enough to hurt him."

"Yeah," Hank said, "but a bad guy every which way you look at him. He used to run extortion in the candy stores by the schools this side of Western, threatening to cut up the kids going into the stores."

"That's the guy."

"Thanks for the tip, Stashu," Marvin said. "How about a highball before we go?"

"Sure, you got it," Stashu said, and shouted to Wally behind the bar, "Bring these two gentlemen a couple highballs, Seven and Sevens."

CHAPTER 11

IN THE KITCHEN the next morning, Hank stood at the stove stirring Margaret's oatmeal.

His daughter liked it dry. She liked it really dry.

She was a wonder to him. Only nine years old, and already she was a kid with taste and opinions. Dry oatmeal? He'd never heard of such a thing. When he was a kid, he ate what his mom put in front of him; whether it was cold or hot, wet or dry, edible or not, it didn't matter. His mom, a farm woman from northern Minnesota, said, "Eat it," and he ate it. She said, "Drink it," and he drank it. And now his fussy little nine-year-old daughter was asking him if her oatmeal was dry yet.

"It's almost ready, Sugar. Just another minute or so."

"I'm going to be late for school, Dad. It's Friday, and I'm going to be late."

"No, you'll be fine."

Hazel came into the kitchen, bent down to Margaret sitting at the table and brushed her cheek. "Hey, Angel, how's breakfast coming?"

"I'm going to be late. Dad's cooking too slow!"

"Don't worry. He knows oatmeal. I don't think you'll be late," Hazel said, and came up to Hank. She smiled at him, placed her hand on his stomach, and kissed his lips.

He liked that, liked her hand there pressing against his stomach, but he gave her his crooked smile, the smile that said, "Let's not fool around in front of the kid." He took a half step back and stirred the oatmeal some more, a little faster. "Hazel, turn on the news. Let's see what's going on in the world."

His wife walked over to the counter, clicked on the Crosley radio, and spun the big brown dial to 720, WGN. A guy talking loud and fast for Polk Brothers was selling a washing machine with electric-powered rollers that he guaranteed would reduce washing time by 75%. He promised to throw in a year's supply of Cheer laundry detergent. It sounded like a good deal.

"Dad," Margaret said, "is it dry yet? I'm hungry!"

"Say, Sugar, did I ever tell you the story about my sister Sandy and the day she complained about our mom's meatloaf?"

"Yes, you did. Is the oatmeal ready?" She drew out the last word, and Hank smiled.

"I'm putting it in the bowl," he said, and started spooning the mushy oatmeal onto Margaret's favorite bowl, a light-blue porcelain with some kind of squiggly Aztec design circling the inside of the bowl, just below the rim.

Hazel was sitting down with her coffee when she suddenly stopped and stood up. "Did you hear that?"

"What?" Hank said, putting the bowl in front of Margaret.

"They said something about..." Hazel stopped herself for a moment. She looked at Margaret and then continued, "...the case in Humboldt Park."

Hank walked over to the radio and turned it up. An announcer with a quick, metallic clip to his delivery was finishing the report. "Suitcases were found near the boathouse. And police report that a suspect is in custody."

"Jesus!" Hank exclaimed. "They probably have him at Shakespeare Station, up on California. I got to get over there."

He looked over at Margaret. She was looking back at him. He figured that she probably felt the same way her mom did: He was always going off chasing some lead, or thinking about some guy who had done something wrong and needed to get bent. She was right.

"Hank," Hazel said, "why don't you finish your breakfast? You don't even know if they've actually got a suspect. You know how they are, always making something out of nothing. They've probably just brought in one of the hoboes who sleeps in the park."

Hank was about to agree with her when the wall phone by the sink rang. He picked it up. It was Marvin.

"I just got a call from O'Herlihy," he said. "Have you heard? There's been another killing. They got somebody."

Hank stared at the wall in front of him for a minute. Then he said, "Yeah, I'll pick you up in ten minutes."

Hank looked at Hazel again. She looked back at him.

"Dad," Margaret complained, "the oatmeal is too wet!"

CHAPTER 12

HANK DIDN'T HAVE any problem parking the Ford near the station. He was surprised. All the way down, Marvin kept yakking about how the place would be jumping with reporters and photographers from all the newspapers, cops from the other stations and the neighborhood, moms and pops, and even TV cameramen, but it wasn't like that at all. It was quiet.

Hank found an easy spot on Shakespeare Street, just off California, and they went into the two-story red brick station house through the back door.

The first person they ran into was Freddy Stern, an old street cop, straight Irish from the old country, though you couldn't tell by his name. He was standing near a couple of gray steel desks set up in the back for report writing. A young cop Hank didn't recognize was standing next to him. The old guy was talking and the young guy was listening, and they were both drinking coffee out of white Dixie cups.

"What's going on, Freddy?" Hank asked. "Marvin and I figured this place would be jumping, swarming with cub reporters and downtown cops."

"You'd think it," Freddy said in a half brogue. "But the chiefs and the bosses fooled the reporters and the lookie-loos too, told them all that the suspect was dragged over to Wood Street Station, so we'd have some room here for the interrogation."

Hank glanced at Freddy when he said the word "interrogation". The old Mick's cop hat was pushed back on his head, and he was just putting his cigarette to his lips. There was a hard look in his eyes. It was the kind of look Hank used to see in his dad's eyes back in the Thirties, when he was out of a job and the family needed money bad and he was ready to do anything he could to get it. It was the kind of look that said, I won't like this, but I'll do what I have to do because I'm a man and I know what that means.

"Where they doing the interrogation?" Marvin asked.

"In the basement, you know, in the holding cells in the front. The brass cleared them all out except for the one the killer's in. Let the bums and drunks go back to the bars they came from. It was something to see. They didn't want anything interfering with the interrogating."

"Two dead kids," Hank said, shaking his head.

"Two? Jesus, it's not two. Three altogether now. The one from the first night and then the two last night."

"*Two* last night?"

Freddy put his coffee down on one of the steel-topped desks and slowly lowered the tip of his cigarette to the cold, brown-gray liquid. The smoke died in the cup.

"That's right. Three babies dead altogether, cut up like chickens." His voice had gone soft.

Hank could see that it was getting to Freddy. The old cop paused for a moment and bent his head down, trying not to cry. Hank looked at the young cop. He didn't say anything, but the way he stood with his head turned away from Freddy made it clear that he wished he was someplace far away, doing anything else. It had to be better than being here with this old Mick cop and his tears for the dead kids.

"It's a terrible thing. Three little babies. They found the two in the park, by the old boathouse, the one they use for summer concerts now."

"How'd they find them?"

"That's a story," Freddy said, pulling himself together. "It seems the guy who collared the killer is a high-school student from DuPage County. Him and his girl came down to Humboldt Park to pet, what they call necking now. That's a long way to drive for a little kissing and petting, but that's what they both said they were doing there in the park, in the big parking lot by the boathouse. They drove a long way."

"Yeah," Marvin said.

Freddy paused and looked at Marvin.

"Sure," Freddy said, "they came from some swank neighborhood on the other side of Oak Park Avenue. Anyway, you know it was raining last night, the rain coming down like dog piss, and they were smooching it up in the back of his daddy's blue Cadillac. They were parked off to the side by the bushes, for some privacy, when the boy looks over his sweetie's shoulder and sees something in the dark rain."

"What did he see?" Hank said. He wanted to move the story along. Freddy had the gift of gab when he had an audience, and he had one now.

"What did he see? I'll tell you what he saw. He wasn't expecting to see anything moving out there in the rain, and when he saw it he jumped, and when he jumped his girlfriend jumped too. Now he didn't say what they were doing besides kissing, but if he's jumping and she's jumping along with him, you got to figure it's more than just smooching."

Hank sat down on one of the desks. "How did the kid see any-thing? The lights stink over there. I think there's maybe one light for the whole damn parking lot by the boathouse."

"I know," Freddy said. "Sure, the lights stink but the kid saw some movement, maybe when lightning flashed. I don't know, and then his girlfriend sees it too. There's some crazy man hauling suitcases in the rain. He's bent double, and he's lugging two suitcases. Working like they must weigh a ton, and the rain is falling fast and loud. The boy, Chris, his name is Chris Wessel, he doesn't know what to make of it. He wants to go back to smooching or petting or whatever else they're doing in his daddy's Cadillac, but she pushes him off and says, 'No, Chris, that's got to be Suitcase Charlie.'"

"Suitcase Charlie?" Hank said. "That's the name we heard yesterday from some kid down by the White Eagle Tap."

"Yeah, it's what they're calling the killer in the papers too. Suitcase Charlie."

The young cop spoke for the first time. He asked, "What did the kid do when his girlfriend pushed him off?"

Marvin chuckled. "He probably shit his pants in his daddy's blue Caddy."

Freddy looked at Marvin and shook his head. "If he shit in his pants, he didn't report it to the investigating officer."

Marvin laughed and sat down on the swivel chair behind the desk.

"What he did report," Freddy continued, "was that he climbed into the front seat and reached under the seat for a tire iron, and then the kid did what a man would do."

"Yeah," the young cop said, "that kid's got a pair on him."

"Yes, sir, that's right. He snuck up in the rain behind the killer hauling the suitcases and whacked him one on the head so good that the guy went down like a sack, and when he was down on the ground, that kid from DuPage whacked him on the noggin again, three times."

The young cop said, "We're lucky the kid didn't kill Suitcase Charlie."

Hank, Marvin, and Freddy Stern gave the young cop a look.

CHAPTER 13

EVEN IN THE quarter-light of the 30-watt bulbs strung on the ceiling of the corridor, Hank saw that the holding cell was almost empty. There was no cot, no benches along the wall, no toilet. There was nothing except the suspect and the three-legged stool he sat on. It was short, and it made the guy sitting there look like a fool. The rough bandages wrapped around his head didn't make him look any smarter. They were crusted heavy with blood, which was still oozing in spots.

When Marvin got a load of the suspected killer, he did a slow whistle and whispered, "Je — sus Ch — rist!"

Hank remembered what Freddy Stern had said about this guy getting some healthy whacks to the head with a tire iron. The kid who beat up this moke had more balls than brains. The kid should have been worried that the moke wouldn't take kindly to the whacking. Hank knew that when you hit some guys across the face or the back of the head with a tire iron, they don't go down. They turn around with a curious look and whack you right back and harder, or they shoot you in the face if they're carrying a gun. A tire iron across the back of the head just gets the attention of guys like that. The kid from DuPage was lucky this guy wasn't that kind.

Hank figured this guy got the worst of it. Looking at him sitting on his stool, he could tell the kid must have pounded the guy's head real good. Hunched over, he looked like he wouldn't be hitting or shooting anybody for a long while. He looked dopey. His ears under the bandages looked too big and floppy for his head, and he seemed like he was about ready to fall off the stool, collapse right onto the gray concrete floor. He was bare-chested too, and the blood smears on his stomach and sides had mostly dried. This guy didn't pack a lot of weight, but there was muscle across his chest. He had the strength to lug some suitcases.

But Hank didn't know if he was Suitcase Charlie. He looked like a working guy who had been punished in spades by a cowboy in heavy boots and spurs. Punished and then left alone to sit and think about it.

Hank could see that plain, and it didn't surprise him. That's the way the cops here liked to play it. If they wanted to get something out of a guy, they made him feel like a mope, a retard. Keep him waiting on a little stool with blood drying in his hair and snot rolling down his lips and chin. Yeah, that was the idea. Make him sit like that for a couple hours on a little stool with his shirt off or his pants around his ankles. It would be a sure thing, a winner any way you look at it. Loosen him up a bit. Get him yakking and ready to yak some more. That would do it, sure. That, and beating the mother with a hard-rubber hose.

If Hank knew anything, he knew that. This guy had been worked over with hoses, and he would be worked over some more before he got out of Shakespeare Station. The hoses had been here, and they were coming back.

But meanwhile, Hank could see that the suspect was shivering. It wasn't warm in the room, and it wasn't cold either. It was just right, Hank figured, but the guy was shivering. Even his teeth were shivering, chattering. Hank wondered why he was shaking. Were these junkie shakes? Were they out of remorse? Guilt? Hypothermia? Maybe he was still cold from trying to lug those suitcases in that long, hard downpour last night. Or maybe it was fear? Or pain?

The rich kid from DuPage County must have whacked him good, if the cuts on his head were still dribbling blood the next morning.

Hank turned to one of the sergeants leaning against the open cell door looking at the guy on his three-legged stool. It was an old Polack cop who had been around since the time of the Flood, Tommy Kowalski from around Logan Square.

Hank nodded to him. "How's it going, Tommy?"

"Pretty good, Purcell," he said with what sounded to Hank like sarcasm. "We've had this guy here since about two this morning, and he hasn't said anything yet. Not one word. Nothing. There was a police medic here earlier. Made sure the killer was breathing. Checked his eyes for hemorrhage. Patched him up some with stitches and bandages too. He's probably got a concussion. Maybe that's why he ain't talking."

Marvin eased next to Tommy and stared at the prisoner sitting on the stool. "This guy's a mess. It looks like he's already graduated from interrogation school."

"Nope, he ain't got his diploma yet," Kowalski joked. "We got to give him a few more lessons. And then there's the final." Tommy chuckled.

"Hard to believe this guy's still in school," Marvin said. "He must be about thirty-five."

"Yeah, in fact, we've been waiting for you and Hank. I guess Lieutenant O'Herlihy figures you two guys ought to do some work around here for a change. Pull your own weight instead of just moping around on the city's nickel."

Hank took his .38 Detective Special out of its holster and handed it to Kowalski. "You hold on to this while I'm working."

"Sure, kid. I got your piece, and I'll hold your partner's too," Tommy said, and stuck his hand out to get Marvin's .45.

Marvin handed it over to Tommy and turned to the suspect. "This guy here got a name?"

"Not as we can get out of him."

"He speaka da English?" Marvin asked.

"That's something else that we haven't figured out," Tommy said and smiled. "That's why you and Professor Purcell are here. To ask the $64,000 questions, the hard ones. And it's not going to be easy. Like I said, this mope ain't talking."

Tommy pushed the cell door open slowly, and Hank and Marvin stepped in. The cell was good-sized for an old station; on a typical Saturday night, the cops could squeeze thirty drunks in, and the drunks would have room to say their prayers and dance a jig or a polka if they wanted to. And right now, with one man sitting in the middle of the cell on a little three-legged stool, there was plenty of room to negotiate around him.

Marvin said, "Mind if I take the first shift, Hank?"

"Sure, go ahead," Hank nodded, and leaned against the wall behind the man on the stool.

Marvin walked straight up to the suspect and stopped when he was a couple of feet away. Hank could see that the guy on the stool had had a bad night. He was shivering and trembling, but he didn't raise his head or moan or do anything else to suggest that he knew Marvin was standing there and ready to start working him some more.

Marvin took off his sport coat and tossed it over the suspect's head to Hank. Then he rolled up his sleeves and knelt down on both knees in front of the guy. He looked up into his face. The guy's eyes were closed, and he didn't do or say anything. Neither did Marvin. He just looked at the guy's face.

Hank moved to the left to get a better look at what was going on. Marvin placed his fingertips on the shivering man's left cheek. Then he curled his palm under the guy's chin and waited for a moment. The guy didn't do anything, didn't acknowledge he knew Marvin was even in the cell. The guy didn't even acknowledge the hand pressing against his cheek and chin. He just sat there on the stool shivering with his mouth and eyes shut. Drooling a bit too.

Then slowly and gently, Marvin's fingers guided the suspect's head so that he was looking down at Marvin. The prisoner was silent and motionless. That's when Marvin shouted into his face, "What the fuck were you doing with them suitcases, Charlie?"

The prisoner's eyes snapped open, and his head jerked back, and his mouth popped wide. His eyes then started blinking, and his breathing came in fast, short panic breaths. He tried to stand and fell on his ass instead, scuttling backwards like a human crab toward the cell's far wall, just missing Hank's legs.

Tommy Kowalski and Marvin started laughing.

Hank looked at his partner and Kowalski. Then he looked at the suspect huddled on the floor. The cops were having a time.

"My turn now?" Hank asked.

Marvin was rolling his sleeves down. "Sure, Professor, enjoy yourself, but don't pussy out on us."

Hank ignored Marvin. Instead, he asked Tommy Kowalski for a couple of chairs, and the cop brought them in, kicked the stool up against the bars, and placed the two wooden chairs in the middle of the cell. "This okay, Chief?"

"Yeah, that's fine, Tommy. Thanks," Hank said, and went over to the suspect and took his right arm and helped him up, and then he set him in one of the chairs. Hank sat down in the other one about three feet away from the guy.

Hank could see there wasn't anything special about him. He was definitely a working stiff. His face was long and narrow with high, bruised-up cheekbones. His eyes were open now, and he was staring at Hank. There was fear in his eyes. Hank could see that, but not much more.

This guy didn't look like a drooler, a moron, the kind of guy who loves rabbits and kills them, like in that movie Hank saw long ago when he was a kid. It wasn't a killer's face either, all unshaved and scared up and snarling. Not like in the cartoons and the funny pages. But the kid from DuPage had found him last night hauling two suitcases in the rain and the storm, and when the cops showed up the suitcases turned out to be packed with two young boys, naked and cut up like chickens. Just like the kid from the night before.

Hank leaned into the guy's face, looked at his open eyes, and the guy pulled back some. Hank smelled the blood and puke on him. The blood smelled like iron and wet grass, dark nights and the air after lightning struck. The vomit smelled of chocolate and shit, sour cabbage and vinegar. They were familiar smells. The smell dead people give off. The detective wondered what the guy thought about it, about smelling like the dead.

Hank said, "Listen, you understand me?" And he waited for the guy to say something, but he didn't. He just sat there, his body shivering and his eyeballs clicking. Hank turned around to Tommy. "What did you get out of his pants pockets? Anything?"

"A wallet, couple singles, thirty cents in change. A key. No driver's license. No ID. No green card or social security card. Nothing with his name on it."

"Does he know what was in the suitcases?"

"Sure, he does. We told him what we were holding him for. Murder."

"Did he understand?"

"Your guess is as good as mine."

"Did you try your Polish on him?"

Tommy put both his hands out and shrugged. "You think I'm an idiot. I've been a cop long as you been a cop. Sure I tried Polish, and Ukrainian and Russian, even Czech. This guy's clamming up. He knows something."

"He knows we're cops," Hank said. "He thinks this is like the old country. It doesn't matter if he talks or doesn't. We'll beat the crap out of him either way. So he won't talk."

Hank looked back at the man on the stool. Tomorrow's papers would be calling him the "Polack Killer." It didn't matter where he came from in Eastern Europe. It was all the same to the papers. The Polack Killer.

Jesus, he was a mess. Blood was seeping through his bandages now. When he fell backwards off the stool, he must have jerked his stitches loose. Three threads of blood from his bandaged forehead were sliding down his face, across both his eyes and down his cheeks.

Hank reached into the left inside pocket of his dark-blue sport coat and pulled out a handkerchief.

The Polack — or whatever he was — stared at him. He wasn't shivering as much now.

Hank lifted the white square of handkerchief and said, "Listen, I'm going to give you this handkerchief. You clean yourself off."

The guy extended his left hand and took the handkerchief. Hank watched him carefully and slowly wipe the blood off his face. When he was done, he offered it back to Hank.

"That's okay," Hank said. "You keep it. I got plenty."

"*Genkuja*," the suspect said in Polish, and then he added, "Thank you."

Marvin smiled at Tommy Kowalski. "Well, it looks like he can talk at least two languages. Polish and English."

"Thanks, Sherlock, let's find out if he's the killer," Tommy said. "Hank, ask him if he did it."

Hank turned back to the guy.

His shivering had stopped, and he sat looking at Hank. "Mister," the guy asked. "Can I have my shirt?" His accented English was thick with hard consonants in weird combinations.

Hank nodded and looked at Tommy. "How about it? His shirt around here somewhere?"

Kowalski returned the nod and left the holding area to find something for the suspect. He returned with an old wool army blanket and threw it to the suspect. He wrapped himself up in it.

It was a funny picture to Hank, the suspect sitting in a khaki-colored blanket on a chair in a cell. Like some old photo of those old Apaches, Geronimo or Cochise.

Marvin came over, lit the Polack a cigarette, and handed it to him. "Here you go, fellow, take a puff on a Lucky." The suspect took a deep drag and coughed some. Hank wouldn't have been surprised if some of the guy's ribs were broken. The kid with his tire iron probably kicked this guy a couple of time in his midsection. That Dooper was a hazard to public health and safety.

"You sit here," Hank said. "I'll be right back." He stepped out of the cell, slamming the heavy metal door behind him, and walked up to Tommy Kowalski.

Tommy looked at the suspect and then he looked at Hank Purcell. "He sure does look cozy in there now. What do you think, Hank?"

"About what?"

"Jesus Christ, man, about this killer, the kids in the suitcases."

"Here's the way I see it, Tommy," Hank said softly. "This guy's walking home from work, cutting through the park because it's raining like nobody's business. He turns the corner of the boathouse and comes across these two fine leather suitcases. What the hell, he figures. They're just standing there, so he starts dragging them home."

Tommy looked at Hank and shrugged. "Come on, son. This skinny mope? He's gonna drag a hundred pounds of suitcase all the way home? He probably lives over on Rockwell or Division Street somewhere, for Christ's sake. That's like a half a mile, maybe more."

"He probably thought they were filled with solid gold or jewelry. I mean, this is America, the place where the streets are paved with gold and the sewers have chips of diamonds lying down there in the muck instead of broken glass."

Marvin said, "He's right. You see these Polacks, and they're always dragging stuff home. I've seen them try to drag home steel trash cans from the alley. I mean, what are they gonna do with those 50-gallon cans? Build pontoon bridges?"

Hank stepped in again, "Sure, Tommy, and what's the alternative? That he was going to drag the suitcases with the dead kids from his home to the boathouse? A hundred pounds of dead weight, across a half a mile in the rain. Why would he be dragging them all that way? Somebody might've seen him, fingered him for Suitcase Charlie. Everybody's on the lookout."

"Maybe," Tommy said, but Hank knew he still didn't believe him.

"Whoever's killing these kids has a car. It's too much dead weight to be schlepping from one end of the park to the other."

"Maybe, but it's you talking. What about this Polack? He ain't saying nothing."

Hank turned back to the fellow sitting on the chair in the khaki blanket. "Mister, you gonna set us straight here, or are we gonna keep fishing?"

The prisoner didn't say anything for a minute. He looked down at his hand, the cigarette cupped there. Hank thought that they would have to bring out the billy clubs and the rubber hoses again for this guy. He didn't want that to happen, and tried one more time: "Come on, tell us what happened."

The suspect looked up and said, "I didn't mean to steal the suitcases." His voice was deep, his English accented.

"That's not half of it," Tommy Kowalski snapped. "You killed those two kids."

"I didn't. Why would I kill kids? You think I'm a killer. I didn't kill those kids. I seen enough of that in the old country, the war."

Tommy rushed up to the middle of the cell and came right up against the prisoner's blood-crusted face. "So what the hell were you doing in the park with those suitcases?" he yelled.

"I was coming home from work. I found the suitcases. I thought there was something I could sell in them. Sell in the hock shops over on Milwaukee by the Congress show."

"Why didn't you open the suitcases there in the park," Marvin asked, "instead of trying to drag them home?"

The Polack started coughing and bent down into himself. He was like that for a moment, and then he looked up at Marvin.

"I guess you never stole nothing."

"What do you mean?"

"You steal something, you don't want to look at it 'til you get home. You're afraid if you look sooner, some guy will see you and take it away. Or some cop will arrest you, maybe."

"Hmmm."

Hank came up to the Polack. "Listen, forget about the suitcases. You steal them, you didn't steal them. It doesn't matter. I want to know if you saw anything last night before the kid clobbered you."

"Saw anything? It was raining. There's not much light there by the boathouse, and it was raining hard."

"Where were the suitcases? Were they just standing there?"

"Yeah, sure, by the statue of the man on the rock."

Kowalski turned to Hank. "That's the Leif Erikson statue. North of the bridge."

"I dragged the suitcases from there."

"And you didn't see anybody?"

"It was raining. I didn't see anything." The suspect pulled the blanket tighter around his shoulders. "But listen. I'll tell you something."

He said that and stopped. Then he started shivering again, his shoulders trembling. A deep cough rumbled out of his chest and spit itself onto the drunk-tank floor. He bent double and clutched his sides. "Oh, Jesus," he moaned.

Hank turned to Tommy Kowalski. "Can you get the medic back here? Take a look at his ribs?"

Tommy shrugged and left the cell again.

Hank waited until the suspect stopped coughing. "You said you were going to tell us something. What was it?"

"I come from Bukovina, the Ukraine, you know?"

"I never heard of it."

The suspect nodded and said, "This, what's happening here? The boys in the suitcases, chopped up, naked? This kind of thing happened in the old country sometimes. Kids disappear, mister, and then they show up dead. Their bodies chopped and skinned or hung upside down in the forest. Sometimes people would find them hanging upside down, hanging from their feet."

"Yeah, like in that Hansel and Gretel fairy tale," Marvin said, and turned to Hank. "This is bullshit."

"No bullshit, mister. I seen it. In the war. A boy. His skin all cut off. His body just blood, muscle and bones. Somebody left him nailed to the church door. I seen this."

Hank believed him. He could see it in his eyes and hear it in his voice, the way the words came out flat, plain, no drama or tears, an emotional weight of zero. He was telling what he had seen, what wouldn't leave him.

Hank asked, "Who did these things?"

"Who did them? Who knows?"

"Fairy tales," Marvin shouted. "I'm telling you, Hank. This guy is fucking with us. Next thing you know, he'll be talking about witches and devils with red tongues nine feet long rolling out of their mouths."

The suspect ignored Marvin and spoke straight to Hank. "Who did it? Maybe it was Gypsies, or Bolsheviks, Nazis, Polacks trying to scare the Ukrainians, Ukrainians trying to scare the Jews. I don't know." Then he started coughing again, the cough rolling through him and lifting and dropping him like a slow jack-in-the-box.

"Jesus, where's the medic?" Hank said. Then he turned toward the cell door and shouted, "Hey, Tommy, hurry up with that medic!"

Marvin said, "Come on, Hank. You buying this act? This guy

ought to be on General Electric Theater."

The Polack's coughing eased up a little, and he tried to sit up.

Hank didn't say anything. He stepped over to the suspect and wrapped the blanket around his shoulders again.

After a minute the coughing stopped, and the prisoner started talking again. "The old country, it was a place where somebody was always trying to scare somebody else, trying to make them leave or shut up or die of fear. One time before Holy Easter, I remember when I was a boy, some Russians stole a kid and told people in my village the Jews did it. Some of the drunks heard this and believed it. They went to the synagogue on a Friday night where the Jews were praying. These men, they took their hammers and nailed the doors and windows closed, and set the place on fire with gasoline. They did this to their neighbors."

The prisoner stopped and turned to Marvin. Hank could see Marvin standing by the door of the cell, shaking his head.

"You don't believe this?" the man from Bukovina asked. "I saw it. My father took me with him. He was one of the men with the hammers and the nails."

"Hansel and Gretel shit, Hank," Marvin said.

Hank turned to his partner. "Come on, Marvin. Give it a rest." And then to the prisoner he said, "The Jews, did they get out?

"Some got out. Some didn't."

CHAPTER 14

HANK CLIMBED INTO the Ford and started the engine.

Marvin had his hand on the door, but his head was turned back to Shakespeare Station and he was saying something to Freddy Stern. As the door opened, Hank heard Marvin give a laugh.

Marvin climbed in, still chuckling.

"What was that about?"

"Freddy was telling me about the Dooper kid, Chris Wessel. His dad had to come pick him up, and he slapped him silly when he showed up."

"That's funny?"

"Yeah. He was ticked off—not because the kid was in Humboldt Park, not because he was smooching or whatever else he was doing, but because he put the tire iron with all that Polack's blood and gore on that crisp, new Cadillac-leather seat between him and his girlfriend."

"That's what you and Freddy were laughing about?"

"Yeah, why not? What's wrong with laughing about that?"

Hank shook his head, eased the Ford into first gear, and moved into the street.

"What do you think about what that bohunk said about the old country?" Hank asked as he rounded the corner and started heading south on California.

"About the Jews getting killed and burned, or about guys framing them for killing kids?"

"Yeah. Both."

"I heard it before. No surprises."

"Doesn't it tick you off? Make you angry?"

"Why, because I'm a Jew?"

"Yeah."

"Hank, my friend, you ask a question like that, and I'm thinking you don't know me. That Jew killing and Jew-killer stuff, that's why I became a cop."

"How's that?"

"So I could pack a pistol and be perfectly legit if any of those anti-Semite motherfuckers came looking to lynch me or set me aflame," Marvin said as he pulled out his .45 and started twirling it around his index finger.

"So why did you give that Mr. Fisch such a hard time, swiping his duck's-blood soup and all that?"

"Why? Because that's the kind of Yid I am. One that ain't got a lot of use for the rest of my brothers and sisters."

"You always been this way?"

"Yeah, I have, Hank. Since the time of the Flood. You want to do something about it, my friend?"

Hank looked at his partner and smiled. "Nope. Just talking."

Marvin laughed and sang out loud, "I'm the Yamaka Kid, the pistol-packing Yid, coming at you with a ti yi yippee and with a ti yi yippee yippee yea. Hi-Ho, Silver Nose!"

"Jeez."

"By the way," Marvin asked, holstering his .45, "where we going?"

"Lieutenant O'Herlihy wants us down at Cook County Hospital, to talk to the mortician down there about something."

CHAPTER 15

WHAT HANK NOTICED first about the hospital was the smell.

That's what a lot of people didn't like about Cook County Hospital, the smell. It was a hospital where, if you had to go, they had to take you; and they took you whether you were Polack or Negro, poor man or rich man, working girl or junkie, hundreds every week. They put you in the waiting room if there was room, and they stuck you in the long, gray corridors if there wasn't. If it wasn't your day, you got stacked up like kindling or pancakes in passageways that smelled of piss and ammonia.

But Hank didn't mind the smell of the hospital. In the war, he had come across his share of bad smells, lots of them. No, it wasn't the smell.

What he hated was the confusion, the maze-like corridors, the fact that they were always moving the mortuary office and the morgue. The place was a nightmare Hank was always getting lost in.

But not this time.

He and Marvin followed Miss Hathaway, the mortuary director, down one corridor and then another. Carrying her clipboard and dressed in a white lab coat, she was moving like a woman on a mission.

Miss Hathaway took a left suddenly, and they came to another corridor. Some rubberized yellow sheeting that looked like the kind of material you'd make rain slickers out of hung across the corridor, and a thick film of dust and pebble-sized pieces of gray plaster lay at the foot of it. Somebody was sure pretending to keep the dust under control here, and Hank wished they were doing a better job. He felt the stuff in his eyes and throat. There was a dryness in his chest too. It felt tight, constricted. He wished he had a bandana he could wrap across his mouth.

Miss Hathaway stepped through a slit in the middle of the yellow sheet and held it so they could follow her.

"Jesus," Marvin said, kicking a book-sized piece of plaster out of the way. "This place is a mess."

"It has been for a hundred and fifty years, Detective," she offered, and started walking when he passed her. "Just a little further."

They soon came to a section of temporary plywood wall with two glassless doors set about eight feet apart. Miss Hathaway stopped at the farther one and turned around, made sure the detectives were still with her, and then she pulled the door open.

As soon as she did, a soft yellow light hit Hank. He didn't like it. It reminded him of the kind of light he used to see in the men's rooms in the subway stations downtown. He always figured the light was yellow so you couldn't see the piss puddled up on the floor. The docs and bone surgeons at Cook County probably didn't want him noticing the stuff on the floors here either, and he walked carefully into the yellow-lit room.

Hank pulled the collar of his blazer up. The room was maybe sixty feet long and twenty feet wide. There were narrow steel carts lined end-to-end along three walls and a double row of the carts in the center of the room. The bodies were spread on what looked like long cookie sheets.

It was cold, almost freezing.

He stuck his right hand in the pocket of his sport coat. The temperature in the morgue was just about 35 degrees. That was enough to keep a body in decent shape for a few days, but not cold enough to stop decomposition for very long. For that, you needed a negative-temperature mortuary, a place where the temperature never got much above zero and the bodies were frozen solid.

He picked up his step to catch up to Marvin and Miss Hathaway as they moved down the narrow aisle between the rows of steel carts and their bodies. Some were covered with black rubber sheets, some weren't. Some of the bodies looked like the guy or gal was just taking a short break, catching a nod and twenty winks. Give them five minutes, and they'll bounce back up and get to work. But some of the bodies weren't like that. They were a mess.

There were faces with their mouths thrown wide open and locked into smiles or screams. Some of the faces were staring up at the ceiling. One guy had both his lids open but only one of the eyes was there. The other eye had been scooped out, Hank figured. More than one of the corpses had started to decompose. Dark blue hands and feet on some of the bodies. Another one had started to give off brown and gray fluids. Hank knew that the cells and intestines must be breaking down already. He could smell the human gases that he learned about at the Police Academy.

Hydrogen sulfide. Methane. Cadaverine.

Yeah, sweet cadaverine.

Walking through a morgue, he always remembered the summer he spent with his dad when he worked for a restaurant just northwest of Lake Geneva, Wisconsin. There was barn behind it, and Hank got stuck in it once. He was nine then, and he couldn't slide back the heavy, twin, wooden doors. They were on rollers, and the doors must have weighed a couple hundred pounds each. The smell of shit and straw and stuff rotting ripped his breath away. He figured he would die of the smell or die of fear. He was crying and pounding on the door when one of the cooks came out looking for some eggs. Hank was blubbering, his face red, his lips shaking, his breath full of gasps and tears. And she just looked at him and started to laugh. It only made Hank cry harder, but she kept laughing and trying to soothe him, comfort him. Later, the cook said she was sorry about the laughing. She just couldn't stop.

Hank didn't know what kind of system they used to place bodies, but it was always the same. It always took too long to get to the ones he needed to see.

Finally, at the end of the narrow room, Miss Hathaway came to another door, the one to the forensic mortuary. Here was where they kept the bodies they wanted to preserve, hold on to for a while, while investigations were going on.

She pushed the door open and they stepped in. Here it was seriously cold, almost down to zero. Hank wished he had brought his raincoat. He pulled his jacket tighter.

This room was smaller, but there were still twenty carts in it. Some had bodies on them, some didn't. Miss Hathaway led them to three carts near the back wall. Each one had an uncovered body. She stopped by the one closest to the door. She checked something on her clipboard and put her hand down on the edge of the cart. "Here are the bodies Lieutenant O'Herlihy wanted you to see. This is Little John Doe #2, and that's Little John Doe #3 on the cart next to it." She nodded toward the third cart, perpendicular to the other two. "That's the first dead boy — Little John Doe #1."

Hank knew this time what he was going to see: kids' bodies cut and broken into pieces, the pieces between six and twelve inches long. Lieutenant O'Herlihy had gone through it all at the briefing after the first child was found. Hank looked at the three carts and saw that somebody, maybe Miss Hathaway, had put the puzzle pieces of the boys together, assembled them back into the boys they were.

Almost.

He thought about Pinocchio, the puppet boy in the Walt Disney movie he took his daughter Margaret to see a couple of weeks ago. He was a boy put together with pieces of wood threaded together with string. His daughter found the movie scary: the puppet that so much wanted to be a boy, the dark carnival town, the boys turned into donkeys, braying and braying. Margaret was only nine, and she wanted to leave the theater, but Hank made her stay, told her to just close her eyes, put her fingers in her ears, and hum a happy song.

Suddenly, he realized that Miss Hathaway was responding to something Marvin had asked, and he shook puppets and Margaret out of his head.

"The three boys were about the same age, Detective — around nine. The two new ones were killed the same way the first boy was killed: the blood drained out of them while they were still alive."

Marvin looked at the nearest boy. "Say, how long you figure it took one of these kids to bleed out?"

She didn't hesitate. "It depends on a number of factors: the health of the body, the condition of the blood, the body's ability to heal. The size and depth of the cut are important factors too, of course."

"What's your best guess?"

She didn't hesitate. "Forty minutes to get like this. Death a while before that."

Miss Hathaway took a long yellow #2 pencil out of the right

pocket of her lab coat and said, "This is what Lieutenant O'Herlihy specifically wants you to see. The boys' cuts. They're almost identical."

With her pencil she turned the two dismembered feet of Little John Doe #2 so that both his soles were facing up. Then she pressed the tip of the pencil into the sole of one of the boy's feet.

Marvin stepped closer and bent his head down toward the foot.

Hank didn't lean forward. He saw it right away. The sole of the left foot had a deep isosceles triangle cut into it, its apex pointing toward the toes and its base facing the back of the heel. The triangle on the right foot was identical to the one on the left, except it was pointing in the opposite direction: the base faced the toes while the tip pointed toward the back.

Hank took a look at the other boys' feet. They were the same.

Miss Hathaway laid the pencil down on the marble slab and picked her clipboard off the steel cart. She pulled back a paper sheet and revealed a black and white eight-by-ten glossy photograph. It was of the soles of the first boy's feet. The photo had been shot under strong lights, and Hank could easily see the depth and shape of the cuts. They looked like they were about a quarter of an inch deep.

"We sent a copy of these photos over to Lieutenant O'Herlihy earlier today, but he wanted you to see the actual cuts. He felt you'd get a better sense of the wounds if you actually viewed them up close."

"Maybe," Hank said as he bent toward the feet and tried to do what O'Herlihy wanted.

After a couple minutes, Hank shook his head and asked, "Why two neat triangles? And why are they going in different directions?"

Miss Hathaway didn't say anything. Hank knew that she knew he didn't expect an answer from her.

He and Marvin were the detectives here.

Chapter 16

HANK AND MARVIN sat at a table in Tony's Little Italy, a bar on Harrison not far from Cook County Hospital and its morgue. The place was long and narrow, dark and empty except for a couple of old Italian grandpas drinking homemade red at the end of the bar and talking about the good old days.

Hank liked the place. It was homey. Blue and green Christmas-tree lights always hung above the bar, and Tony's mother cooked in the back room. You could smell her baked ziti and lasagna as soon as you walked in, and Tony's red wine really was good.

Marvin was holding his Italian beef sandwich with both hands and chomping down on it. Oil and juice dripped down on his fingers and shirt. There was no way to eat one of these sandwiches neatly except with a knife and fork, but the Marvin Hank knew wouldn't be caught dead doing that.

Hank poured some more red from the pitcher into Marvin's glass and his own, and his partner drank it all down in a shot. Hank sipped his. It tasked like a ripe plum covered in dark chocolate, the kind he sometimes found during the war when they were going through those French villages near the German border.

He sipped some more of the red wine and thought about the suitcase he had seen that first night. It had made him puke. He pictured again the bones broken up and pressed together like pick-up sticks.

Hank wondered why somebody would do that. If you went along with what the prisoner at Shakespeare Station said, you'd figure that some gang of foreigners was trying to intimidate another group of foreigners. But stuff like that happened in backwater countries that nobody but the natives had ever heard of. Bielowicza? Bukovina? Yeah, backwaters...and some not so backwater. He remembered the way the Germans in some of the villages he passed through had looked at the freed slave laborers that followed the G.I.'s from town to town. He remembered one time finding the body of a young Polish girl in a ditch beside a road. She had been raped and clubbed to death, probably with lead pipes. There was nothing left of her face. Even after all the killing stopped, there were some people back there who still hadn't had enough.

But why would that kind of stuff be happening here?

It wasn't easy to figure. Probably the killer was crazy, and he didn't need to have a reason that made sense to anybody but his shrink. Hank had seen crazies like that before. There were the harmless ones, like the guy at the big library downtown who went sneaking around under the long oak tables in the reading room pouring Heinz ketchup into women's shoes — a total nut job. When they caught him, he tried to explain to the cops why he had done it, something about the devil and green cellophane. After listening to the guy for half an hour, Hank gave up. He was sure not even God Himself could figure out why that crazy used ketchup.

And there was the woman who decided one New Year's Eve to stab one person in the face in every saloon on Division Street between the Polish Triangle and Humboldt Park. She did it with a fountain pen filled with indigo blue ink.

When Hank and his old partner Frank Flaherty finally stopped her, she had made it to Wood Street. Ten saloons, seven on the north side of the street, three on the south. And the only reason they stopped her there was because that last bar was around the corner from the precinct station and the place was jammed with cops celebrating the New Year between shifts. The last man she stabbed, in fact, was a patrolman — Skinny Eddie Navaretti, who kept the bars on Rush Street safe for the pilgrims from the suburbs.

Hank remembered talking to her in the police station on Wood after she sobered up the next morning. He asked her why she did it, why she stopped those men and stabbed them with a fountain pen on New Year's Eve, 1951. She was sober that morning and quiet in the cell, solemn in fact. She was sitting there like a schoolteacher on the narrow bunk with her hands folded in her lap. She had washed her face and combed her brown hair, and the women guards had put her in a clean, starchy blue uniform dress. If she'd had a rosary in her hands, she would have looked like a nun.

Her own clothes, in a thick paper bag in the evidence room, were heavy with blood from all the men she had stabbed.

It turned out she wasn't a hooker or a junkie, just a pharmacist's assistant at a drugstore near the Crown Theatre up at the Polish Triangle intersection, not far from where she started her rampage. When Hank asked her why she stabbed those ten men in the face, she looked him hard in the eye and said, "I'm not sorry at all. They deserved it."

It didn't make any sense. She didn't know the men, didn't know anything about them.

The last was a cop and the others were working men or bums, Germans or Polacks, Catholics or Jews. They came in all sizes and shapes, but that didn't matter to her. Nothing mattered except that, like she said, "they deserved it."

And that wasn't all of it. He wondered why she only stabbed one guy in each bar. Why not two? Why not one in every other bar? And why did she stab them in the face?

Yeah, she was screwy. But she had a reason. She knew why she did it. She just wasn't going to tell him or Frank Flaherty or Lieutenant O'Herlihy or her lawyer or the priest from her parish who came down to hear her confession that New Year's Day when she finally sobered up. "I got nothing to confess," she said. "They deserved it."

The guy draining the blood out of the little boys probably had his reasons too. He had his reasons for cutting isosceles triangles into the soles of the boys' feet and hanging the kids up by their thumbs and draining the sweet red juice of life out of them like they were calves or geese or pigs, squealing and swinging their heads, trying to break free. Suitcase Charlie certainly felt that he had his own good reasons for that, and equally good reasons for chopping them up with an axe or cutting them up with a saw when he was done with the draining.

Or at least that's what Hank hoped. He hoped the killer didn't start the chopping and sawing until the boys were drained dead.

Yeah, Suitcase Charlie had his reasons, and they were definitely crazy, but Marvin, Hank and O'Herlihy and the other cops had to try to make sense of those reasons, so they could find Charlie and stop him from doing it again. Killing more boys.

Marvin put down the heel of his sandwich and poured more of the red into his glass and Hank's.

"Hank, my friend," Marvin said, taking on an Irish accent, "you're not drinking. Aye, it's true. You take this job too seriously. If I had known this about you, I would have never agreed to partner up with you. I need a partner who knows, like it says in the Good Book, that there's a time to die and a time to live, a time to cry and a time to laugh, a time for working and a time for eating Tony's mother's beef sandwiches and drinking some of that mother's son's excellent red wine."

Hank picked the glass up, swirled the wine slowly, and sniffed it. "I was just remembering how good the wine was that we drank in France during the war."

"Yeah, that's probably why the Krauts fought so hard to hold on to the place."

Hank finished his wine and put the glass back down on the table. "I've been thinking about all the why's in this case," he said.

"Yeah, there are a hell of a lot of them," Marvin replied, and took a French fry. "This isn't your normal 'stop and ticket' crime."

Hank nodded and pulled his memo pad out of his breast pocket. He started to read: "Why's he killing the kids? Why's he draining their blood? Why's he stripping them naked? Why's he packing them in suitcases? Why's he cutting triangles in their feet? Why isosceles ones, and why pointing in opposite directions? Why is it only boys? Why is he only killing nine-year-olds? Why is he doing it around Humboldt Park? And why, for Christ's sake, isn't anybody claiming these kids?"

Marvin shook his head to the beat of Hank's questions. "Maybe we should finish up here and go back to the scene of the crime? Go back there and see if we can trip over anything?"

"Yeah," Hank said. "And we've been spending our time talking to the good people. Maybe now it's time to talk to the bad ones."

CHAPTER 17

HANK BACKED THE black Ford Mainline into a parking space across from Humboldt Park and a half block down from Jimmy's Pool Hall; they figured they'd make this stop and then report to O'Herlihy down at the station about what they saw at the morgue. It was already 7:15 in the evening, and the sun was hanging low in the west over the warm, misty street. Hank wondered what the night would be like. Would another boy be found in another brown leather suitcase?

Marvin got out of the car and headed for the door of the pool hall.

"Not so fast, partner," Hank said.

Marvin turned and said, "What?"

"Take your hat off and hold it in your hands. You need to do something with your hands when we get inside."

"What're you talking about?" Marvin said. "Are you still talking about that stinking ice-cream parlor on North?"

"Yeah, that and the news stand on Pulaski, near the trolley barns."

"Christ, you're like my mother. You never forget."

"Just be careful, be cool," Hank said, pushing open the glass door leading into the pool hall. "You never know what these Outfit guys are carrying."

"The Outfit? These guys are just hoods. The real mob ain't gonna bother with two-bit pool halls on Division Street. Next thing you'll

be telling me about Al Capone. You do sound like my mother, trying
to scare me with that old shit about the Outfit."

"Thanks, I'll take that as a compliment," Hank said, and looked
around. The room was long and narrow like most of the storefronts
on Division Street. A rainbow-topped Wurlitzer jukebox sat sparkling against one of the walls. It was playing a tune that Hank
liked: Jim Lowe, the country-western crooner, was asking the world
if it knew what was behind the "Green Door". It was a song about
a mystery that nobody could solve.

Hank looked down the narrow room to see what was happening.
Three pool tables ran along the middle of the place on a bare wooden
floor. At the back one, a skinny teenaged kid in a leather jacket was
hunched over the table getting ready to take a shot. Hank thought
his form looked pretty good, the way he held his elbow away from his
body. He seemed careful, like he knew how to run a table. Another
young guy in a white t-shirt and black dungarees was watching him
and drinking an orange soda. Behind the last table, Hank could see
the stairs leading up to the second floor. He knew that upstairs was
where the real action happened.

He followed Marvin over to the counter up against the wall by
the middle table.

A little guy perched on a tall stool there. He was wearing
a narrow-brimmed hat and chewing on a soda straw, but Hank
didn't notice that about him right off. Instead, what Hank's eyes lit
on was his build. He looked like a pint-sized Charles Atlas, a real
bodybuilder. He wore a sleeveless, white t-shirt, and Hank could
tell he did serious work with barbells and weights. The muscles on
his arms looked like they were made of flesh-colored ropes that had
been twisted and twisted and twisted until there wasn't anything

to them but tension, coil and rock hardness. His pectoral and neck muscles were like that too. It looked like he was always just about ready to pop right out of the cotton t-shirt.

"Hey, man" Marvin said to him, putting his hands palms down on the glass counter. "We're looking for your boss."

The little man with the big muscles didn't say anything at first. He just sat on his stool behind the counter and looked at Marvin. Then he said, "Hay?"

It was a question.

"Yeah, we're looking for your boss."

"Hay?" Mr. Muscle repeated as he stood up. "Hay? Hay is for horses."

"What?" Marvin shot back.

"You heard me, cops. Hay's for horses."

"What the hell are you talking about?"

"Marvin, don't worry about it," Hank said. "It's some goofy thing the kids say."

The little guy turned to Hank and said, "Goofy? What do you mean 'goofy'? You calling me goofy?" Then he put his hands down on the glass counter and stared at Hank.

Hank could see the guy's spread, tensed fingers pressing down on the glass, his arms tightening up, his neck muscles moving like there was something alive and squirming slowly inside of them, snakes or electrical wires. Hank lifted his hands and turned them palms up to the guy, cocked his head a little to the left and said, "Maybe my partner and I should go out and come back in again. What do you think, Marvin? Because it seems like you and us got off on the wrong foot here. We're sure not looking for any trouble."

"Speak for yourself," Marvin interrupted, and started around the counter toward the guy.

Hank grabbed Marvin's right arm and held him fast. "Come on, Marvin, cool it." Then, turning to the little guy, he said, "Listen, we're not looking for any kind of beef. You know we're cops. We're just here about the kids who were killed. You know, just asking some questions."

Mr. Muscle cooled down as fast as he'd juiced up. Hank could see it across his whole body. It just sort of lost about a tenth of its mass. The coiled muscles went back in to wherever it was they normally lived.

Hank knew things were going to go more smoothly now. The guy reached for his stool and pulled it toward the counter. Then he gave a short hop and sat down on it. Hank pulled Marvin back to the safe side of the counter without much fight.

"Yeah, those kids," the little guy said and shook his head. "Who'd do a bad thing like that? A crazy 8-ball thing like that?"

"Suitcase Charlie," Marvin offered, and put his hat down on the counter.

"Why the hell didn't the kids' parents keep an eye on them?"

Hank shrugged. "Like they say on TV, that's the $64,000 question. Your boss in?"

"Yeah, you want to talk to him about the kids?"

"That's right."

"Sure, he's in," Mr. Muscle said. "I'll ring you in. I bet you know where the stairs are. Up in back."

Hank knew where the stairs were. He'd been there before, like the little guy said. Upstairs was another long, narrow room, but instead of pool tables there were eight card tables scattered here and there, a bar at the top of the stairs, and a line of slot machines along one of the bare brick walls. Julie London was singing about crying herself a river on another jukebox, this one bubbling up rainbow light near the bar. But the place was mostly empty. A guy in a light-yellow sport coat and sharp-pressed black slacks was dropping nickels into one of the slot machines. He seemed to be the only customer. There wasn't even a bartender working, but Hank wasn't surprised. He checked his Bulova: 7:30. It was still early. The poker boys and the drinkers would be around later.

Up front near the windows overlooking the street, the local Outfit boss Alex Santori sat at one of the round card tables with a couple of his guys. They were dressed in sport coats and open-collared knit shirts like they were going out for drinks at some swank place down along the Gold Coast with a bunch of showgirls.

As the two detectives walked forward, Hank looked at Santori's guys. They looked back at him.

"This is just a social call," Hank said to the one who looked smarter, a guy with a cigarette in his mouth. The guy looked at Alex Santori then, and the boss gave him the high sign. The guys stood up and moved back toward the bar.

"Sit down, my friends," Santori said to Hank and Marvin. "Can I buy the Chicago Police Department a cool drink this fine, warm evening?"

Hank looked at Marvin, and Marvin shrugged.

"Sure, Mr. Santori," Hank said. "I'll take a Bud. My partner, Detective Bondarowicz, he'll take a Seven and Seven."

Santori turned to the bright-looking guy. "You got that, Frankie?"

Frankie nodded.

Hank and Marvin sat down on the wooden chairs. Marvin squirmed a bit. "You got something more comfortable?"

"Not tonight, Detective. The seat's not soft enough for you? You must be like the princess in the story about the pea."

"I guess I am," Marvin said, smiling. "I guess if you don't have anything else, this will do just fine."

"My pleasure," Santori smiled back. "You fellows here about the boys they found butchered in the park last night?"

"Well, Mr. Santori," Marvin said, "there's not much that happens around the park that you and your associates don't know about, so our Lieutenant suggested that me and my partner come down here to ask if you've come across anything that might help us."

"You can bet we've been talking about this. Three dead boys in two days. A terrible thing. I haven't seen anything like it since the war. The Japs didn't much care about who or what they chopped up. Stuff they ain't gonna put in the history books, stuff you don't want to ever see again. You know what I'm saying?"

"Yeah," Marvin said. "I saw some of that war myself."

Santori's guy Frankie came up from the bar and set their drinks in front of Hank and Marvin, and Hank took a long sip of his beer. It was cold and crisp, fresh like it had just been delivered from a brewery down in Cicero.

"This beer's pretty good," Hank said, and put the schooner of beer down. "Thanks."

"You're welcome," Santori replied. "So, you got anything on this Suitcase Charlie? Know anything?"

For a moment, Hank didn't say anything. Instead, he wondered if he should tell Santori how little the police knew. Sure, he was a button man for the Outfit, the crime syndicate that dated back to before Al Capone; but then what did any of that have to do with what was going on around the park right now? Hank couldn't imagine it was the Outfit that was killing these boys and chopping them up, and he was sure that Santori and the other Outfit guys in the area would be happy to see the cops solve this one and pull back some of the extra patrols from the local streets.

Hank finally smiled and said, "We don't know much."

"I figured that. You coming around here is a sure sign. So what do you have?"

Marvin put his glass back down on the table. "We know three or four things. The same guy killed the three boys. He killed them by draining their blood. He carved triangles on the bottoms of their feet."

Hank wished Marvin hadn't mentioned the triangles, but he watched Santori's reaction just the same. He didn't blink, didn't swallow, didn't shrug or shake his head. He didn't put his drink down or pick his hand up. He just stared at Marvin.

Finally, Santori said, "Are you jerking me around, fucking with me?"

"Nope, he carves triangles," Marvin said. "Nice neat pointy triangles on the bottoms of the boys' feet. You know what an isosceles triangle looks like? That's the kind with two sides equal and two angles equal."

"Yeah, they look like this," Hank said, and poured a little beer out of his glass. Then he dipped his index finger in it and drew a triangle on the wooden table's glossy top, an isosceles triangle. "He drains the blood through these cuts."

Santori shook his head now. "This is one sick *oobatz*."

Hank nodded.

Santori took a Lucky Strike out of the pack next to his hand and stuck it in his mouth. He shook his head again, cupped his hands around a wooden match, and lit his cigarette. He drew the smoke in deep and let it play out slowly. "You cops got more than we got."

"What do you got?"

"My associates in the area around the park have been checking around, but they haven't seen anything that might be hooked into these killings. They haven't seen any weird guys hanging around the schoolyards. There's been nothing going on in the park except the usual stuff. My associates haven't heard of any kids being snatched."

Hank leaned back in his chair. He looked at the triangle he had drawn on the table. The beer had mostly dried out as he and his partner talked to Santori, but Hank could still see the outline. The two equal angles, the two equal sides, each about four inches long. Three kids dead.

He looked at Santori.

"This is like those killings last October," the Outfit boss said. "Three kids snatched off the street. The boys found over by the forest preserve. Bobby Peterson and the Schuessler brothers."

"Yeah," Hank said. "Three boys this time too, but now the killer is chopping them up and sticking them in a suitcase and cutting triangles on the soles of their feet. This is some new trick."

Marvin looked up from his drink. "Last time, there was nothing we could do to nail him. He snatched the boys, killed them, and was gone before we knew what hit us. He didn't leave a clue."

Santori brushed a curl of cigarette ash off the table. "This time it looks like he's going to be hanging around for a while. Three dead boys spread across two days. Maybe he'll show his hand."

"I hope so," Hank said to Santori. "Where do you think these kids are coming from? How come nobody is reporting them missing? I mean, it seems crazy to me. It's like those Lost Boys in that

Broadway musical, *Peter Pan* — you know, the one with Mary Martin. Those boys get lost and nobody ever claims them."

"I don't know about *Peter Pan*," Santori said, "but lost kids? The world is full of them. I see two or three come through here every week or so. Sometimes they walk in the front door. Sometimes my sweep man finds them in the alley, sleeping behind the trash cans. They see him, they ask for a handout. I've seen these kids as young as five, boys and girls both."

"Why do they come to you?" Marvin asked.

"Listen, my friend, it's not me. It's this place. A pool hall. They know this is one joint that won't turn them over to the cops, make them go back where they came from, the mom and dad who are beating them stupid or making them work when they don't want to. These kids figure they can come here and maybe even get a handout or make a couple quarters sweeping up so they can buy a hot dog and a Coca Cola."

Hank stood up. "What happens to them, these lost kids?"

"You know what happens, Detective," Santori said. "Mostly nothing. They get tired of hanging out here, and they go back home; or they drift off from here and head west or east. They figure that the world is softer or at least different in Montana or New York. They drift until they get older and get some girl in trouble, or get busted by some cop in Podunk, Nebraska, and get sent away to prison. Some of the kids end up dead. Their bodies turn up alongside a river bed or next to some alley cans somewhere. What happens to them isn't that different from what happened to these three boys in the suitcases."

"You know, Santori," Marvin said, "for a mobster, you're not a lot of laughs."

Santori smiled, showed all his teeth. "What can I tell you, my friends? It must be the melancholy side of my Italian nature. You know, like the clown Pagliacci in that opera, laughing on the outside, crying on the inside?"

Hank shrugged and got to his feet. "I guess we're done here, Mr. Santori. Thanks for your time."

"I wish I could do you boys a favor, but really there's nothing more that I know. Whoever is doing these killings is doing it from the outside. I'm not seeing them. They ain't coming through my joint or any of the saloons down here with the cheap broads and penny-ante hoods."

"I guess you're right," Hank said. "One last question. If you were looking for this killer, who would you be looking at?"

Santori laughed. "I hope you boys aren't asking me because you think I'm a killer and I'd know what another one looks like."

"None of us are angels here, Santori," Hank said. "I'm just asking the question because you've been here and there and seen a lot of guys, all different kinds of people."

"Thanks, chief," Santori said and nodded. "Who'd I be looking for? A guy who's got a lot of time on his hands, lots of crazy thoughts bubbling around his brain. I'd look for a guy who knows a good piece of luggage, leather. Maybe a Brit or a German, definitely not a Frenchman. Could be an Italian. But only from the north."

Marvin downed the rest of his Seven and Seven and interrupted Santori. "Say, can I get another one of these to go?"

Santori turned to the bar and signaled the order to Frankie.

"You mention all those foreigners," Marvin said, "but you didn't say he might be an American. How come?"

"Too many clues. A guy like you or me, an American, I mean, when we kill, we like to do it fast. We want to be in and out. A bullet in the head, a shiv in the back. Quick. We don't want to be thinking about leaving a lot of clues laying around. But not this guy. This guy wants to take it slow. He's like a fancy cook. He chops, he cuts, he makes little engravings here and there. He drains the blood, waits — what? — thirty minutes or an hour for it to drain. I bet he bled the two kids from last night separately. First one and then another. It's like he's following some kind of complicated recipe. Maybe he is a Frenchie, I don't know. That's just the way I feel about it. He's doing it cold, he ain't doing it hot."

"Doing it cold," Hank nodded. "Who's the coldest bastard you know?"

Santori moved his head back, just a little, and looked Hank in the eye. "Joe Rosetti. Joey Roses."

CHAPTER 18

LEAVING JIMMY'S Pool Hall, Hank walked over to the Ford Mainline while Marvin headed down to the newsstand on the corner. He said he wanted to get the evening paper, see what was happening.

Hank stood by the car and waited, pulled a Chesterfield from his pack and lit up. He liked the hot drag of the smoke against the back of his throat. He didn't get it, why people started smoking filtered cigarettes. He looked across Division at the entrance to Humboldt Park.

The shadows of the maple trees were lengthening around the statue there on the corner. Hank knew the statue. It was a piece of work molded out of a mound of marble or something like that. Maybe it was carved out of a single big rock. Hank had seen it plenty, and he always liked it. It was there when he was a kid playing ball in the park, and he bet it would be there when he was an old man shooting the shit with the other old guys on the benches. Nobody was going to move that hunk of rock. It must weigh a couple tons.

The statue was called "Home", and it was as simple as its name. It showed a guy kneeling on one leg and hugging his daughter. She looked to be about his own daughter Margaret's age. The guy was some kind of working man. That was clear. He wore a cloth cap with a lantern strapped across the front of it. He was probably a guy working in a mine, although there weren't any mines around

Chicago — not that Hank knew of — and there was a lunch pail set down in front of him and his daughter. He was hugging her like she was the last best thing in a world steaming with shit and smelling of death.

Hank looked at the statue and wondered if maybe the killer chopping up those boys was doing it here in this neighborhood because he knew this statue and hated it, thought it lied about what home was. Maybe the killer never had a home or a daughter or a son and was pissed off at people who had them, and maybe he wanted to make those people suffer like he suffered. And he'd do it by killing their kids.

It was a crazy string of thoughts. Hank knew it, but it was no crazier than what had happened in the park last night when it was raining, and what might happen again tonight. There had been three boys killed in two days. Maybe in the morning, the cops would find another one or two.

Or maybe three. Yeah, maybe three — if the progression kept moving in the direction it had been going. That would make it six dead, and what about the day after?

He turned his head and saw Marvin walking back slowly, reading the evening paper, *The Chicago American*.

Hank took a drag on his cigarette and blew smoke toward the Ford. "Anything about Suitcase Charlie?"

"They found the first kid's parents. It says here, they live up on the North Side, near Wrigley Field. The kid disappeared on his way to the drugstore." Marvin's eyes suddenly went big as he handed the paper to his partner.

"What the fuck, you're smoking?"

"Yeah."

"Where did you get it?"

"I got my sources," Hank said as dropped his cigarette on the sidewalk and took up the paper. He scanned the article quickly. Then he paused for a long moment over a photograph of the boy. It was the kid's First Holy Communion picture. The boy had blonde hair and was wearing a navy-blue suit. His hands were folded and raised in prayer in front of his chest, and there was a rosary with little white beads wound around his fingers.

Hank folded the paper. "Jesus, why didn't the parents report the kid missing?"

"They did. It says so on page two," Marvin said. "When the kid didn't come home that afternoon, they first looked around the neighborhood, checked in with all of his friends. They even tracked down the kids he hated. Nothing. That's when they went to the police station. It says the cops at the precinct house there didn't send the report in until this morning. They were busy with a lot of paperwork."

"Jesus, they waited two days to file the report?" Hank said, and pulled another cigarette out of his breast pocket and lit it with his IMCO. "I bet it's gonna be the same story with the other two boys."

"Yeah, the old lard-asses in the precinct houses are playing pinochle and drinking Schlitz instead of doing their paperwork."

Hank took the cigarette out of his mouth and pinched a shred of tobacco off the tip of his tongue with his thumb and index finger. He looked at the light brown, wet dot of stuff.

He thought about his daughter. She'd be winding down for the night right now, maybe reading in bed, her old stuffed panda Candy next to her, probably sharing the pillow with her. She'd been sleeping with it since she was three years old. She never felt she had anything to worry about if it was with her. It kept her safe. Candy was like a prayer.

He rolled the piece of tobacco between his fingers and flicked it away.

CHAPTER 19

THE LAST BITS of the setting sun were shimmering across the lagoon as Hank and Marvin showed up at the boathouse parking lot. It went down in an orange and gray sauce behind the maple and birch trees and hills that bordered the west end of Humboldt Park.

The park was cooling now, and the big parking lot was empty.

Leaning against the black Ford, Hank lit a cigarette and thought about Joe Rosetti. That's the second time his name had come up. The bartender at the White Eagle mentioned him earlier. And now Santori, the Outfit guy. Hank knew Joey Roses was a cold bastard, but that didn't mean Joey had anything to do with the killings going on around here.

Hank knew Joey. Grew up with him, went to grade school and church with him when he was a boy. Knew his father too. Teddy Rosetti. Teddy Roses. A crazy man. He'd get drunk and tear Joey's pajamas off and whip him naked through the streets. The old guy would do it to his daughter, too. A real wild man. Nobody knew what happened to him. He just disappeared right before the war, leaving Joey and his sister to pretty much make their own way. And they had: his sister turned tricks on Division and Wells, and Joey pimped for her 'til the mob guys broke his hands. Now he ran with a mixed-race gang down on the edge of the color line.

Hank took a couple quick short drags on his cigarette and shook the smoke slowly out of his mouth.

Marvin was off somewhere. Leaving the car, he said he'd be right back, but he wasn't. He said he had to take a piss, so he went down to the men's room in the basement of the boathouse. The toilet was open day and night, every day of the year including Christmas and the Fourth of July.

Hank looked toward the bridge west of the boathouse. He was surprised to see that the police barricades were gone. The cops had set them up earlier when they were searching the area where the suitcases were found, but now they were gone. He wondered why they had been taken down. Were they calling off the search for the killer? It didn't seem likely. He was surprised too that there were no other cops around. He figured there'd be some uniforms searching the grass near the bridge or the pavement in the parking lot where Chris Wessel, the DuPage County kid, got out of his daddy's blue Cadillac and whacked the guy the papers were calling "Suitcase Charlie" and "the Polack Killer" with his tire iron. But there weren't any cops around. The city must have needed the boys in blue someplace else.

Hank turned to the boathouse and listened to how quiet the park was. He remembered back during the 1950 census, reading that the government estimated that more than three and a half million people lived within a ten-mile radius of this park, but tonight Hank found it hard to believe. He could just as easily be in Alaska, in one of those million-acre national forests where the deer and the antelope played. Or on the moon.

There was nothing here. No sign of life, no movement. He couldn't even see a light or hear a sound from the four busy streets that blocked this section of the park off from the rest of the city and the world beyond it. Maybe if there was some cloud cover, he'd hear something or see some reflected light from the four lanes of traffic on the big avenue just north of the park, but without any low clouds there was nothing.

It reminded him of the war, some town he couldn't remember the name of any more, that his squad had come upon late some evening. The Krauts had spilt, left for someplace further east, leaving the town mostly rubble. Hank remembered staring out at the ruins, the bricks, the darkness and silence, and he remembered thinking there were people in those ruins, German moms and dads and kids, all watching him and wondering what kind of evil he was going to bring down upon them the next morning when the sun rose and its light pierced through the slow rising smoke of their homes.

Hank took another drag on his Chesterfield. What was keeping Marvin? What was he doing in that toilet? Reading the funny papers?

Hank hated the boathouse men's room with its broken stall doors and leaking pipes, the crap and brown toilet paper smeared on the floors, its stink of piss and hoboes, its grafitti, its phone numbers and long slimy cocks carved into the wood of the stalls. Faggots too. Plenty of them. Sad old men and sad young men looking to cop a blow or a feel. The city, Hank figured, ought to close the place down and burn the boathouse on top of it.

What was taking Marvin so long? He should have just pissed here behind the car. The city wouldn't mind. Better that than going down into that open sewer of a toilet, but Marvin was probably doing more than just pissing. He was probably taking five for a crap and a smoke.

Hank needed to stretch his legs, so he started walking toward the statue of Alexander von Humboldt, the guy the park was named after. The statue of the German explorer wasn't much to look at — just a self-important-looking Kraut in fancy clothes. Funny that it was still up. He thought that it would have been taken down during the war, melted down and shaped into a bomb the flyboys could drop on Hitler's home town. Guess somebody must have liked it, even though the statue of A. Von didn't ring inside Hank the way the one called "Home" at the park's entrance did.

Besides, this city with its Polacks, Krauts, Wops, and Bohunks had too many of these statues. Maybe some day they would be building them to commemorate the grand work he and Marvin had done for Chicago.

That'll be the day, Hank thought.

The suitcases had been found not far from where Humboldt's statue stood. Looking north along Humboldt Drive, Hank could see the bridge that carried the drive over the lagoon, and he could see the statue of Leif Erikson on the other side of the bridge. That was the statue that the "Polack Killer" had mentioned. It was where he said he found the suitcases and started dragging them home in the rain. Suitcase Charlie must have just dumped them there. Pulled up in his car and dumped the suitcases, then skedaddled.

The Polack must have dragged them across the bridge and just past the statue of Humboldt. That's when the Dooper kid hit the Polack with the tire iron. Was there a clue here somewhere? Did Erikson and Humboldt have something in common? Is that why the killer dropped those suitcases between the statues? Was the killer a Viking like Erikson, or a German like Humboldt? Or a hybrid German-Viking?

Hank wished it was all like it was in the movies or TV. Some Basil Rathbone or Charlie Chan looking at a single square foot of sidewalk and figuring out all the clues that lay there. Like that Steve Wilson on *Big Town*, the show Hazel liked to watch on TV.

And maybe one of those detectives could explain to Hank why the killer dropped those clues here. Two suitcases, each with about 90 pounds of dead boy in it. Those were big clues. No TV detective needed a magnifying glass to find them. And the killer left them there in the open, in the middle of a park in the middle of the second largest city in America, halfway between Leif and A. von Humboldt, a Viking explorer and a German explorer. Maybe Santori was right and the killer wanted the cops to find those clues.

And it was the same with the first suitcase that was dropped off on the corner of Washtenaw and Evergreen, between the convent of the Sisters of St. Joseph and the White Eagle Tap. The guy who was doing this killing wasn't trying to hide what he did. He wanted the cops and everybody else to know he did what he did.

Why?

Why?

Hank was back to that long string of why's he and Marvin got tangled up in over lunch at Tony's Little Italy. Hank looked at his cigarette. It was almost out, just a butt. Thinking about the murders, he had forgotten to smoke it. He flicked it up into the darkness and watched it come rocketing down and smashing into the pavement of the parking lot like a fistful of stars.

Then he started walking toward the men's toilets in the basement of the brick boathouse. Marvin had been in there for too long.

As Hank reached the first concrete step leading down to the toilets, the dark gray wooden door started opening. There was a light bulb in a cage above the door. The light it threw wasn't great, but it was good enough for Hank. He stopped.

Marvin was pushing his way through the door with his right shoulder. Hank saw his partner's knuckles. They were bloody and scraped, and there was a cut above his left eye that was running a red bead down his face. Marvin's army-issued .45 was dangling from his right hand, a handkerchief from his left.

"Jesus, what happened?" Hank asked as he hurried down the steps.

"What happened was a couple fags in there blowing each other. I had to teach them a lesson. Where were you?"

Before Hank could answer, Marvin stopped dead and fell back toward the door. His weight pushed it closed behind him, and he continued falling backward and sliding down the door as Hank grabbed him. Falling, the two of them crashed onto the men's rest room floor. Marvin grunted as Hank's weight collapsed on top of him.

Hank immediately started to rise and pull his partner up. "Come on, man. Get up. Come on."

"The short one was tough," Marvin said, and paused and then whispered, "a hard case."

Hank turned his head to the stalls as he threw Marvin's arm over his shoulder and started to carry him out. He could see the men Marvin had fought. They were in separate stalls, their bodies crumbled against the toilets. One of the men was groaning and starting to move. The other guy was still. He wasn't moving or groaning. Marvin must have busted the guy's leg. It was turned a funny way. He had only one shoe.

Marvin had done a job on them.

"Stupid thing to do, Marvin. You ought to leave those guys alone. They aren't hurting anybody."

"Says you," Marvin whispered through a cough as they stumbled out. "Where to?"

"Let's get out of here and go see Joey Roses."

Chapter 20

IT WAS HOT again outside the park, and Hank had his car window down. He was driving east on Lake Street under the elevated tracks.

Friday night on Lake was a world of flicking yellow neon signs telling Hank to drink and drink some more because tomorrow would probably be worse than today but not as bad as the day after. Here were the bars and the juke joints and dance halls that promised him something better than what he had: Terri's and Long Tall Gal's, Red Rose and Lou's, Memphis Belle's and Lucky Lady's.

Hank didn't think Suitcase Charlie was in any of these places. A guy like that, ready to carve up a little boy and toss him in a pullman case, he wasn't the kind to stop for a Manhattan and a little socializing with the kinds of women, black or white, he'd find in these bars.

Driving down Lake Street, the borderline between white Chicago and Negro Chicago, Hank thought about how, in the end, there really wasn't much difference between the North Side of Chicago and the South Side. The houses south of the Lake Street El track were like the houses north of it, either brick or wood, three-story apartment buildings or two-story single-family houses carved into flats, but there was one big difference. If you were a black man, you couldn't live north of the El; and if you were a white man, you wouldn't want to live south of it, because south of the El was District Five and West Town and Bronzeville: another country.

And in that country, there was Joey Roses and the coloreds, Puerto Ricans, and white boys he ran with. His gang liked to hang out in one of the apartment buildings down there on Washington Boulevard, a big one, twelve units.

Easing to a stop for a red light on California, Hank looked over at Marvin. He was pushed back in his seat, his eyes closed, his head thrown back. He'd been quiet for most of the trip down here, except that once in a while Hank could hear him draw in his breath in a fast jagged whisper. Maybe his partner had some broken ribs. Those guys in the boathouse must have worked him over almost as good as he worked them.

The light flipped to green.

"You going to be okay for this?" Hank asked.

"For Joey Roses and these hoods?" Marvin said and turned his head toward Hank. "Yeah. You got a pint under your seat?"

"I think so. Maybe half a pint, Dewar's."

"Pass it here, daddy-o. It's what the doctor ordered."

Hank gripped the wheel with his left hand and reached under the seat with his right. His fingers found the small flask, and he passed it to his partner. Hank could hear Marvin working the cap off the bottle.

Marvin drank and Hank drove, and both watched the Friday night action in the street. Things were jumping in the southland. Lake Street under the El was the borderland, the place where whites mixed with the coloreds, and the coloreds showed off what they had: juke joints and beer joints. Dark blacks who were picking cotton for ten bucks a week before the war were now strutting around down here with high-yellow babes in mink and red satin. College kids came down all the way from Skokie and Evanston to see what jiving was really like.

It wasn't bad here, not like the real stuff further south, down around 47th Street. There you could hear race music like nothing you heard on the radio. There you could also buy a switchblade, a pistol, a whore, a reefer. Or a shot of heroin.

Waiting for the light to change at the corner of California and Lake, Hank took the bottle from Marvin and finished it off with a long pull. It burned as it went down, but the burning felt familiar and good. Liquid lava.

Hank turned his head to the right.

A white woman in a short blue dress and high black heels was standing there. She had the light, but she wasn't stepping off the curb. She was just standing there. Hank could see that her lips were full and red, and her eyes were dark. She looked at Hank and smiled. He smiled back.

She put out her tongue and fluttered it down and up. It looked like she was lapping milk. She fluttered her tongue again, up and down.

As the car pulled away from the light, Marvin groaned, "Oh, Mama. Pull in here, Hank. I think I know this lady."

"No time for that bullshit."

"Really, man, I know her. I think I went to high school with her. Give me five minutes to catch up on old times."

"We're looking for Joey Roses."

"Come on. Pull over. You call the Lieutenant and fill him in, and I'll reminisce."

Hank's foot eased up on the gas pedal. "Calling the Lieutenant probably is a good idea. I better do it from a pay phone."

"Sure, drop me off here," Marvin said as the car started to slow. "There's a drug store down the block."

Chapter 21

IT WAS ALMOST eleven o'clock, and Hank was calling his Lieutenant at home from a colored drug store on the south side of Lake Street. He knew what O'Herlihy would say even before he picked up the phone to dial. It wouldn't be happy, but he had to make the call.

After a dozen rings, somebody picked up.

There was a long silence, and finally the Lieutenant answered, "What?"

"Sir, I'm just checking in."

"You were supposed to get back to me about those cuts in the soles of those boys' feet this afternoon, Purcell. Eleven at night isn't afternoon."

"Sorry about that, sir. I tried to call the station, but you were gone already."

"I was there 'til after ten."

"Yeah, that's what the desk sergeant told me."

"You should have called earlier. You and your goofball partner think this is like some Mike Hammer caper. Like you're some kind of private dicks chasing leads. That's bullshit. You're part of a team, and if you want to stay detectives you got to play it that way."

Listening to the Lieutenant, Hank nodded. "We got tied up following some leads."

"I bet."

There was a drawn-out silence, and then the Lieutenant said, "You're on the phone. Tell me about the cuts. Did they look like the killer was marking some kind of specific forms, designs? The photos didn't really nail that down. That's why I sent you and your partner down there to see Hathaway at the morgue."

"Yes, sir, the cuts seemed deliberate. Two isosceles triangles on the soles of all the boys who were murdered. The one on the left foot pointing toward the toes, and the one on the right foot pointing toward the heel. All deep cuts, straight, done carefully."

"What do you make of it?"

"The killer is sending some kind of message."

"Purcell, I expected a comment like that from your partner, but I thought you were smarter than that. What the hell kind of message?"

"Well, sir, I'm no expert, but the triangle is sometimes seen as a religious symbol. Going all the way back to the Egyptians. The pyramids are triangular, and I think what the Egyptians were trying to do was connect with their gods, or maybe show their godliness. The Masons use the triangle as a symbol of the eye of God. That's what you see on the dollar bill."

"Hmm. But that Masonic triangle is one with equal sides. You said the ones the killer is carving are isosceles ones."

"Yes, sir, two longer equal sides and a short one."

"So where does that get us, Purcell?"

"I don't know. And maybe the triangles aren't symbolizing God or gods. Maybe they're symbolizing other things. Maybe like a mountain or a woman's femininity?"

"What the hell? Femininity?"

"Sure, an inverted triangle looks like…"

"Yeah, I get it."

There was silence again. Hank looked around the drug store. It was empty except for a pharmacist way in the back and a clerk sitting at the cash register reading a paper. Hank wondered if there was anything new about Suitcase Charlie in it.

"Purcell, we got too many clues and not enough. And I'm worried that the morning will bring us another killing. Better call it a day now. By the way, where are you two?"

"We're following some leads. Two of my regular informants mentioned Joey Roses, a local grifter. So we're looking for him."

"I know Rosetti. Small potatoes. But maybe he knows something. Where you at now? Where you calling from?"

Now it was Hank's turn to be silent.

Finally, he answered, "We're in an all-night drug store on Lake just west of California."

"South Side?"

"Yes, sir."

"What the hell are you doing in the ghetto?"

"Following leads."

"I know Bondarowicz. If he's there, you guys aren't following leads. Put him on."

"I can't sir. He's out in the car."

"And I bet I know what's he's doing. Listen, Purcell, I want both of you guys out of there before you get into some kind of trouble that has me explaining why two of my detectives are working the colored area."

"Yes, sir," Hank said as he heard the phone click on the other end and then go dead.

He checked that his wallet was in his pocket and walked toward the front door. He thought for a moment about calling Hazel. It sure would be nice to talk to her. Ask how the kid was. Hear what Hazel had been watching on TV.

But he didn't make the call.

The clerk was still reading the paper, and Hank stopped at the counter and looked down at it. It was the colored paper, *The Chicago Defender*.

"Yes, sir, can I help you?" the clerk asked.

"Sure, anything in there about Suitcase Charlie?"

"No, sir, the *Defender* is a weekly paper and the killings are too recent. There hasn't been a new edition since the bodies were found."

"But you know about the killings?"

"Of course I do. I may be colored, but I follow the white news in Chicago. Hard to ignore it."

"White news? Why do you call it the white news?"

"No colored man would have done it. Colored man do a lot of bad things, but nothing like this. It's a white man cutting up these little schoolboys."

Hank looked at the clerk. He looked about 40 years old, working the late shift. Educated. Smart too.

"Why do you say it's a white man?"

"All the evil in the world come from the white man, sir."

Hank said, "Hmmm," nodded, and continued out into the street to find Marvin.

It had been a long night, and it was going to get longer. The Lieutenant wanted them to head back home, but he and Marvin were still looking for Joey Roses.

CHAPTER 22

HANK STOPPED AT the third-floor landing and waited for Marvin to catch up. The staircase smelled of urine and fried onions, rotting cabbage and garbage. It was mostly dark, too. A little light filtered through from the bottom of the apartment door in front of Hank. A little more came from the skylight in the ceiling above his head. It was just enough so that he could see Marvin moving up the stairs slowly, holding onto the wooden banister and hauling himself forward and up. At least he wasn't groaning.

Not that it would make much difference.

Hank figured that Joey Roses and his friends knew they had company coming up the stairs. They knew it before Hank and Marvin even got out of the Ford and started up the wooden front steps. Only one kind of white man came out here south of the Lake Street El late at night: a cop.

Everybody knew that the cops were here, and the jig was probably up for somebody. The kids on the street, the juvenile delinquents and their debs on the corner, even the old dolls sitting by their windows with nothing to think about but their pet canaries — they all knew the cops were here, and they were all getting the word to Joey and his friends that the cops were coming up the stairs after them. Huffing and puffing, and getting meaner with each step.

Waiting on the landing, Hank reached his right hand under the lapels of his jacket and felt the wooden grip panels of the revolver in his shoulder holster. The Colt .38 Detective Special was a short-barreled piece, the kind that his partner liked to call a snubby. Marvin was always joking that Hank should just leave the revolver at home and let him take care of business with his .45 automatic. Hank's response was always the same. He'd shrug. He didn't care what Marvin said, and he didn't care what kind of heat Marvin carried. The little .38 felt right.

Marvin turned the corner and started up the last flight of stairs. His breathing seemed steadier to Hank now, and his climbing wasn't as raggedy as Hank thought it would be. That was good.

"How you doing there, pal?" Hank whispered.

"I'm coming, Pops," Marvin whispered back. "Don't stop 'til you get to the top."

Hank nodded and waited for him to get to the landing and catch his breath. He could see that his partner was doing better now. The scotch he drank in the car must have pushed back some of the pain, and the reunion with his high-school sweetheart beneath the El tracks must have done the rest. When he got to the third-floor landing, Marvin pulled his bloody handkerchief out of his back pocket and mopped his forehead.

"Ready?" Hank asked.

"Absolutely, two times."

There was enough light for them to see that there was no name on the door. Hank moved toward it and pressed his ear against the wood for a moment, listening. He thought he could hear some voices, but he couldn't make out what they were saying. Someone laughed. Someone else shouted, "Bastard." In the background, a radio or a record player was on, mixing a tune with the talking. Hank knew the song, recognized the melody.

It was the one with the crazy lyrics that had just come out — "Be Bop a Lula". Now Hank made out some of the words: "Be Bop a Lula, she's my baby. Be Bop a Lula — I don't mean maybe."

He took a step back and knocked on the door.

The door didn't open for a long moment, and then when it started opening, it opened slow. A thin rectangle of light grew wider and wider on the floor of the landing until it took in Hank, his partner Marvin, and the landing behind them completely. Hank blinked in the light and looked at the guy who was pulling the door open.

He was something. A light-skinned Negro, and tall, tall as you get. He looked seven feet tall, maybe taller. His wavy conked hair was piled about four inches high on his head, and there were three parallel vertical scars on each cheek, cut deep. In his left hand, the Negro held a length of chain, maybe five feet long.

Hank heard Marvin behind him say, "What the…!" And Hank himself took a step back from the door. Here was trouble; Hank reached into his jacket for his shoulder holster and started pulling his revolver out.

But the tall Negro didn't flinch or go rigid or look startled. He didn't do anything. He just looked at Hank, staring at him blankly. After a moment, the colored man pursed his wide, cracked lips. It was like he didn't know what he looked like, or what effect the chain in his hand would have on his cop visitors, the kinds of questions it would cause them to consider. He seemed lost in thought like he was some wavy-haired African Albert Einstein contemplating his own deep and solitary thoughts about the molecular structure of time, mass, and gravity.

Hank stared back at him with his revolver's wooden grip in his right hand, ready for the man's next move.

When the Negro finally spoke, it seemed to come as a surprise to all three men standing at the door — Marvin, Hank, and the tall wavy-haired Negro himself. He looked at Hank again and then noticed Marvin and said to the two detectives in a soft, dreamy kind of voice, "Oh, you here for that white boy? That Joey?"

Hank eased his body toward the door and said, "Yeah, that's right. We're here to see Joe Rosetti. The guy they call Joey Roses."

"I gets him for you," the tall Negro said, and then after a pause, he turned and walked down the long shadowy corridor toward the back of the apartment. As he walked, he dragged the chain across the bare wooden floor; it gave off a long, loud clanking sound that must have been hell on the neighbors below.

"Some kind of greeting," Marvin said behind him.

"Yeah," Hank replied, and stepped into the apartment. Marvin followed him.

Under the two-bulb ceiling lamp, Hank could see pretty well. He was sure this was supposed to be the dining room, but there was no dining-room table or china cabinet here, just a card table with three wooden folding chairs around it. The table had some newspapers and beer bottles on it. The only other thing in the room was a radiator with a yellow plastic table-model radio sitting on it. This was what Hank must have heard from the other side of the door. The radio was tuned to a rock-and-roll station cycling through the hit parade. He cocked his head toward the radio. They cued up a song he liked, "In the Still of the Night". It was soft and yearning.

Hank sniffed. The apartment smelled as bad as the staircase. Piss and sour cabbage.

He looked left toward the living room. It was all pretty sparse. There was a TV set in a blond wood cabinet in one corner, and a stack of mattresses piled four feet high up against the wall. Partially-filled paper shopping bags were scattered under the windows and beside the mattresses.

Marvin tapped Hank on the shoulder, and Hank turned around.

"Where's everybody?" Marvin asked. "I thought I heard voices in here."

"Yeah, me too."

"You think they split?"

"I didn't hear any doors, but it looks like it," Hank said, and walked into the living room.

It was darker there. The only light was coming from the ceiling light in the dining room. There was another shadowy hallway that led from the living room to the back of the apartment. Hank could see three closed doors along the hallway that led to a door with a glazed window that probably led out to the service corridor. Beyond the window, there was a dim yellow light.

"In the Still of the Night" ended with a "doo shooby doo" and another song started. Hank didn't know this one, and he didn't like it. It was fast and loud and had a guitar on it that sounded like the guy playing it was strung tighter than a leather whip, like he was on bennies or jap speed. The singer was shouting about Louisiana and New Orleans and colored boys and being good.

Hank figured Marvin probably didn't like the song either. He walked over to the radio and turned it off.

"Hey, I hope they don't mind," Hank smiled.

"Hell with them," Marvin whispered.

"Why you whispering? They know we're here."

"I got a headache."

Hank shook his head and pointed toward the hallway that led to the door with the glass window. "You follow the man with the chain, because I don't think he's coming back."

"Right."

"I'll check out this end of the flat."

"Right," Marvin said again as he turned to follow the big colored man.

———

Hank walked up to the first of the three doors along the hallway and checked the knob. It turned easily, and he shoved the door open. The room had a bare mattress on the floor and a couple of woven Navaho blankets folded on top of it. About a dozen cardboard boxes were scattered or stacked around the room. Hank moved over to the nearest one and opened it up. The box was filled with black-handled switchblades. Hank took one and pressed the button. As advertised, the blade zipped out of the handle fast as a fish. Most of the other boxes had switchblades too. There must have been a couple thousand shivs. Hank pushed the blade back into the handle and dropped the knife into his pants pocket. He figured Joey and his pals were going to sell these to school kids for a quarter apiece.

Hank turned to a box in the corner. It was labeled Cutty Sark, and contained quart bottles of the whisky. He grabbed a bottle for Marvin and walked over to the window and lifted the shade.

There was nothing to see but a brick wall and, above it, some dark, un-starry sky. Next to the window there was a closet door. When he turned its knob, nothing happened. He tried applying pressure, but that didn't do anything either. It was probably locked. He turned around and looked at the door that led in from the hallway. There was a key in its lock. He pulled it out. If he was lucky, this key was the master that would fit all the doors inside the apartment.

He was lucky.

He turned the key and the lock tumbled open. He pulled the knob. The door gave a little and then stuck. He pulled harder, and the door shot open and smashed him across the bridge of his nose and his forehead.

Then a fist hammered his forehead. Hank's head snapped back and snapped forward, and the fist hammered him again, hammered him good. Tumbling backwards, he saw the face at the other end of the fist. It was Joey Roses.

And then Hank's eyes filled with stars and clouds and his hearing gave way. He collapsed quick and hard against the boxes of switchblades.

———

That was all Hank knew for a while — until Marvin lifted his head and poured a thin stream of Cutty Sark over his lips.

The stinging stirred Hank, and he slowly came a little bit awake. The scotch burned his lips, but he couldn't open them. It was like he had forgotten how to open his lips and how to swallow. Marvin poured more of the booze over his partner's lips, and it streamed down his right cheek for a moment. Hank tried to shake the Cutty Sark off his face then, but that just made more of a mess, spraying and dribbling booze down past his cheeks and neck and onto his sport coat. He blinked his eyes open but couldn't see much, just what he had seen before he passed out, stars and clouds, and a fist power-driving into the bridge of his nose.

Then Marvin started baby-slapping Hank's cheeks, and Hank started seeing things clearly again, more or less. The stars were losing their glow, and the fist drifted into the clouds, and the clouds started to drift back to where they came from.

Hank could see again, and he realized his hearing was coming back too, little by little, at least in his left ear. The right was still ringing like there was a crazy drill in a permanent state of electrical agitation going on and on in there. But the left ear was being sensible.

"Hank," Marvin shouted.

"Yeah, I can hear you. Not so loud. Headache."

"What the hell happened?"

"I opened a door and got hit. Two or three times. Then I was down, crumbled across these boxes. He was on top of me and beating me silly."

"So you saw him? Did you recognize him?"

"Yeah, it was Joey Roses. Before he hammered me, I saw him."

"If it was Joey," Marvin said, "he's gone."

Chapter 23

MARVIN REACHED HIS hand out, and Hank took it and pulled himself up. He was wobbly at first. Vertigo from the punches to his ears, he figured. He felt like his head was going to slam into the floor or one of the walls any minute, but he kept moving, bit by bit, with his partner's help. The world was a crazy carousel on the edge of an abyss.

"You sit on these mattresses here," Marvin said. "I'll take a look at some of the other rooms."

Hank nodded and let himself be led to the stack of mattresses in the living room. He sat there holding onto the edge of the top mattress, his head doing a figure eight, and watched Marvin go back to the other end of the apartment, down that corridor that probably led to the kitchen. Hank saw him open a door and disappear, and then in a couple minutes he reappeared. Moving down the corridor, his partner disappeared into and reappeared three more times, and each time Hank's head was less dizzy, more stable.

And then Marvin shouted his name and kept shouting his name, in a weird way that made Hank think at first that Marvin was pulling his leg, but then he realized that not even a jokey cop like Marvin would be shouting for the joy of some gag when his partner was as beat up as Hank was. He was saying "Hank!" over and over, and Hank knew he had to stand up regardless of the tricks his head was pulling.

He pushed himself off the mattresses and collapsed right back down, and he fought not to let his head crash into the mattress the way it wanted to. He then realized he couldn't rush it. He tried getting up again, this time inching up along the wall until he was standing, but standing didn't seem to be what his body wanted to be doing. His head felt like it was carrying the weight of his whole frame, and that weight wanted to get down onto the floor as fast as it could. Hank fought to keep his face from slamming against the wooden floorboards. He stuck his arm out and propped himself against the wall and let the wall give him the balance that he couldn't find any other way. Holding onto the wall, he followed the sound trail of Marvin's crazy wailing.

He was calling "Hank, Hank!" someplace down in the darkness of the back of the apartment.

Hank made it through the dining room and into the hallway, past the doors that Marvin had opened and closed, past the kitchen into the last room that opened off the kitchen.

There was a bedroom there, off the kitchen.

A couple of full-sized mattresses were stacked there like in the other rooms, and not much else in the way of furniture, just some bags and some boxes, some opened, some closed. The closed boxes had junk on them, cups, plates, ashtrays. Whoever was using this room used the boxes for end tables. The room was pretty well lit up, too — a three-bulb ceiling fixture threw a lot of light, pushed back a lot of shadows. Hank wished there were more shadows.

He stood in the doorway, a hand on each side of the frame, but he was still shaky. Now it was mostly in his legs. They were like noodles. Marvin stood in front of him. He had stopped calling Hank's name in that crazy way, with that off-beat modulation, a sort of low, husky tremolo. Marvin must have known Hank was there behind him on his noodly legs because he wasn't saying anything now, just sort of looking at the mess on the mattress. That's what it was, a mess, covered in blood.

A full-sized mattress holds a lot of stuffing, but the dead girl had bled out into it, and the mattress looked like a giant red sponge. Hank was wobbly, and he felt like he needed to put his head somewhere fast, or it would fall down under its own weight, but he didn't know where he could put it. Not on the mattress. Maybe on the floor.

He looked around and wondered how this mess fit in with the other, bigger mess, the one Suitcase Charlie was making.

There weren't any suitcases in the room, and the girl wasn't chopped up into six- and twelve-inch sections like the three boys were. She was all in one piece, but she was naked like them, bare as God made her except for a blue scarf with tiny white flowers tied around her neck. And those boys, they were white, and she was black. Older, too, than they were, Hank figured. They were nine years old, and she was eleven or twelve. It was difficult to tell with girls, colored or white. Some seemed to mature faster than others. This one, she had breasts coming in already; and if she hadn't been stabbed so many times in her belly and crotch, Hank would probably have seen the start of pubic hairs coming in down there.

She was a mess. Hank could see that she had been beaten a lot, too, around the face and breasts. Dark bruises showed through her dark skin, a thick brocade of purple, blue, and green pain. Her open eyes were yellow, and they were staring at the ceiling with its bright light.

Hank turned to Marvin and expected him to say something funny. He was always saying stuff, joking about this dead guy or that one. Hank remembered one time when they found a drunk frozen dead in an alley off of Western Avenue on a cold New Year's Day: his partner went up and shook the man's stiff hand because he was the first corpse of the New Year. But Marvin wasn't joking tonight. He wasn't saying anything.

"We better call this in," Hank said. "Did you see a phone?"

Marvin made a soft sound, a "hmm", and said nothing else.

"Marvin, we got to call it in. Did you see a phone?"

"Yeah, I mean no."

"Which is it?"

"No, I didn't see a phone."

"I'm still dizzy. Do you think you can call this in on the car radio?"

"Yeah, I think I can. Yeah, sure."

"I'll wait here with the girl. You call it in. Just go down the stairs and call it in."

"Yeah, thanks, I'll call it in," Marvin said, and turned around and left the room.

Hank eased down on the floor near the mattress. His head wanted to press against the floor, but he wouldn't let it. He knew he had to sit there watching the dead girl, keeping her company until help came.

CHAPTER 24

AN HOUR LATER, the cops and a couple of forensics guys were already moving through the apartment, and Hank was back in the living room, sitting down again on the edge of the mattresses stacked against the wall. They seemed thinner and dirtier than he'd noticed before. If he were to turn around, he knew he would see stains and the outlines of stains. Some of them would be brown. The older ones would be gone to yellow. He didn't need to turn around to see them.

In the bedroom off the kitchen in the back of the apartment, the dead colored girl still lay on the blood-soaked mattress. The stain there was dark red, almost purple, but Hank knew it would turn brown finally, a safe dry brown. If someone put a sheet over the mattress then, no one would see the stain or smell it. They wouldn't remember the girl who died on the mattress either. She would be the thing no one remembered.

Hank wasn't as dizzy as he had been earlier. He figured he could stand up if the detectives working through the apartment asked him to. He also noticed that his hearing was starting to come back in his right ear. The agitated ringing there was coming and going, and if he didn't think about it, it went away for a while. He could hear the cops opening and shuffling through the cardboard boxes and shopping bags scattered through the apartment. Things were getting clearer in his head by the minute.

A couple of feet away, Marvin slouched against a wall with his hands in his pockets. He wouldn't look up, couldn't look up. He looked miserable, and Hank felt pretty much the same way.

In front of them, Lieutenant O'Herlihy sat on one of the folding chairs. He was leaning back, his right leg crossed at the knee over his left, his hands clasped and planted on his neatly creased pants leg. In his thin mustache and brushed Homburg, his beautiful black Italian loafers and his Brooks Brothers suit, he looked natty, Hank thought. Natty. An old-fashioned word, but it fit the Lieutenant, even rousted out of his bed late at night.

He was natty, and he was chewing them out.

"Why'd you fellows drag yourselves into this place? I don't understand that. You're looking for a man who's butchering up white boys all over the Near Northwest Side of Chicago, and for some reason you drag yourselves down here to the South Side. The South Side! To the colored belt, where you're getting hooked up with dead colored girls and guys who are selling knives and booze to colored people. I just don't understand. I thought you guys were working for the Chicago Police Department and I thought I was your supervisor."

"Lieutenant..." Marvin began.

"You? I'm not asking you. I'm asking your partner. If I was asking you, I would be addressing you, but I'm addressing your partner, that's why I used the expression 'you fellows'. I'm talking to you two fellows as a unit of police law enforcement, and as such a unit only one of you has the authority to speak in response to my asking 'you fellows', and Detective Bondarowicz, you're not the one."

"Sorry, sir."

Lieutenant O'Herlihy stared at Marvin and lifted his index finger to his lips and whispered, "Shhh."

"Yes, sir."

Hank pressed his hands against the mattress and steadied himself. He looked at the Lieutenant and knew it was his job to come up with the explanations. "Sir, as I told you earlier, we were following some leads."

"They must have been pretty slim, if they brought you down here south of Lake Street. Bad leads, in fact."

"Well, sir, they were the leads we had. The two people who mentioned Joey Roses to us were the bartender at the White Eagle across from where the first suitcase was found, and then Alex Santori, who operates the Outfit pool hall on Division near California. They're both smart guys who know a lot."

Lieutenant O'Herlihy nodded and began again, "That's all fair and good, but I need to point out two things to you fellows. First, you could have tracked Joey Roses down on the North Side. He must have hangouts up there. There's no point in dragging the department down to the South Side. It's a distraction. We're looking for a killer who's carving up little white schoolboys. We're not looking for a murderer carving up colored girls. Honestly, gentlemen, this butchery here — no matter its brutality — doesn't concern us. Even if Joey is the one doing all the carving of the boys as well as this colored girl, I don't want to be adding her name and her situation to the concerns of this department. It's a colored crime, one of the crazy things that happens down here. It doesn't concern us. Is that clear?"

Hank nodded and looked over to Marvin. Marvin nodded too.

"Good," O'Herlihy said. "Let's keep it on the North Side. Now that was the first point I wanted to make clear. Here's the second: When you called and told me that you were heading south, I told you not to. I made that clear, just as I made it clear that this dead colored girl is none of our business. Isn't that right, Purcell?"

Hank looked up at the Lieutenant from his dizziness and nodded. "Yes, sir, you made it plain."

"Good. I wanted to be sure you understood me that time and this time."

"Yes, sir, we're clear."

"Good, because you boys have used up all the good will I ever had for you. One more mess like this and you're back in uniform rousting drunks out of the shit on Maxwell Street. Got that?"

Hank nodded again. Marvin was about to say something, but then ended up nodding like his partner.

"Now why don't you fellows get out of here and get some rest? We'll clean up this mess."

CHAPTER 25

HANK UNLOCKED THE door and pushed it open quietly.

It was 2:30 in the morning, and the house was dark. That was good. His head still hurt some from the beating Joey Roses gave him.

He walked toward the back of the first floor of his house. There was a staircase there leading down to the basement, and that's where he was planning to sleep, on the old blue couch. He didn't want to wake Hazel. She'd be getting up in just a few hours and preparing Margaret for her Saturday. Hazel would be the one trying to explain to Margaret why Daddy didn't come home until after she had fallen asleep and why he couldn't take her to story hour at the library.

He walked into the kitchen and turned on the small light above the stove. Like always when he was late, Hazel had left him a dinner plate wrapped in cellophane. This time it was a piece of chicken breast and some mashed potatoes with a side of peas and carrots. He wasn't hungry, but he picked up the plate anyway. There was a note from Hazel under it.

"Dear Hank, don't sleep in the basement! Come lie down with me. Love."

He carried the plate over to the Frigidaire and put it on one of the bottom shelves next to a covered saucepan. He didn't feel like eating chicken, or anything else, really. He had seen four dead children in three days, and each killing was terrible. He wondered if each horrible killing was more horrible than the last one.

Maybe it was.

He wondered how that could be.

When the first boy was found in the first suitcase, Hank had thought it was the work of a crazy person who had gone off and done one terrible, crazy thing, and he figured the killer's madness would somehow suddenly dissolve and he'd never do such a thing again.

Hank was wrong.

That one terrible thing had happened again, and this time it happened to two boys. The terrible become more terrible. Then the murder of the young colored girl, an act of rage rather than coolness — an anger so extreme that not even the death of the girl could stop the killer from killing her some more. The forensics technician in his white lab coat who first saw the colored girl's body at the apartment told Hank he thought she had been stabbed thirty times, maybe more. The guy explained that he couldn't be sure because the first time through a crime scene he had to move fast, and maybe he had missed some of the knife work.

And this crime against the colored girl, according to Lieutenant O'Herlihy, wasn't related and shouldn't be connected to the other deaths, the deaths of the three boys. It was a terrible death too, but the others were more terrible because they had happened to white boys. The coloreds were on their own there on the South Side, taking care of each other or killing each other. Either way, it wasn't the concern of Lieutenant O'Herlihy or the Chicago Police Department or the City of Chicago or the United States of America, or of Detective Bondarowicz and Detective Purcell. At least that's the way the Law saw it.

Hank took out the gallon bottle of milk. It was half full, half empty, and he poured himself a tall glass. The milk was frosty, fresh and creamy. He wondered how the Mid-City Dairy could manage to make something so simple taste so good. Maybe they didn't do anything, just let it be. He drank it down fast and poured himself another glass and sat down at the table in the kitchen.

Hank took a long, slow sip of milk then, and put the glass down. He wondered if he and Marvin and the other cops would ever catch the guy who was killing these boys and packing them into suitcases. It would be a good thing if they did catch him, of course. Hank didn't need to pick up a newspaper or watch TV to know there was fear in the city. He knew parents were keeping their kids indoors even though the kids were moaning about wanting to go outside to play, and he knew too that the parents were watching one another, keeping an eye on all their neighbors because they were figuring maybe the guy standing next to them on the bus was Suitcase Charlie going off to do another killing more terrible than the last.

Hank was one of those parents too, could feel and understand the fear everybody was feeling. But what if the killings stopped and they didn't find the killer? What would happen to that fear? Would it evaporate? Go up in smoke and gray steam? Drift away like a balloon on a windy Chicago day? Drift east, maybe, 'til it was over Lake Michigan? Drift west 'til it was lost somewhere over the prairie that extended on and on 'til you got to the Rocky Mountains and the Continental Divide?

Yeah, Hank figured the fear would slowly dry up. If the killings stopped with the boys that the Polack Killer was hauling home in the middle of Humboldt Park a couple of nights ago, if they stopped with those two killings on top of the first one, then the fear would stop, sure as anything. People would forget the suitcases and the bones chopped up into short and long pieces and the isosceles triangles carved on the soles of the three boys' feet. People would forget the horror of what had happened. They would forget the fear that kept them behind doors and away from windows.

People would forget like they forgot the killing of the Schuessler brothers and Bobby Patterson last year.

But Hank would remember.

He was the great rememberer. That's not what he got paid for, but that's what he did. He'd remember the kids who were butchered and the fear people felt and the fear he felt for himself and Hazel and Margaret. He was the great remembering machine for all the fear and horror in the city of Chicago.

Hank picked up the tall glass of creamy, fresh and cool milk and drank it all down. The milk was good, and the fear was fresh and cool. It lay around him in this kitchen in this bungalow in this city. Fear and the image of chopped, bloodless bones and a black belly with too many stab wounds. Thirty, maybe more. Punctured so often and so hard that all the blood the belly contained had spilled away from the young black girl 'til she was just another dried-out corpse nobody wanted to pay attention to.

Nobody but Hank.

He heard something behind him, and he turned around. Hazel was coming down the dark hallway from their bedroom. She had her blue bathrobe on. Her eyes were barely opened, and she was rubbing her cheek with her hand. Hank could tell she was mostly asleep.

"Why don't you come to bed, Hank? What time is it?"

"Late, really late," he said. "I'm just going to drink some more milk, and then I'll come."

She sat down across from him at the kitchen table. "Such a long night. When'd you get home?"

"Just a little while ago. Maybe fifteen minutes. I've been drinking milk, thinking about the job."

"You ought to come to bed."

"Yeah, don't worry. I'll be there soon as I finish this milk. You go and keep the bed warm. I'll be right there. Promise."

She raised her head, opened her eyes wider, and looked at him. "No, I'll wait right here until you finish your milk and you're ready to sleep."

"Okay," Hank said, and gripped her hand.

CHAPTER 26

HANK STOOD ALONE waiting at the door of one of the three classroom buildings at St. Fidelis School. Lieutenant O'Herlihy had sent them out here; he'd received a call from one of the nuns about some kind of mysterious letter that had been found, and he wanted Hank and Marvin to check the lead out. Right now, his partner was checking out the buildings at the back of the schoolyard, and Hank was waiting.

The Lieutenant said that the letter was important, but Hank thought different. This was probably just a little lesson to teach Hank and Marvin something about following orders.

Hank looked at his watch. It was close to 3:30 in the afternoon, and the school day was over for most of the kids there, the good ones at least. The only people still around were a handful of the nuns, and some of their problems.

Sister Mary Philomena was inside her first-floor classroom with one of those problems, a bad boy. Hank could see the two of them through the window next to the door. The classroom was empty except for the kid and the nun. The kid had a crew cut, and he was short, maybe a third grader. The crew cut made him look tough, like one of the punk hoods you saw smoking cigarettes by Mandel's candy store down on Potomac Avenue.

But the nun glaring down at the kid made him seem a little less tough. He was sitting at a small desk staring at his hands on the desk. She stood over him looking at a piece of paper the boy had probably given her. The boy's hands were thin and white, his fingers knotted together.

Hank couldn't hear what she was saying. She must have been talking softly, whispering. But he sure could see her talking. She was upset in the way only nuns get upset. Her flushed, sweating face was pressed against the stiff white borders of her squared-off wimple. She was gesturing with one hand and pointing at some paper on the boy's desk. Occasionally, she pounded it with her knuckles and made big rolling motions with her head, roiling it back and forth like she was trying to scare out a handful of bees that had got lodged in her headdress.

Hank had been there himself as a kid, and he knew the nun's drama was just starting. He figured he'd save the kid a little misery, so he knocked on the classroom door and stepped in.

Seeing Hank, Sister Mary Philomena nodded, then turned back to the boy.

"You're dismissed," she said.

The boy quickly started toward the door.

Hank wanted to smile, but he knew the kid didn't feel like being smiled at. He'd had a time of it. Hank could see the boy was sniffling and working his cheeks to force back the tears. He wondered if the Sister had cracked him a good one with a ruler across the knuckles. Nuns were like that, and worse. Hank had learned that lesson long ago.

He looked at the Sister. She was staring at the whimpering kid rushing out of her classroom. Her white hand was holding tight to the rosary that hung at her side.

"Yes, good day, Detective Purcell. Please come in."

For a moment, Hank panicked and thought that now it was his turn for the ruler, but then Marvin walked into the classroom and Hank figured he was probably safe. Marvin winked at him, pressed his hand against his shoulder holster and the .45 he carried there, and whispered, "No sweat, man. We'll be okay."

———⁓———

Standing behind her desk, Sister Mary Philomena motioned with her right hand toward two chairs positioned near a window. "Please bring them to my desk and sit down," she said.

Hank walked over to the chairs and carried them to the desk, carefully so they wouldn't scrape on the floor or knock into anything. He pushed one toward Marvin, and he sat down on the other.

"Sister," Marvin started, "Lieutenant O'Herlihy said that you had something for us, a letter you think has something to do with the case we're working on."

"Yes, the Suitcase Charlie killings. But it's not really a letter; rather, it's a sheet of paper. One of the girls, Elizabeth Zak, brought it in after the lunch break. She was passing it around to the girls in the back of the room. The girls sit there because the boys generally need more guidance." The Sister said that and stopped. She looked at Marvin, and there was silence for a moment.

Finally he looked up from the hat on his lap. "Yes, Sister," he said.

Hank could tell she seemed happy with Marvin's response, and she continued, "The girls were passing it around, and there was some chatter back there. I won't stand for chattering chit-chat, so I told Miss Zak to stand up and explain herself. She said she had found a letter on the way to school after lunch. I told her to bring it up."

Hank nodded and waited. Sister Mary Philomena opened her desk drawer and pulled a sheet of paper out. She placed it squarely in the center of the green blotter that occupied much of the desktop.

Hank leaned toward the paper. It looked like a standard sheet of typing paper, white, 8 ½ by 11 inches. It was folded in thirds, the way you would fold a letter you were going to stick in a regular business envelope. He picked the paper up by one of its corners and held it up to the fluorescent ceiling light. He was looking for some kind of clear marking on it, but after a moment he realized there was nothing like that on the surface of the sheet.

Sister Mary Philomena sent him a quizzical look and asked, "You're not worried about smudging any fingerprints on it?"

"No, Sister, not at all. I think the prints at this point can't help. By this time, what with being passed around the classroom by a group of students, I don't think there's much the fingerprints can tell us."

She nodded, looking disappointed.

Hank smiled back at her and said, "But let's see what we do have."

He stood up, unfolded the letter, and spread it flat on the green blotter.

The letter was divided into three equal parts by the two folds, and there were five images drawn on it in black ink. To the left of the fold on the left side, there was an isosceles triangle pointed to the top of the sheet. To the right of the fold on the right side, there was a similar triangle. It pointed to the bottom of the sheet. In the middle, between the two folds, was a big, crudely-drawn question mark. A black "equals" sign was drawn in the middle of each of the two folds.

Hank turned to his partner.

Marvin shrugged and stood up to get a better look at the letter lying on the blotter. "Isosceles triangles," he said. "Hmmm."

"Yeah, the triangles again."

"I read about them in the *Sunday Sun-Times* yesterday," the Sister said. "The reporter said the three boys all had such triangles cut into the soles of their feet."

"That's right, Sister," Marvin said. "But that question mark. Why's it there? What do you make of it?"

Sister Mary Philomena didn't say anything. Instead, she walked quickly up to the blackboard at the front of the room and picked up some yellow chalk with her right hand and held it tight. Without pause, she drew an isosceles triangle pointing up, just like on the sheet, and then on top of it, she sketched the second, downward-pointing triangle. The two overlapping triangles together formed the image of an elongated, narrow star, a six-pointed star, the Star of David.

The nun turned around and looked at Hank.

He knew what she wanted. She wanted him to tell her that there was some kind of logic here, some kind of meaning behind the two triangles and the elongated Star of David. She wanted him to show her the codebook that spelled out in simple words what these hand-drawn images had to do with the three little schoolboys who had been found in suitcases in her neighborhood. Those boys were just like the ones she saw every day in class, and she wanted to know why someone would hate them so much as to cut them and bleed them to death. Hank knew this was what she wanted him to tell her, but he couldn't because he didn't have the codebook and he didn't have a clue.

What he had was three dead boys, a dead girl he wasn't supposed to think or care about, and a letter that said something and told him nothing.

CHAPTER 27

STANDING ON THE porch of the two-story brick building, Hank pressed the doorbell and waited. Nothing happened, and he pressed again, leaning into it. The bell didn't give off any kind of sound. It must have been broken, so he knocked.

Elizabeth Zak lived just about a dozen houses away from the school, and it had been a quick walk up Washtenaw. It had turned out to be a nice late-spring day, and the kids who lived around the school seemed to be enjoying it. Most of them were blowing off steam, getting over a day spent in school listening or not listening to the Sisters and the lay teachers. Some of the kids were wheeling their bikes up and down the street, others were stringing yo-yos or running, arms pumping, around the rectangular plots of grass in front of the houses, and others were sitting around on their front porches chewing the fat or grumbling about homework.

Passing them, Hank wondered if any of these kids were thinking about the boys who had been butchered and stuffed into suitcases that were found not far from here. Did the kids on Washtenaw worry that maybe they'd be the next ones caught and killed? Or were they just thinking kid thoughts about teachers who busted their chops, what they were going to have for dinner, and what they would be watching on television after that?

Walking, Hank didn't see any fear in their faces, but that didn't mean anything. It was easy to hide what you felt, bury it under a laugh or a curse or what the kids called a bad word. Especially fear. Hank knew fear was easy to hide. He had seen a lot of kids hide it when he was a beat cop working the neighborhoods after the war. He had hid it himself, too, plenty of times. Even now, he hid it.

The door finally opened, and a young girl stood looking up at Hank. She reminded him of his daughter. The two were about the same height and had the same coloring, brown hair with a bit of auburn, pale skin that probably freckled easily. Hank gave her a smile and showed his badge. Then he said, "Excuse us, Miss, I'm Detective Purcell, and this is my partner Detective Bondarowicz. We're with the Chicago Police Department. Are you Elizabeth Zak?"

The girl answered without hesitation, "Yes, I'm Elizabeth, officer. How can I help you?"

Hank was surprised. Except for her size, she didn't seem like a kid in second grade. She seemed older.

"Sister Mary Philomena sent us," he said. "She told us that you found a letter today, and we'd like to talk to you about it. We've got some questions. Are your parents home?"

"Yes, sir, my mother's home, but she's in bed sleeping. She works the third shift, from midnight to eight in the morning. Do I have to wake her?"

"Well, Miss, we'd like to ask you some questions about the letter you found, and it would be a good idea for your mom to be there when we ask them."

"Will we have to go to the police station?"

Hank could see a slight smile on her lips as she asked that. The idea of going there seemed to make her happy. He figured she had been thinking all day about going there and telling her girlfriends about it during recess tomorrow.

"No need for that, miss. We can ask our questions here."

"Oh," she said. Hank could see she was disappointed as she pulled the door open and went to wake her mother.

Hank and Marvin followed her into the living room. It was a boxy space, small and overstuffed. A light-green couch took up most of the far wall. A couple of easy chairs, a coffee table, and a television in a maple cabinet rounded out the room. The TV was on, but the sound was turned off. It didn't matter much — it was showing an old silent picture. A fat man in a Keystone Kops suit was running down a busy street against traffic. He was chasing a goat. Trolleys and taxi cabs kept whizzing past him, but he kept running in that sort of jerky way they did back in those old films, his arms pumping.

Marvin sat down on one of the easy chairs and smiled. "I like these old silent movies," he said.

"I think this one has the flatfoot's life down pat," Hank said as he took the other easy chair. He wasn't interested in the movie. He felt like he knew it as well as he knew his own life.

There was a newspaper turned face down on the coffee table, and Hank picked it up. It was the *Dziennik Chicagoski*, a Polish daily. He couldn't read it, but he thumbed through the paper, looking at the pictures. Boy Scouts bunched around behind a Polish flag flapping in the wind. A priest saying something over a coffin draped in white roses. Four well-dressed couples, the men in suits and the women in frilly dresses, dancing at some gala ball.

Hank turned to the cover. It was a photo of the two suitcases the DuPage kid found by the boathouse. They were closed up and standing in a room somewhere. He couldn't tell if they were empty or not. He glanced at the caption and wished he could read it. He wondered what the Poles made of these murders. Did they scratch their heads, wonder why they came to America where there was such brutality, where every place seemed to be a slaughterhouse?

He heard footsteps from the back of the apartment, and saw Elizabeth and a woman walking toward the living room. The woman was attractive, a brunette, middle-aged and carrying some weight but still looking pretty good in a black dress sprinkled with small yellow polka dots. She had gotten dressed up and put on some makeup. He wasn't surprised. He knew these women from the old country. They had some kind of pride. You wouldn't catch them in a bathrobe and curlers, even if they were sleeping off a shift at a factory where they were making fifty-six cents an hour.

Hank stood up with his hat in his hands. Marvin followed his lead.

"Ma'am, we've got some questions for your daughter," Hank said. "And we're obligated to have one of her parents present."

She nodded and sat down next to her daughter on the couch. "I understand, but my English is not so good."

"That's not a problem," Marvin explained. "It's just standard procedure."

Hank saw the woman give Marvin a questioning look and shake her head slightly from side to side. He could see she didn't understand.

Elizabeth turned to her mother and said something in Polish. It was quick and precise, and her mother nodded and turned to Hank and said, "*Tak, Tak.*"

"My mother understands now," the girl said.

Hank put his hat on the arm of the easy chair and said, "Good. Here's what we need from you, Elizabeth. Can you tell us where you found the paper you passed on to Sister Mary Philomena?"

"Oh, I didn't find it, officer. A man gave it to me."

Marvin looked up from his memo pad. "Excuse me. What do you mean, a man gave it to you? The Sister says you found it."

The girl didn't hesitate. "Sir, a man gave it to me. When he gave it to me, he said he found it and asked me to take it to the Sisters at the school." Elizabeth paused and then said it again. "He found it. I didn't find it."

"Did he say anything else?" Marvin asked.

"Yes, sir, he said 'Thursday.'"

"Thursday?"

"Uh-huh."

"I don't understand that," Hank said. He shook his head and looked at Elizabeth's mother. She was leaning forward, her hands clasped together and resting on her knees. He said, "Crazy."

"*Tak*," she nodded, "*głupstwo*."

Hank turned to the girl again. "What did this fellow look like? Did you ever see him before?"

"No, Detective, I never saw him before, and I don't think he was anybody from this neighborhood. He looked like a movie star."

"What do you mean?"

Elizabeth didn't say anything for a moment. Hank could see she was thinking. He didn't press her. He waited.

"The mothers and fathers around here, the grownup people, you know, they all work. People in movies, they're not like that. They don't have jobs. When my father comes home in the evening, he looks tired. He moves slow. His face looks dark. I guess he needs a shave."

"And that's not what this man looked like?"

"No, sir, he didn't look tired. He gave me a big smile and his eyes twinkled, and he had a nice soft voice, like a movie star."

"Do you remember anything else?"

"His hands were so white, and the fingernails were clean and long. All of them."

"Did he have an accent? Did he sound like an American?"

Elizabeth paused again, looked at her mother, and said, "No.... He didn't sound like my mother or father when they talk English, but he didn't sound like an American either, the people on TV or the radio."

Marvin stopped writing and nodded. "You've been a big help, Miss, and I want to ask you only a few more questions, and then me and my partner will be leaving. Do you remember anything about the way he was dressed or how he moved?"

"A dark blue suit just like the one my father has, but I think it was newer — the back wasn't shiny at all. And I remember one thing about the way he walked. He didn't seem to be in a hurry. He didn't run away."

Elizabeth looked at her mother, and her mother nodded and put her hand on her daughter's cheek and pressed it for a moment. Then she turned to the two detectives and said in her broken English, "The man who's killing these boys. You find this son-of-a-bitch, you kill him."

"Yes, ma'am, we'll try," Hank said, and stood up.

Marvin nodded too, and added, "We'll do to him worse than he did to those boys. You can bet on it."

"Thank you," the woman said, and shook their hands.

CHAPTER 28

THE ALLEY WAS dark, and rain was falling in big loud drops on their unmarked Ford. Behind the wheel of the parked car, Hank stared down the alley at the puddles here and there. They looked like black mirrors lying on the wet asphalt. The temperature had dropped; the rain had cooled the day off. He liked that.

Earlier, leaving the Zaks' apartment, Hank had looked at the sky, and it wasn't blue and clean anymore. A strong steady wind was moving gray clouds in fast and low from the lake. Most of the kids who had been playing outside were gone. The wind or the damp chill had scared them, Hank figured, or maybe it was the fact that evening would be coming on soon, and after that there would be night, and night would bring Suitcase Charlie back into the neighborhood. Or maybe the kids weren't thinking about Charlie, but Hank would bet their parents were, and maybe they were the ones who hauled their kids in.

The Ford was parked in the same alley Hank and Marvin had parked in that first night, before they knew a thing about what Suitcase Charlie had dropped off on the corner between the convent and the White Eagle Tap.

Hank thought back to that night as he listened to the Ford V8's soft hum. It reminded him of some quiet days in Germany. One minute the world is a bright sunshiny place, and you're like Fred

Astaire in one of those MGM musicals. You're strolling through Central Park and whistling a happy tune, and the next minute the devil is creeping down your throat and up your asshole at the same time.

It's funny how one thing can change everything. It was like what Hank's mom used to say. She was a superstitious pessimist of the first order, and when he was a boy whistling a happy tune, she'd look him in the eye and say, "When you whistle, Buddy, you whistle up the devil."

Hank knew that the man filling suitcases up with dead schoolboys wasn't the devil; Suitcase Charlie was just a twisted pervert or a mental midget with some kind of grudge against kids. But even if he wasn't the devil, he would do until the real one came along.

Hank looked at his partner sitting next to him. His head was thrown back, and he was chugging a long, hard drink from a pint bottle of Smirnoff vodka. Hank knew that a bottle like that, sixteen ounces of juice, had around seven or eight Marvin-sized pulls in it. Marvin was in the middle of his third. He hadn't offered Hank a drink so far, and that was okay with Hank. He was still feeling the wobbles from the beating Joey Roses gave him down in the black belt south of Lake Street. Besides, with a crazy case like this, especially on a gloomy night, he knew one of them had to stay reasonably sober, and he knew tonight that it was him.

Hank could barely hear the Ford V8's steady murmur through the rain splashing on the roof of the car. He reached over and turned the police radio up, but it wasn't worth the trouble. It was the same old bullshit.

Through the humming static and sizzles, a voice would sometimes pop a word into the mix, and Hank could almost parse out a syllable. But even if he listened closely and wrote down every word he heard, it still wouldn't make any kind of sense.

It was just like this case: "The Case of Suitcase Charlie and his Three Leather Suitcases."

Hank wished that he was reading about it in the *Tribune's* comic strips or watching it on TV instead of having to solve it. He and Marvin and all the cops on the force were looking, and there wasn't anything even close to a solution. He felt this case needed a better detective than he was. Maybe Dick Tracy or Fearless Fosdick could pull it all together and slap the cuffs on Charlie.

Sitting behind the wheel, Hank pulled his pack of cigarettes out of his shirt pocket and slipped out a Chesterfield. He lit it with his Nazi lighter and pulled the smoke into his lungs. He let it sit there for a while, getting comfortable. Then he blew the smoke out his lips and watched it swirl out the cracked window into the falling rain and the darkness.

The blue-gray smoke in the alley's half-light coiled there for a second, taking up space in the wet night, and then it wasn't.

Hank and Marvin hadn't talked much in the car since leaving Elizabeth Zak's apartment, just smoking and staring at the rain, listening to the snap, crackle, and pop drifting up from the police radio, each thinking his own sweet thoughts.

Hank felt Marvin poking his elbow and looked down. His partner was passing the vodka to him. Hank hesitated for a second, then he took it, lifted it to the glow of yellow light coming down from somebody's kitchen, tipped the bottle to his lips and pulled down a good shot. Maybe a double.

Vodka. There was nothing else like it. A cool burning, an acid that stung and then suddenly didn't. This stuff was the real white lightning, not that moonshine stuff that hill folks and farmers talk about. Hank remembered an old song some hillbilly in his outfit overseas used to sing about cocaine. How did it go? "Some people say it will kill you, but they won't say when. Cocaine, running round my heart and brain." Vodka was like that. It snuck up on you like a guy with a blackjack.

Hank shook his head and handed the bottle back to Marvin.

His partner looked at it, and then he glanced back at Hank. "You on the wagon tonight, chief?"

Hank didn't say anything, just shrugged. Marvin threw his head back and took another pull.

"You know," he said as he screwed the cap back onto the bottle, "this case is fucked up."

"Yeah. That's right."

"What we got here?" Marvin asked. "In three nights, we got three dead, and what else we got? Not much. Three brown leather suitcases, me and you and a walk in the park, a Polack Killer who ain't a killer getting brained by a kid from DuPage who just happens to be in the park when suitcases start popping up like mushrooms after a flood, a letter with a stupid diagram that a nun thinks could be a recipe for a Jewish Star, and a mysterious stranger who a little girl thinks looks like a movie star. Is that what we got here?"

"Yeah."

"And don't let me forget the dead girl on the mattress down in Bronzeville. And what about Joey Roses? Where does he come in?"

"I don't know," Hank said, pulling another Chesterfield out of his pack.

"You'd think that we'd be able to put something together here. I mean, get some kind of direction. If we laid the pieces out on a table, we should be able to see some connections. But we got nothing.

I don't see any kind of lines running between these bits. We got puzzle pieces, but none of the edges fit — like the pieces are from half a dozen different puzzles, all smooshed together."

Hank flicked his thumb over the wheel of his Nazi lighter. There was no flame. Maybe the flint was loose. He slapped the IMCO against his palm and ran his thumb over the flint wheel again. This time, he got a flame and lit his cigarette.

"You know," Marvin said, "my dad wasn't a thinker. He was just a short mouse of a guy, a real Jew, who spent most of his life working a shit job in a shit factory. That is, when he was working. There were times when he couldn't get work, times when nothing was working for him. During the Great Depression, for instance. You know? So what did he do then?"

Hank shrugged and watched the cigarette smoke roll out the window and disappear into the rain. He didn't say anything.

"Hank! I'm asking you. What did he do?"

Hank turned to Marvin. "I give up. What did he do?"

"He used to say, 'When they knock you down, you got to get back up, and start all over again.'"

"You're right. Your dad was no Albert Einstein."

"Are we down, right here? Sure we're down. We ain't got a pot to piss in when it comes to clues and seeing where they lead, but we can't give up."

Hank tapped the ash off his cigarette. It floated down, settling on his pants leg. He brushed it off with his left hand and took another deep drag.

The rain was picking up. Earlier, he could almost see the big drops hit, hear their rat-tat-tat-tat on the Ford's roof and windshield, but now it was coming down so fast and hard that he couldn't. The rain was falling steadily, and it was washing over everything. Even the yellow light from the kitchen a few houses down seemed almost gone. It was just a wet glow now rather than a clear, firm light.

"You're not listening to me," Marvin said.

"You're right. I'm not."

"What the fuck?"

"Marvin, listen to me. I've been thinking. About the letter and the dead boys. What connects them up is those triangles. The isosceles triangles that form a six-pointed star."

"Yeah, and that Zak girl, she's connected too. She talked about a movie star. Maybe he's a six-pointed movie star."

"That's crazy. You're drunk. You've had one too many pulls on that Smirnoff's."

"What you want me to do about it?"

"Next time buy the small bottle. The half pint."

"Okay. So where were we?"

"The triangles and the stars," Hank said. "Remember when we went to see that old Jewish guy, Mr. Fisch? He mentioned stars. A crazy conversation. Out of nowhere, he was asking me about stars, about the kind of stars that sheriffs wear in the movies and the kind of stars that Chicago cops wear."

"I don't remember. What're you talking about?"

"Stars, Marvin. Stars. Mr. Fisch was talking about five-pointed stars and six-pointed stars."

"You sure?"

"Sure I'm sure. Look it up in your memo pad. That damn memo pad's a better cop than you'll ever be."

Marvin reached into the breast pocket of his sport coat. He was looking for his notepad and not finding it. Then he started patting down his pants pockets. Hank could see it wasn't there either.

"Come on. Forget about the memo pad," Hank said, and rolled his window down and flicked his cigarette butt up into the rain. Its glowing tip arced into the wet darkness and disappeared.

Marvin looked at Hank and shook his head. "So you think we need to talk with Mr. Fisch again?"

"That's right."

"You know, I think I still have that duck's-blood soup, his jar of *czarnina*, in the trunk."

"You want to give it back to him?"

"Ahh...no, I don't think so."

CHAPTER 29

IT WAS ABOUT 10 PM when Hank parked the Ford a couple of doors down from where Mr. Fisch lived on Evergreen Street. The rain was still coming down in a hard and steady fall, and the streets were empty. Hank could see that most of the apartments up and down both sides of Evergreen were already dark.

But not Mr. Fisch's apartment. His front room had a light on, a faint one. Through the Ford's windshield, Hank could see some kind of gray-green glow through the big picture window that fronted the street. Maybe the light was coming from Fisch's television set where the old guy was watching wrestling or some old movie, or maybe that pitchman Marty Faye from Brooklyn hawking something. Hank tried to remember if Mr. Fisch had a TV, but he couldn't. It didn't matter much, he figured.

Slouched down in his seat, Hank smoked and waited for Marvin. His partner was in a gangway somewhere between two of the narrow apartment buildings nearby, taking a leak. He said he couldn't wait, and he had to go, but the piss was taking him forever. He was like an old man. Hank hoped Marvin hadn't gone off on another of his adventures. Maybe he was just trying to pass a stone.

Hank shook his head, stepped out of the Ford, and started running through the rain toward Mr. Fisch's door. Marvin would know to look for him there.

Standing on the porch, Hank knocked and didn't have to wait long. "Yes?" Mr. Fisch asked through the closed door.

"Sorry to bother you again. This is Detective Purcell. We've got some follow-up questions for you."

"Yes? What kind of questions, Detective?"

"Can I come in? It's like Noah's Flood out here. I'm getting soaked."

"Yes, of course, I'm sorry," Mr. Fisch mumbled, his high, whiny voice sounding soft and far away. Kind of a fruity voice, Hank thought as he stepped in. He could see that the old guy was getting ready for bed. He was dressed in an old bathrobe, a yellow one with dark blue vertical stripes. It hung down to the floor, and Hank thought it must have been bought for a taller man, or maybe the old guy had been taller when the bathrobe was new. Now the bathrobe just showed how short he was. Like a gnome, Hank had thought the first time he saw him, and he still thought so now.

Stepping inside, Hank shook the rain off his raincoat. He took his hat off and shook it also. "A hard rain out there, Mr. Fisch."

"Yes, yes, as you say, it must have been this way in the time of Noah. The great Flood that swept away the whole world. A terrible thing. So many people died. But what am I thinking?" Mr. Fisch said, reaching for the detective's hat and coat. "Let me take your wet things."

Hank handed them over to Mr. Fisch and thanked him, and the old guy hung them on a coatrack near the front door.

"My partner, Detective Bondarowicz, will be here soon. We've got some things we want to talk over with you."

"Please make yourself comfortable. Can I get you a cup of hot coffee? A night like this, maybe you need something to warm you up."

"Thanks, Mr. Fisch. I think my partner will want a cup too when he comes in."

"Of course, of course. Sit down, please. I'll just heat the coffee up," Mr. Fisch said as he walked to the kitchen at the back of the apartment.

———✥———

Hank didn't want to sit down. The legs of his black slacks were wet from the short jog from the car to the door of Fisch's apartment. Instead of sitting, he walked over to one of the pictures Fisch had hanging on the wall of the front room. Hank remembered trying to figure it out when he was here last time. He was beat that night, from the heat and the work and seeing that boy chopped up like a chicken. And he was a little beer-drunk and sleepy that night too, and he remembered that he could barely keep his eyes open by the time they spoke to Mr. Fisch. Sitting on the couch here in Mr. Fisch's living room that first night, Hank had kept looking at that one picture; he couldn't tell if the white blotch on the top left of the canvas was a cloud or a cow. He figured now would be a good time to check it out, while he waited for the coffee and waited for Marvin to stop pissing and find his way back here.

He turned on one of the table lights and walked to the wall. The light helped. The painting was about two feet tall and a little less across. The frame was beat up. Hank could see where the thing had been nicked here and there, but that wasn't what surprised him. It was an old frame, and the painting was old too. Standing close to it, he wondered how he ever could have thought that it was a picture of a cloud or a cow. It was a painting of a violinist, a fiddle player, and it looked like it had been painted by a drunk or a very talented twelve-year-old. Some of the painting was clear and made sense. The fiddle player was standing and playing in front of a log cabin. There was white snow on its roof. That must have been what Hank thought was a cloud or a cow — just some white snow on a roof. Just behind the fiddle player there was a boy holding a cap. He was extending it forward, like he was collecting money for the fiddle player, to get people to pay for his playing. So far, no problem.

Then the painting started to get weird. First, the colors were all wrong. The snow on the roof was white in places and blood-red in others. The fiddle player's face and hands were sort of green, and he was wearing clothes that didn't seem to be any one particular color, just dabs of all different colors. Then the painting got weirder. In the street behind the fiddler and the boy, there was a big-breasted woman in a black skirt with some kind of roses scattered across it. She was smiling and hugging a man with a white briefcase. Maybe the guy was an accountant, but the really weird thing was that she didn't have a blouse on. She was just standing in the road with her right arm thrown across this accountant's shoulder, and her breasts were there for all the world to see.

Hank began leaning closer so he could get a better look at the snow on the roof. It was almost like there was a face in the snow, or maybe it was a cow's head or something. He was leaning into the painting when Mr. Fisch came back with the coffee.

"Here you are, officer," Fisch said, and handed Hank a cup of black coffee.

"I was just looking at this painting, Mr. Fisch. It's really something."

"Yes. I bought it in Paris before the war. It's by Marc Chagall."

"Chagall? I don't think I know him."

"You don't know Chagall?" Mr. Fisch shrugged slightly. "Well, he's a Jew, like me, but he was from Russia, a village there somewhere."

"He likes to mix up his colors."

"Yes, I think you're right. I think you can say that. You know, I met him once, in Paris before the war, and I asked him about his colors and about how what should be white in his paintings is red sometimes, and vice versa. You know what he said? He said, 'There is only one color, and it's the color of love.' How do you like that?"

Hank smiled and sat down on the burgundy couch. "The color of love? That's a funny thing to say. A mystery. I guess I'll have to think about that when I get a chance."

"Yes, a mystery," Mr. Fisch repeated, and sat down on the chair across from Hank. "A playful mystery. One meant to get us scratching our heads and wondering about this and that. Art gives us mysteries that don't hurt. Not like these other mysteries, the murders here. I read in the newspaper today that there were two more boys found, this time in the park just up the street, by the boathouse. I know the place very well."

"Yes, sir. Two more dead boys, and we were wondering if you might help us."

"Of course, but what can I tell you? I'm not a sleuth, a detective. I'm just an old man, a language tutor living on a small pension."

Hank took the sheet of paper from Elizabeth Zak's movie star out of his inside breast pocket and handed it to Mr. Fisch. "We came across this today, and I wonder what you make of it."

The old man pushed his wire-rimmed glasses up on the bridge of his nose and looked at the paper. It was still folded in thirds like a letter, and he examined first one side and then the other. Then he unfolded the sheet and held it tight with his hands.

Hank sipped some of the black coffee and watched him. He could see Mr. Fisch's large gray eyes move slowly from the right side of the sheet to the left. It was almost as if he were studying some complicated text or equation, rather than simply taking in the five figures on the sheet: an isosceles triangle pointing up, another pointing down, and between them a large black question mark and a couple of equals signs. Then he turned the sheet over and examined the back side. There was nothing there except the faint outline of the figures on the other side, Hank knew. He had looked at the paper as carefully as Mr. Fisch was doing now.

"Before I tell you what I see here, detective, may I ask you why you came to me with this paper?"

"You said something last time we were here."

"What was that?"

Hank shook his head and smiled. "Maybe I'll tell you later. But for now, what do you see in the drawings?"

"Sir," Mr. Fisch said, returning the smile, "policemen all over the world are exactly the same."

"I guess you're right." Hank paused. "What do you see?"

Mr. Fisch didn't say anything at first. He turned over the sheet so that the blank side was facing up, toward him. Then he folded the thirds of the sheet together and pressed them so they would stay that way. He handed the re-folded letter to the detective.

Hank put his cup down on the coffee table and took the letter. He already knew what he was going to see. With the light shining through the paper, the two isosceles triangles came together to form a six-pointed star.

"Thank you, Mr. Fisch."

"Did you come to see me because this drawing suggests that two triangles form the Star of David, and I'm a Jew?" the old man asked as he adjusted his glasses again.

"Not necessarily, sir."

"I'm not the only Jew here, you know, in this neighborhood. There used to be many of us here before the war, but now not so many. On this side of the street there are maybe three others, elderly women, you know. They live at 2728 Evergreen. They make wonderful pastry. But we're almost the only ones left. The Poles have taken our place, the new refugees."

Hank listened but didn't say anything.

"You know," Mr. Fisch said. "I read about these triangles. They found them carved in the feet of the boys who were killed. You think a Jew did this?"

Hank could hear the rain hitting the picture window behind him. It was a bad night. The wind must have picked up. He wondered for a second about Marvin, wondered what had happened to his partner. He wanted a cigarette bad, but figured that Mr. Fisch wouldn't be crazy about someone smoking in his apartment.

"I don't know who did it," Hank said. "Jew or Christian? I don't know. Me and my partner were sitting around trying to connect up the pieces we have in this case. We were trying to see what fit and what didn't, and you know, the star was one of the only pieces that seemed to connect with any of the other pieces. We remembered you said something about stars when we were here last time. That's why we came back."

Mr. Fisch leaned forward, and Hank noticed again how really short the old fellow was. His feet in his furry slippers didn't even touch the floor when he was sitting.

"But Detective, believe me please when I say that I don't remember saying anything to you about triangles and the Star of David."

"Maybe, but you asked me about badges, the kinds of stars on badges."

"If I did, I must have just been making conversation."

Hank nodded. "I'm sure that's all it was, but it was the kind of goofy link that the police have to track down. And it brought us back to you."

"And now you're here."

Hank leaned further back into the couch. "In some kind of odd way, Mr. Fisch, you don't seem very surprised that I'm back here talking to you. I show up on a dark night in the middle of a rainstorm and start talking about three murders, and you don't seem surprised. You bring out hot coffee and tell me about the one color of love."

"You're surprised that I'm not surprised?"

"I guess."

"Can I get you another cup of coffee?"

"No, thanks. If my partner ever shows up, he'll probably want some. But tell me something about why you're not surprised."

"I'm a Jew. You know about the war, I'm sure. Six million of us died there in the ovens and the concentration camps and the ghettoes and the forests because some people thought we were vermin. And long before that there were people who thought we were trying to get our hands on all the money in the world and control everything. And people still think we start the wars and disrupt the peace and poison wells and bring bubonic plague into the world. So I'm not surprised that somebody would think a Jew would kill some little boys. In the old country, there was a lot of such talk."

"What kind of talk was that?"

"What kind of talk? Talk. You heard it even in a sophisticated country like France. Talk of ritual killings. Of course, the Nazis loved to publish these stories, but so did many others. Jews kidnaping a Christian child, tying him to a cross, stabbing him in a way to

simulate the crown of thorns that Jesus wore at the end, and draining the child's blood off. We Jews call such stories the Blood Libel."

Hank leaned forward. He looked at the question mark on the
sheet of paper the man who looked like a movie star had given the
little girl, Elizabeth Zak. "Why would people do this?"

"Why? Which why, detective? The why that asks, 'Why would
someone say that Jews are doing this?' Or the why that asks, 'Why
would Jews do this?'"

"Yeah, let's hear the second one first. What reason could anybody
give for why a Jew would do this?"

Mr. Fisch didn't answer right away. He seemed agitated. His
left cheek was twitching slightly, and the fingers of his right hand
were bunching up and then stretching and stiffening out. Hank
remembered that first night he and Marvin had met him. Fisch
seemed perturbed then, bothered by something. He kept going on
about boys and girls, children in the neighborhood streets chasing
him, boys calling him wicked, dirty names. Mr. Fisch was agitated
back then, and he was agitated now.

That's what Hank wanted. He wanted the old man to be agitated.
He told Mr. Fisch what he had said before to a lot of people in similar situations, both the innocent and the guilty: "There's nothing
to worry about here. Nobody's accusing you of anything or trying
to rough you up."

"I'm sorry," Mr. Fisch said, his voice a high whisper. "You ask me
why some people would think a Jew did this. I will tell you plainly.
Maybe they would say, if the Jews could kill Jesus, our Savior, the
son of God, they could do anything."

Mr. Fisch stopped to take a breath and brush a film of sweat off
his upper lip with his index finger. Then he began again, "I saw

things there in Germany and France before the war, heard things. Accusations. It was terrible. The anti-Semites, the ones in Germany and the ones in France, they talked about us as if were demons, devils with horns and foot-long tongues, ready to feast on the blood of the Christians they said we envied and hated. As if all the great villains that the world has produced — Attila, Nero, Dracula, Genghis Khan, Ivan the Terrible — all were nothing compared to the greatest monster, the Jew. The flesh-ripping Jew with his razor knives and heavy hammers, his sharpened teeth."

Mr. Fisch paused again. His body had tensed, gone rigid; his hands on his knees were pressed into small, round fists.

Hank didn't want to rush him. He sat there and waited for Mr. Fisch to start again. He had heard some of this before. In Germany toward the end of the war, he met a woman, a university professor, a historian who had been educated at Oxford. She and her two young daughters were hiding in a barn, afraid that the Russian soldiers coming into the area would find them and rape them. Hank's squad took the woman and her children in and gave them food and safe passage through the snow to the American lines. One time, in the shelter of some trees when they were taking a break, he asked the woman why the Germans had started the war. He thought she might be angry with his question, but she took it seriously, answered it the way a scholar would. She talked slowly and carefully, in the English she'd learned from the Oxford professors, about what the Jews did to Christian children, how they cut them up and drained their blood to use in secret rituals.

Hank thought at first that she was kidding him, trying to scare him with some kind of Hansel-and-Gretel stuff, and he looked at her and said as much.

But she said, "No, I won't lie to you. You saved me and my daughters from the Russians who would have raped and killed us as they did my mother. I'm telling you the truth. Maybe because you're American, you don't see the Jews the way we do. Your country has the innocence of a young nation. But trust me, in years to come, when the Jews and their Communist puppets come to destroy you, you will learn what the Jew is."

Twelve years later, Hank's reaction was the same as it was that night in the forest in Germany: She might be an educated, intelligent woman who spoke English prettier than he did, but she believed a lot of complete crap, and he told her so.

Mr. Fisch cleared his throat then and began talking again in his high-pitched whisper. This time the whisper was fast. "You see, it was never enough for them to believe that we controlled all the world's money and politics and wars, all the big things. It had to be more personal — something they could imagine happening to their own children, something so terrible that we must be monsters, not really human beings at all. And it had to be secret, so they could believe it even if we looked and behaved just like anyone else. So: the Blood Libel, what the Jews supposedly did to those Christian children. And what did we do to them? I'll tell you as plain as I can. In some secret place that nobody ever found, we drained all of the blood from the Christian child's body, causing the poor child as much pain as possible, of course, and mixed the blood into the dough for matzos, unleavened bread. Then, every year at the Passover feast, we Jews all ate this bread."

"Hmm," Hank said, and then he asked, "Why?"

"Why? Why? We're night monsters, devils, Asiatics, God-killers, strangers in every sense of the word, strange to ourselves and to all others. Some say that there is a curse on us, and the only way we can lift this curse is to drink the blood of Christian children. They say we are vermin, ghouls, vampires even."

"The people, the ones who say this about you Jews, why do they say it?"

Mr. Fisch leaned forward and put his hands on his cheeks. "Why do the anti-Semites say it? They hate the Jews. Why do they hate the Jews? You might as well ask me, 'Why do we live and why do we die?' There are easy questions, and there are hard ones. Why anti-Semites hate the Jews is one of the hard ones. It's like what I told you before, about the children who scream and rush past my house, and come up my stairs to ring my doorbell. Why do they do it? I say they lack discipline, but that's no answer. They do what they do, that's all."

"That's no answer either, Mr. Fisch."

"Yes, absolutely, you're right. That's no answer."

"So, let me ask you, Mr. Fisch. What do you think is going on with these boys in suitcases and the triangles cut into the soles of their feet?"

"What do I think is going on? I'm a Jew. Here in America, it's pretty good for Jews. The Christians don't let us into their country clubs in the suburbs like Oak Park and Evanston, but they don't burn us in ovens either. That's good. What kind of reason would someone have for killing little boys and draining their blood? Maybe they want it to be here a little more like it is over there, in Germany, in France, in Europe. Maybe they want to paint blood on the hands of the Jews and get people afraid of us, angry at us. You read your history, Detective Purcell, and what do you learn? First there's suspicion toward the Jews, fear, then hatred, and then there's pogroms and ghettos, and then Auschwitz and the ovens."

"So you think maybe somebody wants there to be concentration camps here and all the rest?"

"Yes, sure, maybe. Why not? Have you heard of Chmielnicki? No? I'm not surprised. He's from a long time ago, far away. But let me tell you about him. He was a leader in the Ukraine three hundred years ago, long before Hitler and Auschwitz and all of that bad business. This Chmielnicki, he told his people that they had been sold to the Jews, sold as slaves. And what did his people do? They believed him, and they killed the Jews. They killed thousands, tens of thousands, maybe a hundred thousand Jews, maybe more. Nobody knows for sure how many. It was a long time ago."

"It's crazy to think that anything like that could happen here."

"And it wasn't crazy then? Yes, it's crazy, but I think maybe somebody would like to see it."

"Who would do a thing like that? Kill children so that people would hate the Jews?"

"A crazy man. A crazy man to do a crazy thing." Mr. Fisch said that, sighed, and then pushed himself back and put his arms on the arms of his easy chair.

Hank didn't say anything for a while. He watched Mr. Fisch, and Mr. Fisch watched him back. The room was quiet and Hank noticed that the rain wasn't falling and plinking off the windows anymore. It must have stopped or turned into a drizzle while he and Mr. Fisch were talking.

He wondered again where Marvin was, and then he thought about Suitcase Charlie, the crazy man doing crazy things for crazy reasons. How do you find a guy like that? Hank figured that just about every cop in Chicago was looking for him, trying to find some kind of clue that would pry the bastard out of the woodwork.

How many cops was that? Ten thousand, more or less? And then all the firemen, bus drivers, school teachers, newspaper guys, and office and factory workers. Everybody in the city, men and women both, was looking for this Suitcase Charlie, and nobody was having any luck. How do you find a crazy guy? Maybe he wasn't crazy so you could tell to look at him? Could someone crazy enough to kill little kids like that somehow manage to seem more or less as sane as the next guy? Everybody was trying to track him down, but he still wasn't showing up on anybody's radar.

Sometimes what surprised Hank the most was not that the cops didn't always catch the bad guys. The surprising thing was that anybody ever got caught for anything.

He shook his head and said to Mr. Fisch, "Let me ask you another question."

"Certainly."

"Anybody ever try to rough you up because you're a Jew? I know that you've had some trouble with the kids. Did their parents ever try to give you any kind of hard time?"

"No, the parents here are nice people. Most of them came from the old country, and most of them had enough with hating before they came here. A lot of the people around here, they came to America as refugees. Some of them spent years in the camps in Germany doing slave labor. Like I say, they're polite. And the ones who didn't come here as refugees, they don't give me any trouble either. They work, they come home and eat, they go back to work. They're people like you and me."

"Sounds like you see a lot of people."

"I don't know if I see a lot, but I do see some. I have my tutoring, and when I'm not tutoring I like to walk around the neighborhood.

Go to the park or the library, do a little shopping on Division Street or North Avenue. I visit my friends in the Jewish old folks' home on the corner of California and Hirsch, too. Just across the street from the park."

"Tutoring? You talked a little about that when we were here the last time. You mentioned tutoring kids and adults."

"Yes, some children. They come because their parents think they need help with their reading and writing. The nuns tell them they will be held back if they don't learn English. That Sister Mary Philomena is a hard one, very demanding, I hear."

"Yeah, we met her a couple of times. I know what you mean. And the adults?"

"I see some adults also. Some want to become citizens, and they need to be able to read and write English. Others come because they want to learn another language, or want to practice one they already know. I speak some Hebrew, and I know German, Polish, Russian, French, Hungarian, and Yiddish quite well."

"How much tutoring do you do?"

"Less now than before. As you can see, I'm not getting younger, and I don't have the strength I used to."

"And these people you tutor, they aren't all from around here, I imagine."

"Mostly from around the neighborhood. I have a sign in the window — maybe you saw it? But sometimes they come from other parts of the city. Evanston, Oak Park, even Hyde Park, the University of Chicago."

"The University of Chicago. That's something. A professor?"

"Yes, of physics. He's the one I mentioned when you were here before. His name is Professor Zcink. He studied under Professor

Werner Heisenberg before the war."

Heisenberg? Hank knew that name. He had heard it before, somewhere, and he tilted his head slightly forward.

"Yes, Heisenberg, one of the main scientists in Germany's attempt to build an atomic bomb."

"So this guy's a Kraut?"

"Heisenberg?"

"No, I mean the professor, the one you tutor."

"No, no, he's a Hungarian."

"So what do you tutor him in? English?"

"Yes, that's right. English."

"That's strange. This guy's a professor at one of the greatest universities in the country, and he comes up to Humboldt Park to learn English."

"I thought so too, Detective Purcell. I asked Professor Zcink about it once when he first started coming. He laughed. He said he came because he remembered reading about me in an article published in Munich before the war, about English tutors working in Strasbourg. So I was a familiar name, he said. Also, he said that he knew I could speak every language he could speak, so if I couldn't explain what a hot dog was in Hungarian or German, I could surely do it in Polish or Russian."

Having said that in a serious tone of voice, Mr. Fisch suddenly began bobbing his head, and then he started laughing, a high whispering sort of laugh. He looked like a happy troll from one of those kid's stories Hank used to read to his daughter Margaret. The top half of Mr. Fisch's body was rolling from side to side while the feet at the ends of his short legs tried to find the floor. It was a funny scene, Hank thought, and he started laughing too.

Chapter 30

LEAVING MR. FISCH'S apartment, Hank looked up and down the block.

It had stopped raining, but the sidewalks and the street were still wet. Hesitating on the top of the stoop, Hank could feel the chill pressing in on his face. It must be a front moving in. He watched the poplar trees and maples lining the street sway slowly in the wind. He pulled his hat lower over his eyes and started walking to the Ford. He wondered where Marvin was.

He stopped wondering when he got to the car. His partner was spread out, asleep in the back seat.

Hank knocked on the glass above Marvin's head, but he didn't wake up, and Hank knocked again, harder. Still nothing. Then he thumped the back side door of the Ford with his open palm. That woke his partner up. Marvin's head jerked forward and his hat flopped to the floor. His eyes darted around, and Hank could hear him mumbling "Jesus Christ" through the window.

Hank said, "Roll down the window," and Marvin did.

"Where you been?" Marvin asked. "I've been looking for you."

Hank shook his head. "Yeah, I've been here. Where you been, buddy?"

"Like I said, looking for you. Or maybe not. Like the song says, 'had a little drink about an hour ago, and it went right to my head.'"

"I guess," Hank said. "Come on, let's get out of here. I'll tell you what Mr. Fisch said about Jews and ritual murder and the Blood Libel."

Marvin cleared his throat and spat out the window. "You were up there with him for a long time. Did you ask him who he thought did the killing?"

"Yeah, I did."

"What did he say?"

"He didn't have a clue."

"Maybe he should get a job with the Chicago Police Department."

"Maybe he should," Hank said as he put his key into the Ford's ignition. "Oh, yeah, I almost forgot. He thought it might be a crazy person doing these killings, trying to frame the Jews."

As the engine turned over, Marvin started chuckling, and then he stopped.

CHAPTER 31

IT WAS AFTER eleven o'clock when Marvin finally climbed out of the back seat and into the front and Hank turned the key in the ignition, easing the black Ford away from the curb and into the quiet, empty street.

The evening storms that had spilled their heavy showers on the city had stopped, but the city was still covered with a dark glaze of rain. Drops falling from the maple leaves above the street drizzled across the windshield. Puddles were scattered up and down the streets and sidewalks, and streams of fallen rainwater skimmed along the gutters. Hank turned on the windshield wipers.

This was the part of a storm that Hank always liked best. The world felt scrubbed clean and cool. Everything was clear as crystal and summer creeks. There were no mysteries in a world like this.

Driving north on California, Hank wondered about the professor Mr. Fisch had mentioned, Professor Zcink.

Zcink sounded like one of the people who lived along Lake Shore Drive, facing Lake Michigan. They were the rich and powerful ones — the politicians and movie stars, the doctors and lawyers, the professors and archbishops, the judges and newspaper publishers, and the crime bosses and racketeers. They ran the city and the state, and they went to the opera and the museums in the Loop. They ate at the fancy restaurants along Michigan Avenue and Jackson Avenue: The Pump Room at the Drake Hotel, Berghoff's, a world of fancy food and fancy entertainment, with fancy women in diamonds and mink, and fancy men in tuxedos.

Why would a guy like that come looking for a tutor around Humboldt Park, a place nobody who lived along the lake would ever want to come to? He'd have to have a reason a hell of a lot better than learning how to say "hot dog" in English or Hungarian or anything else. "Hot dog"? It didn't make a lot of sense.

Their Ford was approaching North Avenue when Hank suddenly felt his partner's sharp elbow jabbing his side. Marvin started yelling, getting louder and louder, "Jesus, slow down, man. We just passed him. We passed him!"

"Passed who?"

"Joey Roses!"

Hank looked and didn't see anything. There was no traffic coming toward them and none going away.

"I don't see him."

"He's riding a bike," Marvin said. "We drove right past the bastard."

"A bike? What the hell would Joey Roses be doing on a bike?"

"Yeah, yeah, a fucking bike. Slow down, buddy. We'll sneak up on him."

"The Lieutenant's not going to like this. He gave us hell about that colored girl, and this is just gonna be more of the same or worse."

"Come on, Hank, you're sounding like my mother again. We got a chance to get Rosetti, find out what he knows. Get you some payback for the shit he gave you."

Hank shook his head. Then he clicked off the car's headlights, eased his foot down on the brake, and made a slow but sharp U-turn.

Hank looked down California. On the west side of the street, there were just the same tall bushes that bordered Humboldt Park on all four sides; on the east side of the street, there was a library, a hotel, and some bars.

Hank wondered if Marvin was still drunk. It was hard to see anything at all in the street. With the Ford's headlights switched off, the streetlights at each intersection didn't help a lot. What little light they gave off didn't go much beyond a narrow circle of yellow-pink light at each corner.

"You're crazy, man," Hank said as the car crawled down California.

"I know what I saw."

"Yeah?" Hank said. Then he spotted something entering the little cone of dim light at the intersection half a block down the street. He couldn't tell what it was. It was just a lighter smudge of darkness against the darker smudge on the right hand side of the street, the park side. Then the smudge became clear for a moment: It was a guy hunched over a bicycle.

Hank eased his foot off the gas.

He knew he had to play it slow. He didn't want whoever was riding the bicycle to hear him or suspect that the cops were pressing down on him and about to crawl up his backside. The unmarked black police car was coasting forward toward the smudge, gaining on it slightly every second. Hank glanced at Marvin and shook his head again. There was nothing about the smudge on the bike that reached out to Hank and shouted, "Hey, I'm Joey Roses."

When the car was about twenty yards from the guy on the bike, Hank gave the Ford just a touch of gas. The big engine rumbled and pushed them forward a bit faster. The smudge on the bike didn't appear to notice them. It was hunched over the handlebars, and it didn't turn around. Whether it was Joey Roses or it wasn't, the guy just kept pedaling his bike steadily toward Division Street. Hank pressed a little bit more on the gas pedal. He couldn't believe that Joey hadn't heard them. With its 272 cubic inches of horsepower, the Ford Mainline wasn't built to be a quiet car, a prowler.

Five yards away from the smudge, Marvin drew his .45 out of his shoulder holster and started cranking down his window. Then, without turning away from the guy on the bicycle, Marvin whispered, "Let's get the son-of-a-bitch."

Hank fed the engine a burst of gas, and the car surged forward toward and beyond the guy on the bike. When the car was three yards past him, Hank threw the steering wheel hard to right and smashed his foot on the brake. The back tires shrieked, and the Ford's rear end spun and slid forward on the wet pavement. The car's high black hood stopped just short of the guy on the bike, but the guy wasn't so lucky. He couldn't stop in time. He swerved to his right and slammed into the curb on the park side of the street. His hands shook loose of the handlebar grips. The front tire of the bike shimmied for a moment, and then he and the bike crashed onto the wet grass.

A second before the car stopped, Marvin threw open the passenger door and jumped out. His pistol raised high in his right hand, he was running toward Joey Roses, the car's momentum whipping him forward. As soon as his feet hit the grass, he was moving faster than his feet could keep up.

For a second, Hank smiled. His partner looked like some character in one of those old Daffy Duck cartoons that Warner Brothers used to make, feet spinning like a sparkly pinwheel while the body didn't seem to be moving an inch.

Then suddenly Hank saw his partner slipping and sliding on the wet grass and going down and crashing into the guy and his bike. Marvin looked like a runner coming into home base head-first on a botched play.

Hank whipped the door of the Ford open and shot out.

As Marvin smashed into the bicycle crumpled up against the curb, the guy leapt up and away from the bike, the unmarked police car, the curb, and the detective fouled up in the twisted spokes and wheels of the old bike.

Hank saw him plainly now. He was Joey Roses after all.

Rushing toward him, Hank could see Joey running into the park like a man on fire. His arms were cutting through the darkness, and his head was thrown back. Right in front of him was a tall hedge, about ten feet thick, planted parallel to the sidewalk, and Joey jumped into it. He was waving his arms like crazy and smashing the limbs and twigs away from his face. In a second, he had disappeared into the hedge. He was gone, goner, gonest.

Hank shouted for Marvin to cut Joey off from the other side, but Hank didn't have time to look back and see if his partner had freed himself from the wreck of the bike or even heard him shouting. Hank was too busy plunging into the bushes after Joey.

Slapping the foliage away from his face, pushing aside loose branches that got knotted up with his sport coat, kicking his feet over roots and low branches, Hank fought through the bushes, yanking and pulling himself forward. Joey must have gone straight through. It wouldn't make sense to try to move along the length of the hedgerow. It would take forever.

The bushes were like a sea of hard twigs and leaves that were trying to drown Hank in their wet and cold immovableness. He couldn't see

Joey Roses, and he couldn't hear him either. Maybe Rosetti was already out of the hedge and into the open spaces beyond. Maybe not. Maybe he had flown up to Heaven. Hank didn't know, and it was hard to think with all the brambles, vines, and twigs cutting at his face, jabbing themselves into his nostrils and ears.

Hank had to get out of the bushes. He hurled his body forward through the last foot.

When he came out, he was fighting for breath. He bent over with his hands on his knees, his lungs pumping for air, dragging the wet, cold air in and pushing it out, again and again. It was a solid two minutes before he could raise his head and breathe half normally, and then he started feeling the cuts on his face and hands, the stinging sweat mixing with the blood. He turned his head and looked around, but he couldn't see Joey or Marvin or anything but the wide lawn of this section of the park. He could see the perimeter loop road just beyond it, and more wide lawn on the other side.

Suddenly, fifty feet to his left, he saw Marvin running into the park toward the kids' playground on the far side of the perimeter road. A few yards ahead of Marvin was that dark smudge Hank had seen earlier on California: Joey Roses.

Rain was beginning to fall again from scattered clouds, a thin drizzle this time.

Hank had to get to the car. He ran along the hedge until he found a sidewalk that cut through it, and ran back to the Ford. Jumping back into the car, he started it up. There was no street running through this section of the park, so Hank did like they'd taught him in cop school. He positioned the Ford's axle parallel to the curb and gave it just enough gas so that its fat black tires crept slowly onto the curb and then over it.

Once he got into the park, seeing shouldn't be too much of a problem, he hoped.

Driving slowly, he again found the sidewalk that broke through the hedge, and he started searching for his partner and Joey Roses. The last time he'd seen them they were running toward the kids' playground, about a block away. By this time — if Marvin hadn't stopped Joey by the slides and swings — the hot pursuit was probably heading to the ball field beyond the playground, just this side of Humboldt Drive, the street that cut a north-south axis through the middle of the park.

Once beyond the curbs on the perimeter road, Hank drove through the park at a steady five miles per hour. It was raining a little harder, and the ground was already soft from the earlier storm, so he tried to keep to the sidewalks as much as he could. They wound through the park this way and that and slowed him down, but he didn't want to see his tires stuck in a set of muddy ruts. Hunched over the steering wheel, he peered through the windshield looking for Marvin. His partner was fast even after a pint of vodka, and Hank knew that drunk or sober, he could catch up to Joey Roses or any junior-grade punk.

Hank drove past the empty swings and jungle gyms at the kids' playground and headed toward the ball field. Just as he came up to it, he slowed the car down and then stopped. Before him was a big sunken treeless area. It gave Hank a good view, but he couldn't see anything moving — not Joey Roses, and not Marvin either. Hank wasn't feeling good about this. It was a big park with lots of places to hide or get lost in. Especially at night.

Then, in front of him and to the right, Hank saw a flash of light near the bushes at the edge of the field. Just as fast, he heard a hollow sound through the rain, a distant boom. It was Marvin's .45.

Hank eased down on the gas pedal again and watched the speedometer creep up to five and then ten miles per hour. He kept his eye on the spot at the edge of the baseball diamond where he had seen the muzzle flash. He didn't want to lose it.

Driving up a slight rise, he followed the sidewalk between two sections of hedgerow. These were even thicker than the earlier one he'd gone through, but this time he wasn't trying to bulldoze his way through with his face leading the way. He knew where he would end up. On the other side of the hedge on the right was a parking lot, the same one where the Polack Killer dragged the two suitcases and got clobbered a couple of days ago. Across the parking lot was the massive boathouse where Marvin had mixed it up with the two homosexuals. Hank stopped the car and looked around.

He didn't see Marvin or Joey.

Hank got out hoping to get a clearer look, but that didn't help. He still couldn't see either of them. He knew Marvin had a pistol with five or six shots left, but he didn't know if Joey was carrying. Maybe he was. Maybe Hank was wrong about what the shot sounded like. Maybe Joey was the one who had gotten one off.

Hank climbed back into the Ford and switched on the police radio. He hoped the reception was better than it usually was.

And this time it was. Holding the black metal microphone close to his lips, he told the gal on the other end that there had been a shot fired, and he needed backup. Then Hank stepped out of the Ford again and started looking for his partner.

The parking lot was empty, and he could pretty much see all of it, but there was nothing to see. The big hedges behind him made it impossible to see anything in that direction, so he ran in the direction Marvin had been going, across the parking lot and Humboldt Drive. Beyond it, the ground started to slope down gradually toward the lagoon and the tennis courts and ball fields on the other side of the water.

Hank slowed to a walk. It was darker in this part of the park. There weren't many streetlights here, but there was one straight ahead of him, and Hank saw that there was an army-green wooden bench underneath it. He could see someone was sitting there, and he walked toward him.

The rain was still falling steady, and he was glad it was. It was washing his face, easing up the stinging that he had been feeling. The scratches from that first hedge were deeper than he'd thought, and the sweat made the scratches smart.

When he got to the bench, Hank saw what he wanted to see. Marvin was sitting in the rain. His hair was wet and matted, and Hank could see the water dripping down his forehead into his eyes and his open mouth. His head was thrown back and his mouth was open as wide as he could open it. He was letting the rain in.

"Where's your hat, Marvin?" Hank said.

"What's your hurry?"

Hank nodded. Marvin was okay. It was an old vaudeville routine, maybe burlesque. One guy is trying to get the other guy out of his house, so he gives the guy his hat and says, "Here's your hat. What's your hurry?" It was a funny bit on stage. Hank asked him again, "So, where is the hat?"

"Jesus, I must have lost it someplace back at the kiddy swings and slides, maybe earlier during my encounter with that bicycle. I'll try to remember. Have a seat."

Hank sat down on the wet park bench. Even in the rain, it was a nice view. He looked at the dark lagoon and the boathouse across the water. It was like a baronial mansion on the Scottish border in some English movie. He glanced up into the brightness coming from the streetlamp above their heads. Its light made each drop seem distinct, clarified.

"Did you get a shot off?" Hank asked.

"Yeah, I did, but I don't think it did Joey much good. I was trying to kill him, but I only winged him."

Someplace far off, maybe on Pulaski Road, a siren started up its long, electric wail. Hank listened for a moment. It was far away but getting gradually louder, heading toward them.

"So, what happened?"

"Well, I cornered Joey about thirty yards from here," Marvin nodded over his left shoulder. "Back there by the concrete-and-stone water fountain. Joey stopped to get a drink. That guy was running like a son of a gun, and I was maybe ten feet behind him, and that's when he stopped for water. It's probably the low-life life he's living, the late nights and bad food that knocked him out. He didn't have a lot of staying power. Anyway, he must have needed a drink of water real bad because he stopped running to take a drink. Imagine, with me only three or four yards behind him."

Marvin stopped talking then. He turned his face up again to the darkness and light above the bench and opened his mouth to the rain. Hank watched him close his eyes and breathe it in.

After a moment, Marvin started talking again, but this time he talked more slowly, more carefully.

"Joey's sucking in big gulps of water from that water fountain, and I tackled him around the waist. Brought him down hard with me on top. I bet I busted some of that punk's ribs. Anyway, I had him down on the ground under me, and he whipped out a knife. It must have been a sheath knife, a hunting knife, because there was no way for him to open a clasp knife or even work the buttons on a switchblade with me on top of him. He jabbed that thing at me, but I saw it coming and tried pulling away. I guess it could have been worse."

Marvin pulled back his sport coat slowly, and Hank saw the blood on his partner's white shirt. The blot was about the size of a small pizza. It covered most of his left side. The stain seemed almost purple in the shadow of the coat and under the yellow light of the streetlamp.

"I don't want to see how bad the cut is," Marvin said. "You take a look."

Marvin unbuttoned his shirt and peeled it carefully away from his chest and stomach. Hank knelt and took a look. The good news was that the blade had cut Marvin, but it hadn't stabbed him. The wound was six inches long but not deep. It was bleeding some, a slight seeping that seemed to pulse with his breathing.

Hank glanced up at his friend and said, "I think he got you."

"Yeah, but I think I got him better. The shot I got off hit him in the arm, maybe the shoulder. After he stuck me, he twirled around and was running for the lagoon. I got him as he jumped in the water. He jerked and froze for a moment, and I figure I had him, but then he was gone. Swimming away. Who would have thought that bastard could swim? With a bullet in one wing."

Hank nodded. He knew what a slug from a .45 would do even if it just winged a guy. It didn't sound like Marvin got him. He was probably just talking to make himself feel like he hadn't screwed up too bad. Hank knew a guy smacked in the arm or shoulder by a gun like that wouldn't be swimming.

"Can you walk?" he asked.

"Sure, about as well as I can dance the polka," Marvin said, and stuck his hand out.

Hank pulled him up. "We got to get you to a doc, get you sewn up."

They began walking back to the parking lot by the boathouse. The police siren sounded like it was coming from someplace on Humboldt Drive north of them now, maybe on the far side of North Avenue. The cops were taking their time getting to the park, but as Marvin and Hank crossed the drive to the parking lot Hank looked up and saw an ambulance coming up from the south end of the park, probably from the Norwegian American Hospital just beyond it.

The cherry-red light on the roof of the ambulance was twirling like a kid's toy top.

CHAPTER 32

THEY DIDN'T CATCH Joey Roses that night, and they didn't catch
him the next, but what they did catch was hell. When Hank got
to work that morning, there was a note on his desk telling him that
Lieutenant O'Herlihy wanted to see him in his office upstairs. Hank
figured his boss was going to chew him out, and he was right.

When he got to O'Herlihy's office, Hank knocked on the
open door.

"I'm not the Pope," O'Herlihy said, looking up. "You don't have
to knock, Purcell. Get in here."

As soon as Hank sat down on one of the two chairs in front of
his desk, O'Herlihy began staring at Hank, and Hank knew how
he was supposed to feel. Uncomfortable. Like a bad dog that had
pissed on his owner's pants leg.

But he didn't feel that way.

You don't go through fourteen months of combat and a bunch of
years in the Chicago Police Department and feel uncomfortable when
your Lieutenant wants to chew you out. But Hank also knew that
he was supposed to feel uncomfortable, so he pretended to feel that
way. He made believe he didn't know what to do with his face and
eyes. He let his eyes roam for a moment, and then he settled in, just
staring ahead at the Lieutenant as the Lieutenant stared back at him.

And like with a lot of pretending, after a while the pretending became the real thing. Hank became uncomfortable. After a moment or two, he almost felt like he was back in basic training, back in grade school, back in his parents' kitchen on Hamlin Street with his father staring him down because he had done something stupid like breaking the frame of the couch by leaping on it too hard. Hank knew what the Lieutenant was going to say, and he wondered how long the Lieutenant was going to keep up the staring business.

Hank figured that pretty soon his throat would get dry, and right after that he'd start sweating. He knew the feeling and had made other people feel it, but still he didn't like it, being made to feel like he was just some shit-pants kid waiting for the hammer to come down, the leather strap to be pulled. He was about to say what O'Herlihy wanted to hear about how sorry he was about the whole mess when O'Herlihy said, "How's Bondarowicz?"

Hank relaxed some and pushed his chair back a little from the desk. "Thanks for asking, Lieutenant. The cut wasn't too bad. It took thirty-seven stitches, and the emergency room doc at Norwegian told Marvin to take it easy today, so he's out, at home."

"Thirty-seven? Mmm. That's something. It must have been deep. Did the blade reach his ribs?"

"No, sir, the guy who did it didn't get a clean hit. They were fighting, and Marvin had him on the ground. The guy couldn't get a good swing at him no matter how hard he tried."

"That's good. And how's Bondarowicz feel?"

Hank shrugged.

"The report says he got the guy, winged him. You buy that?" Lieutenant O'Herlihy asked.

"Maybe. Bondarowicz says he got a shot off that caught the guy in the arm or shoulder, and then he said that he saw the guy swim across the lagoon. It's not wide at that spot, but I figure it'd be hard for a guy to swim even a short distance after taking one in the arm."

"You know, Purcell, this isn't the first time your partner got a shot off that maybe hit and maybe didn't. There was that thing that happened last summer, in July, when he shot at a cat burglar and almost hit an old man walking his dog."

"Yeah, I remember. It was dark, and the old man lost the heel of his shoe. Nobody was hurt."

"That's not the point," O'Herlihy said, and glanced down at the file on his desk. He wrote something across the top and closed it. Then he looked at Hank again and said, "Marvin's a real Nervous Norvus. You know what I mean?"

"I think I do."

"Like in that song 'Transfusion' where the guy sings about the 'line-crowding hogs and speeding jackasses'?"

"Yeah, I heard it. 'Transfusion'."

"That's right. There's good advice there at the end of that song. Advice you and your partner Bondarowicz both ought to consider taking. What's Nervous Norvus say there at the end? Hey? He says that those speeding jackasses better learn to slow down. He's talking about you, Hank. You and your Jewish buddy Bondarowicz. You guys are bringing me a lot of grief this week. First, with you two busting in to that colored place over south of the Lake Street El. You've been a cop for a long time. You know it's no business of ours if a Negro girl gets killed on the South Side. Then this thing with him getting cut up and shooting at some punk in the park."

Hank interrupted O'Herlihy. "That was Joey Roses."

"So Bondarowicz says, but you don't know who this kid was. Did you eyeball his driver's license? Take his picture and compare it to what we got downtown? Cuff him and look him in the eye? I don't think so. Bondarowicz and you are cruising around on a wet Monday night, probably drinking too much booze trying to keep the blues away, and you see a kid riding a bike and you take after him. You got no idea who that kid is, and you chase him into Humboldt Park and start shooting, real cowboys-and-Indians stuff. You think this is the Ardennes, the fucking Battle of the Bulge?"

Hank didn't say anything for a moment. He remembered the Bulge. Snow falling as the guy in the trench next to him bled out. He kept weeping and whispering something about sand and water, but Hank couldn't make it make sense.

"Lieutenant," he said, snapping out of it, "Marvin took thirty-seven stitches. This was not exactly some innocent little kid."

"But you don't know who the kid was, exactly. Joey Roses, Moey the Plumber, Sammy the Tailor who made your pants too long? And so what if he was Joey Roses? He's just a small-time hood with some kind of connection to the colored rackets, switchblades, and Negro prostitutes. Didn't I tell you that I don't want you bringing that stuff into our department? That stuff belongs south of the color line. Didn't I make that clear?"

"Yes, sir, you did. But we thought we had a chance, and we knew we only had a minute to decide. Joey Roses won the coin flip."

"Bad call for you guys. Not only for your partner with his stitches, but you too. You're coming across as a rogue cop, a maverick. Any chance you're thinking of promotion is getting flushed down the toilet."

"Yes, sir."

"And you're not making the City of Chicago happy. You ripped up a heck of a lot of grass between California and Humboldt Drive. I've been getting reports all morning about how much it's going to cost the Parks District to fix the ruts you cut with your Ford's heavy-duty cop tires."

Hank looked at the window behind O'Herlihy. The morning grayness was getting darker. Some of the rain that dumped a couple inches on the city last night seemed to be lining up again for another try at sinking the Good Ship Chicago. Hank let Lieutenant O'Herlihy roll on for a couple more minutes, let him tirade about wasted resources and cowboy cops. He'd heard it before. He'd hear it again, more likely sooner than later. The Lieutenant jawed on, and Hank waited for him to run out of spit and steam.

O'Herlihy finally clammed up and picked up the pack of cigarettes leaning against his ashtray. Hank watched him fish a Pall Mall out of his pack and light it with a wooden match and take a deep drag. He held it in for a moment, and then he let it out.

That's when Hank lifted his hands and said, "Lieutenant, I know you don't believe it, but we got this feeling about Joey Roses. We think he's tied in to the Suitcase Charlie stuff somehow. His name's come up a number of times during the investigation. The Outfit guy Alex Santori mentioned him, and so did Stashu Dombrowski, the bartender at the White Eagle, the bar across from where the first suitcase was found. And Joey was in that apartment down on Washington Boulevard where we found the dead colored girl."

"Yeah, Purcell, you and Bondarawicz always got a story to back up your screw-ups."

"Lieutenant, I don't see anybody else finding any kind of leads you can believe in on this case. You know that most of what we do is track down stuff and see where it takes us. Sometimes it doesn't take us anywhere. But sometimes it does."

O'Herlihy took the cigarette out of his mouth and streamed some smoke out of the right side of his mouth. "Listen, Purcell, I'll be straight with you. You're not the problem. It's your partner. He's a sad sack, a screw-up. I know you guys are pals, so you better do what you can to keep him in line this time. He's got a smart mouth and not many friends around here."

"He's a good cop."

"Yeah? Since when?"

Hank didn't say anything for a moment. He wondered where this was going, what the point of it all was. Everybody knew what kind of cop Marvin was. Sometimes he was shaky and sometimes he wasn't, and all in all he wasn't that much different from the other detectives and patrolmen, the harness bulls, Hank had partnered up with over the years. Something was bugging O'Herlihy, and Hank didn't have a clue what it was.

"Yeah? So? You going to keep him toeing the line?" the Lieutenant asked.

Hank didn't say what he wanted to say. He said what the Lieutenant wanted to hear: "Yes, sir."

"Good. Now let's talk about Suitcase Charlie. You know that suitcase?"

"You mean Charlie's suitcases?"

O'Herlihy nodded. "Yeah."

"There were three of them, Lieutenant."

"I know there were three of them, Purcell. I'm not a complete idiot. I'm talking about the first one. The one they found between the convent and the White Eagle Tap. That one."

"Yeah?"

"We finally got a report about it from the crime-lab boys downtown. The lock on the first suitcase was different from the locks on the two suitcases that were found the following night. The first one was manufactured in Hungary, but the next two were made in America."

"How do they know that?"

"How do they know anything? They're whiz-kids down there, college boys. Take a look at these photos," O'Herlihy said, and pushed a folder across the desk to Hank.

Hank opened it to find a bunch of eight-by-ten black-and-white photographs. There were ten of them, and Hank wanted to lay them out but there was no room on the desk. He looked up at the Lieutenant.

"Let me help you make some room," he said as he pulled his ashtray and the stacks of folders back so that Hank could spread the pictures out on the desk.

Hank nodded his thanks and arranged the ten shots in two rows. The top row was just medium shots of the three suitcases. In three of the photos, the suitcases were closed and standing up. In two others, they were open and lying on the floor. The remains of the murdered boys had been removed, but Hank could still make out some blood stains. They looked glossy black, deep and solid as plastic. He picked up one of the photos and turned it in his hands slightly to see if he could cut down some of the glare, but he couldn't.

It was like all there was, was glare and blackness.

That's right, he thought, that's all there was, glare and blackness and the memory of that boy's body chopped up the way you would chop up a rabbit or a chicken. It made Hank want to throw up again, the way he had when he saw what was in the first suitcase.

He glanced at the window behind the Lieutenant's head for a second, and then he looked back at the photographs. The bottom row consisted of five shots, extreme close-ups of the inner workings of the suitcase locks. The metal casing from the top of each of the locks had been removed neatly, exposing springs, coils, and tumblers. Three of the photos were of the lock on the first suitcase, and the other two showed the locks on the suitcases the Polack Killer was lugging near the boathouse in Humboldt Park when that kid from DuPage County smacked him with his tire iron.

Hank lowered his head and studied the locks for a minute. They seemed identical, flat, metallic, each about an inch and a half square, with the same mechanisms. Even in black-and-white, they looked identical down to the color. Their casings were probably covered with the same kind of fake gold flake.

He picked up the close-up of the lock on the first suitcase and held it close to his right eye.

"I don't see it," Hank said, finally putting the picture down. "The difference. I don't see it."

"Neither do I, but the science-fiction boys say it's a big deal. What they say is that the lock from the first suitcase is the real thing, a major clue."

Hank leaned back and looked at the Lieutenant.

"What's the clue? What's it tell us?"

"They say that the kind of mechanism on that first lock only comes from one place. Hungary. That's right. Not the U.S., not anywhere else in Europe, not anywhere else anywhere. Hungary. It looks like the Hungarians manufacture their locks in a way that's as mysterious as their language. You can't even buy a suitcase with a lock like this anywhere in Chicago. Probably not even in New York."

"How the hell did it get here?"

"Yeah, Purcell, that's the question. There's not a lot of back-and-forth right now between Hungary and the West, at least not since the Soviets took over the country back during the war, in '45. Like they say, you can't get there from here. And neither can your suitcase."

Hank didn't say anything for a moment. He looked at a photo of the first lock, and then he looked at the photos of the other two. He shook his head.

"Maybe the killer bought it second hand," Hank said, "on Maxwell Street, down by the flea market. You can get just about anything you want there."

"You're a smart boy," the Lieutenant said. "I was thinking along the same lines. There's a team of detectives working the luggage stores around Maxwell. There's a couple on Halsted, and some more just off of it, on the side streets. The old Jewish guys running those stores might be able to help track down where this suitcase came from. We'll see what our guys turn up."

"I hope they find something soon."

O'Herlihy looked at Hank. It was a look Hank understood.

"Yeah, me too," O'Herlihy said. "I hope they find something before we find another suitcase with another body, another dead boy."

Hank nodded.

The Lieutenant picked up the photos and shuffled them back into the folder.

Hank knew the meeting was over, and stood up to go.

"One last thing, Purcell, and you aren't going to like it. I'm roping you and Bondarowicz in. You guys are keeping too many late nights, pulling too hard on the bottle. You know what I mean?"

Hank shrugged.

"I want you two to step back, do some cool time. You and your partner are going back to school. I want you to canvass the ones in the Humboldt Park area. Boost morale by showing off your badges and making the civilians think the Chicago P.D. is worth all the heavy dollars the taxpayers are laying out."

"Lieutenant, us going to the schools? That's not going to do anybody any good."

"Well, I'm not so sure about that. Having two big tough detectives like you and your partner going into the schools might shake some of the fear out of the kids, make them feel more comfortable. That'll be something."

The Next Day: Wednesday, June 6

CHAPTER 33

HANK AND MARVIN were sitting outside the principal's office at
Goethe Elementary School down on Rockwell and Lyndale when
they heard the news about the next killing.

Goethe Elementary was their first school visit together. Hank had
spent most of Tuesday working alone, visiting the schools south and
west of Humboldt Park. Marvin's thirty-seven stitches were enough
to keep him out of work for one day, but today they were both on
the job; and the job, Hank felt, was pointless. The previous day, he
had visited four schools, shook hands with principals and teachers,
eaten some bad cafeteria food, and walked up and down corridors
that smelled of pea soup and kids who were just starting to have
their own unique body odor. It was like being in the army except
without the shooting.

Hank didn't know if he was making the city's school children
feel safer, but he sure hoped so, because the assignment was putting
him to sleep. He felt like a Mickey-Mouse politician running for
chairman of the school board.

Right now, he and his partner were sitting on hard-backed chairs
waiting for the Goethe Elementary principal to finish chewing out
some kid. The kid, a third-grade juvenile delinquent with a ducktail
haircut, had sassed a teacher, told her to "take a hike on a spike." Hank
had never heard that expression before, but he figured it wasn't the

best thing to say to a teacher because the principal wasn't happy. Every couple seconds, they heard him shout "No!" and slam his palm against his desk. He was gnawing the kid out real good, telling him he'd end up in the state penitentiary if he didn't start flying right.

Hank looked at Marvin. His partner was sitting up straight and staring forward. He hadn't said anything for a while, and Hank thought his wound was bothering him. Hank was about to ask him how he felt when the principal's phone rang.

First there was silence, and then Hank heard the principal say, "Oh. Oh dear."

The kid who was being lectured stepped out of the principal's office, looked at Hank and Marvin, and stopped dead for a couple of seconds. Then he turned the other way and hurried off down the gray corridor.

Hank hoped the kid had made him and Marvin as cops, and that from now on the kid with the ducktail would stick to the straight and narrow. Yeah, that and get rid of the ducktail. If anything would make him develop into a full-fledged juvenile delinquent, it was that ducktail.

Hank was about to stand up when the principal came to the door. His face was yellow-gray, and he was shaking his head. It wasn't the kind of shaking that indicated anything complicated, like acceptance or rejection. Hank had seen this kind of shaking before. It was the look of surprise and fear that comes when you've been slammed by something terrible you don't understand and figure you'll never be able to understand.

Hank stood up, and the principal turned to him.

"There's been another," he said, putting his right hand up to his cheek.

"Another what?" Hank asked.

"A dead child. In a park on the South Side."

The principal said that and nothing more. He suddenly looked faint. His breathing was shallow and quick, and Hank thought the guy was going to keel over. Marvin looked at him and stood up. He took him by the shoulder and arm and eased him into one of the chairs outside his office.

"Here, you sit down," Marvin said, and the principal sank into the chair.

Hank bent over and began undoing the guy's tie.

"You'll be okay, pal, just take some deep breaths," Marvin said to the principal. Then he looked at Hank. "We got to get down to the South Side."

"Marvin, you're nuts. O'Herlihy wants us checking the schools out and reassuring the kids."

"Talk about nuts? That's nuts. They don't need us walking around the schools and making the kids feel safe. That's bullshit. They pull us off this case, and as soon as they do, suitcases start popping up again. We got to get down there and straighten this out."

"The Lieutenant isn't going to like this. Especially on the South Side."

"Hank, we're not here to make the Lieutenant happy," Marvin said as he hurried toward the stairwell that led to the door that opened onto Rockwell Street.

CHAPTER 34

BY THE TIME Hank and Marvin drove down to Washington Park, the suitcase was gone, but they could tell where it had been.

Getting out of the car, Hank saw the wooden Chicago Police Department barricades ahead of him. They looked like yellow saw-horses, sectioning off a wide, lopsided, circular area on the east side of Grand Boulevard just south of Burke Elementary School. The circle took in a section of the park that included about a dozen benches, some hedges, a cement water fountain, and three sidewalks that intersected near the water fountain. Inside the circle formed by the police barricades, a ragged line of uniform cops, a dozen or so, walked outward, taking slow baby steps away from the cordoned-off area and staring at the ground.

Hank knew it looked like some funny kids' game, but the cops knew what they were doing. They were searching for evidence, bits of this and that, blood, pieces of clothing, scraps of paper, cigarette butts, anything that might lead to something bigger. He wished them luck. With the morning sun hidden behind a thick layer of gray clouds and a rainstorm coming up, Hank figured it would be hard for them to find anything much, but maybe he was wrong. He sure hoped so.

Nearing the barricade, Hank saw one of the policemen who was walking the search line stop, lower his head, and stoop down. This might be it, Hank hoped. Maybe here was the luck he had wished for, for the cops who were searching.

The officer who had stopped brushed the grass back with a pencil he held in his left hand. Then he stooped lower, reached down with his right hand, touched the dirt, and sat down on his haunches. Something must have caught his eye, and he stayed that way for a couple seconds, first looking straight down in front of him, then to his left and right.

But finally, he straightened up and pushed his patrolman's hat back. He looked to the cop a few feet to his left who was moving slowly forward, and then he started forward too. He hadn't found squat.

A long peal of thunder cracked just south of the park, and a thin, slow drizzle started even before the thunder had echoed off over Lake Michigan.

Hank stopped watching the cops do their work and looked for his partner. Marvin was just in front of Hank at the barricade. Standing with his hands on it, Marvin was talking to a detective in a yellow rain slicker. Hank came up to hear what the detective was saying to his partner.

"Yeah, they think it's the same guy," the cop said. "Same size brown leather suitcase. Same chopped up body."

Marvin shook his head.

"I don't see it," he said. "It's not the same this time. It's a girl, for Christ's sake. The kids found up by us were boys."

The detective in the raincoat looked at Marvin for a moment and then shrugged. Hank could see the guy was tired. The eyes in his long face seemed heavy, the lids on the brink of sliding shut. "Maybe the killer got tired of boys. Maybe he ran out of boys. I don't know."

Marvin shook his head and looked up. The drizzle was growing into rain.

"Where'd they take the suitcase and the body?" Hank asked.

"Up to Cook County Hospital. The Chief of Detectives figured it would be best to keep these bodies together in one place, and they didn't want to have to haul the boys downtown to the South Side crime labs. The Chief also figured that County was sort of midway between Washington Park and you guys up near Humboldt Park."

"Who found the body?"

"A colored boy and his sister going to school. He saw the suitcase and ran up, probably figuring he would beat his sister to it. It was standing up and closed, I heard, and he pushed it over before his sister got to him. They were excited, supposedly felt they were doing the cops a favor, solving a crime. The two of them together finally got it opened up. I was surprised they were able to, but they did it."

"What happened?"

"What happened? Soon as the little boy sees what's in the suitcase, he gets hysterical, goes nuts. Screaming, running around, shouting 'oh no' over and over, blubbering snot and spit. The patrolman who got here first was telling me that he'd never seen anything like it. Most times, a kid's pretty cool, but not this time. Before the cop was able to quiet him down, the colored boy jerked away and ran into the street. A milk truck got him. Smashed him."

Hank could see Marvin wince. "Jesus," he said.

"Yeah, sweet Jesus. Poor kid. He was lucky the cops were here when it happened. They picked him right up and drove him to the hospital with their sirens screaming."

"How's he doing?" Marvin asked.

"The kid's not doing so great. Breathing, but unconscious."

Hank shook his head and motioned toward the dozen cops searching in line for evidence. "The boys find anything yet?"

"Not enough to convict," the detective in the raincoat said.

"What've they got?" Marvin asked.

"The suitcase didn't come in from the street here, Grand Boulevard. The killer must've dragged the thing over from the park street east of here, Ellsworth Drive. That's about three hundred feet away, maybe. He left a trail where the grass was matted down from the weight of the body. A long haul. He must be pretty strong. A big boy with a lot of muscle. Real beefcake."

"Yeah," Hank said, "he probably didn't want anybody seeing him parked on Grand and dragging the suitcase out of his car."

Marvin chuckled. "Cops all over the city are keeping track of anybody dragging, carrying, or lifting a suitcase. Just yesterday, me and my partner Purcell here apprehended a couple heading up to the Wisconsin Dells for their honeymoon."

The detective in the slicker didn't cut a smile. Instead, he gave Marvin a cold look. The rain was falling harder now, and Hank could hear it slapping off the rubberized yellow fabric on the guy's rain slicker. The guy didn't want to hear any jokes about a guy chopping up kids and leaving them scattered like garbage in the city parks. This cop just wasn't in the mood. He was tired and had seen enough stuff he didn't know what to make of.

"Bondarowicz, you're an asshole," he said.

"Can't take a joke, chum? Maybe you've been on this job too long. Maybe you need a little vacation. What do you say? I'll loan you my pullman bag."

The cop didn't say anything else. He just turned and walked away, back toward the line of uniform cops staring at the grass and moving slowly through the falling rain toward Ellsworth Drive.

Marvin looked at Hank, and Hank looked at Marvin. After a moment, Marvin shrugged.

"Well, that's that. I don't think we'll be getting much information from our colleague in the schoolboy-yellow rain slicker," he said. "What now, my friend?"

"You're a hard guy to partner with, Marvin."

"Hmmm. That's a fact. My last three wives said pretty much the same thing to the judges when they made their pitch for the alimony."

"Let's drive up to Cook County Hospital and see what we can find out about the girl who was killed," Hank said, and started walking up the block toward their car.

"Nah, it's too early for that," Marvin said, following him. "I bet they're still doing the admission paperwork. It takes forever. We'll be sitting on our asses for hours there. Let's kill some time down here on the South Side. You said the gnome, Mr. Fisch, told you about some professor he tutors who teaches in Hyde Park, at the University of Chicago. It's not far, around the corner. Let's go see this Herr Professor, Dr. Zcink. If he's not in, we can check out the Museum of Science and Industry. Have you been there since they set up that captured Kraut submarine? The U-505? We can take a tour through it."

Hank stopped and waited for Marvin to catch up. "You know, you really are an asshole."

"Yeah, I know. So's the guy in that girly yellow slicker. What kind of rain gear is that? He ought to be ashamed, and him a grown man and all."

CHAPTER 35

HANK STOOD IN FRONT of the two-story brownstone on Dorchester Avenue and shivered. The steady, hard rain had slackened off into a drizzle, and a cold front must have rolled in behind it. A week ago, it had felt like high summer, the middle of August, and now it felt like it was coming on to late winter or at best early spring. Hank was cold and wet, and he wished he had a yellow rain slicker like the one the detective over by Burke Elementary had. Even an umbrella would be nice, but the city didn't want its cops walking around with umbrellas. Hank remembered reading the memo about it last fall. It seemed to make sense at the time — they didn't want Chicago cops looking like flitty London Bobbies, after all — but it didn't make sense now with all this rain.

He turned around and looked back at the Ford parked at the curb. Marvin was just pushing the door shut. He had gone back to the car to find his memo pad.

Hank couldn't believe that it had only been a week since the first dead child was found. Now there were four. Five if you counted the colored girl he and Marvin stumbled across in the apartment on Washington Boulevard. How many more would there be by next week? Hank couldn't believe that so many kids could just be snatched off the streets without anybody noticing. He shook his head and turned his collar against the rain and wind.

Marvin slapped him on the back and said, "Hank, why are you standing around here on the sidewalk like a moron? It's raining, come on."

Hank's partner started toward the building and took two concrete steps at a time. Before Hank reached the first step, Marvin was in the small lobby, holding the glass door open for him.

Hank stepped in and shook the rain off his overcoat and hat. It would be good to be inside for a while. He looked at the mailboxes set in the wall. There were three of them. The two-story brownstone probably used to house a single prosperous family, but that was a while ago. Like a lot of these old buildings, the brownstone had been cobbled up into two above-ground apartments, with a third in the basement.

The name of the guy Mr. Fisch tutored was on the brass nameplate above the middle mailbox, the one for the first floor: Professor Domokos Zcink.

Marvin underlined the name with his finger and looked at Hank. "Hell of a fine name."

"Yes, it is, Bondarowicz."

Marvin smiled.

"So, this was your idea," Hank said. "You got a plan?"

"A plan? Yeah, yeah, I got a plan. Sure. Napoleon's Famous Two-Part Battle Plan."

"What's that?"

"Part One, we show up," Marvin said, and paused.

Hank humored him. "What's Part Two?"

"Part Two?" Marvin said, and smiled again. "We see what happens."

"Hmm. Sounds better than your usual plan, I guess," Hank said, and pressed the white doorbell button next to Zcink's name.

CHAPTER 36

FOR A LONG moment, they stood waiting for somebody to come to the door, but there was no answer, and Hank pressed the doorbell again.

He could hear it ringing deep inside the apartment. A soft, tinny echo, like a kid far away rattling a teaspoon in an empty soup can. Maybe the apartment was big, and the professor couldn't hear the bell's small metallic sound. Hank waited again for a moment, and then he knocked on the wooden door. Nothing. He put his ear to the door and listened. He didn't hear a sound.

"Well, lucky us," Marvin said. "It looks like we're going to see the Kraut sub exhibit down at the Museum after all. Come on. Nobody's home."

Hank said, "Just a second," and tried the doorknob. It turned easily, and he pushed the door back a little. "It's open."

"You're kidding," Marvin whispered.

Hank didn't say anything. He slowly pressed the door farther back and stepped into a large living room. To his right, three windows bayed out toward the sidewalk and the street in front of the house. To his left, a deep-blue couch and a couple of matching easy chairs sat in the room's gray shadows. Paintings and framed photographs filled all the available wall space. The guy had quite a collection.

Hank heard a sound at the back of the apartment and glanced at Marvin. His partner heard it too, but he didn't flinch.

"And now, we see what happens," Marvin said and smiled.

Hank nodded, turned toward the back of the apartment, and shouted, "Hello? Anyone here?"

There was nothing for a long moment, but then a tall, thin man in a floor-length brown robe stepped through a doorway at the far end of the living room. When he saw Hank and Marvin he stopped and smiled.

"Gentlemen," he said, "what can I do for you?"

"Professor Zcink?" Hank said.

"Yes?"

"I'm Detective Purcell, and this is Detective Bondarowicz, of the Chicago Police Department. We rang and knocked. Nobody answered."

"So you came in? I don't mean to be rude, gentlemen, but doesn't that seem a little strange?"

"Yes sir, Professor, strange is what it seems," Marvin said, stepping into the living room. "The door was open when we got here, and we were just checking to make sure there wasn't a burglary in progress or something worse. We're always worrying about crime, it's part of our job. But of course, we didn't mean to come in without your say-so."

Standing across the room facing Marvin, Zcink didn't say anything for a moment.

Hank wondered what Zcink was going to do. Call the police, tell the dispatcher that two men who say they're detectives broke into his house? Scream for the Hungarian Ambassador? Rush toward them and try to push them out of his apartment? Hank took off his wet hat with his left hand and held it dripping at his side.

The Professor turned from Marvin and looked at Hank.

Hank nodded.

Zcink smiled then and asked, with his first hint of an accent, "So, detective?"

Hank smiled back. It was almost like a scene in some creepy old horror film he had seen when he was a kid. One about vampires, or maybe werewolves. Zcink's English was clear and clean, but there was a Hungarian lilt to it that reminded Hank of the way that Dracula guy, Bela Lugosi, used to talk.

In a quiet, even tone, Hank said, "Professor, we're sorry if we startled you. We didn't mean any offense. We just stopped by to ask you some routine questions. Mr. Fisch, your language tutor, he gave us your name and address."

"Samuel Fisch? Yes, of course, I know Mr. Fisch. He gave you my name?"

"Yes, sir. He gave us your name."

"Hmm, that's interesting. May I ask in what context he mentioned my name, and for what reason?"

Zcink's voice was light, but Hank could tell he was suspicious.

"We're working on a case up around his neighborhood, near Humboldt Park."

"I hope Mr. Fisch is not in any sort of trouble. He's a good teacher, and, more importantly, a good man."

"Yes, sir, he is. A good man. We've spent a lot of time with him this last week. He's sort of helping us with our case, in fact," Marvin said. "Mind if we sit down?"

"No, no, of course not. Please, do sit down."

Hank took one of the two easy chairs across from the blue couch. Marvin took the other one.

Professor Zcink, however, didn't sit down. He switched on an overhead light, and then he put his hands together and asked,

"Gentleman, I know, of course, that you are on duty, but there's a cold rain falling this morning, and it would be inhospitable not to offer you something to fight back the chill. May I offer you a drink? Perhaps a small glass of French brandy? Sadly, one cannot find proper *pálinka*, the brandy of Hungary, here."

Marvin straightened up. "That would be great, Professor. It is cold out there today."

"Thanks, but just a short one for me," Hank said, lifting up his right hand and measuring out a small space with his thumb and index finger. "I'm driving."

"Of course, that's quite sensible. I'll be back shortly."

When Professor Zcink turned and walked to the kitchen at the back of the apartment, Hank stood up and walked over to the wall behind the two easy chairs. He wanted to see the paintings and photographs — he felt like he was becoming quite a connoisseur. Mr. Fisch had that Chagall painting. Hank wondered what he'd find on Professor Zcink's walls. A Picasso? Or maybe something by that crazy guy with the long, waxy mustache, Salvador Dali?

What Hank saw made him wonder even more. A number of the paintings showed blotches of red and brown cut across with streams of yellow. He had seen this kind of painting before; it was what *Life* magazine was calling Abstract Expressionism, a fancy name for colorful red-and-brown blotches with streaks of yellow.

After a couple of seconds Hank had seen enough Abstract Expressionism, and turned to the photos. They were small black-and-whites, and much more interesting. About a dozen were arranged between two of the blotchy paintings. He ran his eye across them; it seemed like every one was a picture of a bombed-out church. Collapsed walls, piled bricks, missing roofs, broken crucifixes dangling from ceilings. In one of the photographs, there was a statue of Mary holding Jesus after he was taken down from the Cross. Behind the statue, a damaged wall cut across the photo, slashing the picture in half. Where the wall was, there was darkness; where the wall had come down, there was light. Mary held the body of her son Jesus so that it ran almost parallel to the top of what was left of the wall. There was light above the body in her arms, darkness below it. Jesus was headless, and Mary had lost her right arm. Quite a picture.

Hank was about to look at another cluster of photos when Zcink returned, carrying a bottle and three small cut-crystal glasses on a silver tray.

"Admiring my photographs?" Zcink said, setting the tray down on the coffee table. "I took them in Berlin toward the end of the war. I thought someone should try to preserve the churches before the Allied bombers finished pounding them into nothing more than dust and gravel."

"You were in Berlin?"

"Yes, and I was lucky to get out just before the Russians came. The Allied bombing was dreadful, almost apocalyptic. For months, the British came by night, the Americans by day. Yes, it was something to see. Not a stone was left upon another, but when the Russians came it was worse. Even the stones bled then. We thought the world was coming to an end."

Hank nodded his head and watched Zcink pour two fingers of brandy into each of the three tulip-shaped glasses. Then he handed one to Marvin and one to Hank.

"Egészségedre!" Professor Zcink said, raising his own glass. "To your health!"

Marvin tried to say "Egészségedre!" in response, but slipped up somewhere in the middle of the toast, just after the "szs" sound.

Zcink chuckled and quickly covered his mouth with his hand. "Forgive me. Hungarian is a difficult language. If you shift the accent just a little, 'to your health' becomes 'up your arse.'"

Marvin smiled, mispronounced *"Egészségedre!"* again, and threw back his brandy.

The professor laughed, and Hank joined him. Then Hank said, "To your health," and drank down half the brandy in his glass. It was sweet and thick, a burning syrup streaming down his throat. "Thanks, Professor Zcink. That'll keep the chill off."

"You're welcome," the professor said, and walked over to the couch and sat down on the right side.

Hank put his glass on the tray on the coffee table and glanced at Zcink. The Professor seemed comfortable, Hank thought. A nervous man would sit in the middle, but Zcink didn't appear anxious about anything. He stretched his legs out in front of him and rested his left arm along the back of the couch.

"Now, gentlemen, what can I do for you?"

Hank put his hat on the floor and leaned forward slightly. "Like I said, Professor Zcink, Mr. Fisch is helping us with our investigation, and he mentioned your name. He said you might be able to help us out some."

"Of course. Is it about the terrible killings near Humboldt Park? I was reading about them this morning in the *Tribune*. Are the police any closer to finding the perpetrator?"

Marvin cleared his throat. "We're not really at liberty to pass around that kind of information, Professor, but I think we can tell you honestly, without divulging any real secrets, that we've come a long way on the case."

"Thank God," the professor said.

"One of the things we wanted to ask you, sir," Hank said, pulling his memo pad out of his breast pocket, "was about that Wednesday night when the first body was found. We're questioning all the people who might have seen or heard something. So far the Chicago Police Department has interviewed about thirty thousand people."

"That many?"

"Yes, sir, pretty much everyone on the force is looking into this, and that's why we're here today. Mr. Fisch mentioned that you were there at his house that night, Wednesday, May 30, the night when the first body was found."

"Oh, yes, I was there. I was coming for my usual tutorial session. Mr. Fisch has been my tutor for five years now, since 1952."

"And as we understand it, you arrived late that evening."

"Yes, I had some car trouble on the drive up from the university."

"Mr. Fisch mentioned that. Could you tell us what happened?"

"Certainly. I stopped for a light on California and Roosevelt Road, and my engine died suddenly when the light changed. Honestly, it was more than slightly unsettling."

"Why's that?"

"I'm sure you know the neighborhood. Working class, poor, much unemployment. Many of the residents are new arrivals here in Chicago from the Deep South — Mississippi, Louisiana.... ou know what they think when they see a white man stuck in a respectable car. They reason that they can profit somehow from another's misfortune."

"Yes, sir," Hank said, nodding his head. "So what happened?"

"First the expected, and then the unexpected. The cars behind me were honking. Some colored people on the sidewalk were stopping to look at me. I was worried, of course, about getting out of my car, but then I realized that if I didn't do something soon I could be there all night long, and something worse might happen then. So I stepped out of my Plymouth and raised the hood. I don't know anything about cars — or rather, I know why they work but not *how* they work — but I started inspecting this wire and that to see if anything was loose. It was no use, futile. The car wouldn't start and I saw nothing I could fix. I was about to see if I could find a phone to call for a tow truck when a polite young colored man came up and offered me his assistance. I happily said 'Of course,' and immediately he enlisted some of the other colored men walking by to push my car to the curb. Then, when it was safely out of the street, he began looking at my engine. I really don't know what he did, but after thirty minutes or so he told me to see if my car would start. And it did."

"I'm glad to hear your story had a happy ending."

"As am I. You hear stories about terrible things happening — like what happened to these poor boys near Mr. Fisch's home — and you imagine the worst."

"You sure do," Marvin smiled. "I never go down to the colored parts of town without my pistol and a police escort: my friend Detective Purcell here."

"Well, Detective, I mean no disrespect, but to be frank with you, that young colored man showed me that one should not be so ready to pre-judge people, no matter what their color, race, or religion. We are — as your Declaration of Independence states — all created equal."

"Professor, let me ask you one more question," Hank said. "After your Plymouth was running again and you drove up California to Mr. Fisch's house, did you see anything out of the ordinary, anything suspicious, especially as you drove nearer to Humboldt Park?"

"No, no, I don't think so. I offered the young colored man some money for helping me, but he said that all he wanted was a ride up to the North Side. I said I would be happy to do that, and drove him to a house on California, just on the other side of North Avenue and the park. After that, I drove back down to Mr. Fisch's. It was dark by then, and honestly, I didn't see anything out of the ordinary on California, coming or going. And nothing unusual on Mr. Fisch's street either."

"Thanks, Professor Zcink. By any chance, did you get the colored fellow's name?"

"Yes, Detective, I did. I asked him his name before I let him get into my car. He told me his name was Pascal Stoop. An unusual name, so I remembered it. I can also tell you which house he entered on California: a two-story frame house just north of the alley, right after the tavern on the corner there. It's on the west side of the street, a grayish house."

"Thank you, Professor Zcink, what you told us helps," Hank said, writing the name and the location down in his memo pad. "It gets us one step further in our investigation."

"Say, Professor," Marvin cut in, "like just about everybody in the world, I'm interested in the Atom Bomb, and Mr. Fisch, he said something about you working on it. I got to hand it to you guys, you sure did some job. During the war I was in the Pacific Theater of Operations, on a ship waiting to invade Japan with about a million other doggies when they dropped the big one on Hiroshima and its little brother on Nagasaki. Those A-bombs fried a lot of Nips and ended that god-awful war. Honestly, I couldn't be happier."

"Thank you, Detective," Professor Zcink said and smiled, "but I can't take any of the credit. I didn't work on your country's Manhattan Project. I worked on the German Bomb with

Professor Heisenberg in Berlin. If we had successfully completed our project, we would have used it to destroy communists in Moscow rather than Japanese civilians in Hiroshima."

"Can't blame you for that, Professor. In fact, it would've probably been a good thing if you had flattened Moscow. Saved the world a whole lot of trouble later."

"Yes," Zcink said. "The world has become an even more complicated place since the Russians developed their own Bomb."

"Complicated, and mysterious too," Marvin said. "And one of the big mysteries for me is how you managed to get here. I mean the U.S., not Chicago. There you were, in the rubble of Berlin, taking pictures and working on the A-bomb fast as rabbits, trying to throw it together before the Reds beat the living bejesus out of you and your Kraut friends, no offense, and now here you are sitting in the comfort of a long, plush bathrobe on a couch — a beautiful couch by the way — here in Hyde Park. It must have been quite an adventure. I mean, I would have thought the Reds would've shipped you and this Professor Heisenberg and all the other A-bomb scientists someplace north of Siberia where the best you can get is like the worst anyplace else. I know I would have if I was the Reds. By the way, would you mind if I had another small drink?"

Not waiting for the Professor's answer, Marvin stepped to the coffee table, poured himself a double shot of Zcink's French brandy, and carried it back to his chair.

"Detective, would you like some seltzer water with the brandy?"

"No, that's fine," Marvin said. "Why dilute it? You know, it just occurred to me — today is June 6, the anniversary of D-Day. Maybe we ought to toast all the lucky bastards who managed to survive Normandy."

Hank nodded his head and poured himself another shot too.

"To D-Day," he said, "and the guys who survived it, and the guys who didn't."

"Yes, of course," Zcink said, and joined the detectives in drinking the toast.

"Now, Professor," Hank said, placing his glass down on the table, "You were telling us about how you got to the States."

"Yes, you're right. It was an adventure. We were at the Max Planck Institute for Physics in Berlin until January of 1945, a cold winter, when the orders came to move out. The generals were afraid that the Russians would capture us, so the Waffen-SS put us in cars and drove us all to Hechingen and Haigerloch in Baden-Württemberg, in southwestern Germany. They had a place there prepared for us where we could continue our research, and we did work on the Bomb; but as everyone knows, we were not successful. Hitler wanted a miracle weapon, a doomsday bomb, but by that time in the war there were no more miracles, at least not for us. Heisenberg knew it, too, although of course he did not tell his superiors. He was a brave man. Just before the end, when the Allies were finally coming close to us, he told us that he was leaving, just like that. And he did: he found a bicycle somewhere, and early one morning when the French tanks were pushing into Haigerloch from the west, he started riding east to his home in Bavaria. Hundreds of kilometers — can you imagine? He was forty-four or forty-five then. I had no bicycle, but I was strong, a good walker and climber, so I headed for the hills, to the south. Where was I going? I thought I might get somehow to Italy, and maybe from there to Africa. I was thirty, a dreamer."

Zcink paused and reached across the top of the coffee table for the bottle of brandy. Hank watched him pour his glass half full and lift it to his eyes. Zcink gazed at the brandy, turned the glass, gently swirled the golden-brown liquor around, and sniffed it. He put the glass down without taking a drink.

"Some story, Doc," Marvin said. "What happened then?"

"Then? The Allies captured us, of course. All of us, from the janitors to the secretaries to the lab technicians to the great Professor Heisenberg himself. They brought us together in Germany and decided which ones were worth keeping and which weren't. The ones they thought were worth keeping were taken to a farm in England. The ones who weren't were given to the Russians or simply left in Germany."

"And you were one of the lucky ones, the guys worth keeping?"

"Yes, I suppose so.... the lucky ones. They sent eleven of us to Farm Hall in England so they could find out what we knew about atom science and the weapons one can make. When they found out how little we really knew, they told us we could go home. Heisenberg and the others returned to Germany. Me? I had no home to return to. I am Hungarian, and Hungary was occupied by the Communists whose puppets still rule over her. In England, the Americans asked me if I was interested in coming to America and working on some projects for them. I said yes, and they brought me here to the University of Chicago."

"Well, Doc," Marvin said, "it sounds like you're quite a celebrity. What are you working on here?"

Zcink looked at Marvin's face and didn't say anything for a second. All of the animation that had filled his face was suddenly gone. He looked serious. Then he leaned forward, put his finger across his lips, and said, "It's hush-hush. Top secret. *Sshhhh.*"

Then Zcink leaned back and laughed.

And so did Marvin and Hank. Laughed and laughed.

CHAPTER 37

DRIVING NORTH ON Lake Shore Drive toward Miss Hathaway and Cook County Hospital, Hank watched the rain splashing across the windshield. The day was getting uglier and uglier. The wind was churning up black waves in Lake Michigan, and Hank could see whitecaps forming just beyond the shoreline. The tall maple trees along the street were swaying wildly in the wind. It looked more like November than June.

"That Professor Zcink, he's not such a bad guy," Marvin said, "for a Nazi."

"You're just saying that because he gave us that brandy in a pretty crystal glass."

"Well, you know, it didn't hurt his reputation with me to stand me two double brandies. Good brandy, in fact, and he seemed like an all-right Joe. No hard feelings about the war, the bombing, any of that shit. I wouldn't mind visiting him again."

"You're a real humanitarian, Marvin. Open to all the possibilities of embracing your former enemies. Me? I'm not ready for that just yet."

"Come on, man. Be cool. The war ended eleven years ago. Who remembers? The Krauts are our brothers now, and the Russkies are the bad boys, the villains with a capital 'V'. What's this Zcink done to you lately?"

Hank pulled a cigarette from his pack. "Zcink? He reminds me of some of the Germans I knew at the end of the war. Pleasant, smiling, ready to give you their right arm if you asked, happy to do business with you and hungry for your trade. Those Krauts all had a lot of charm after they lost, but you know what? I didn't trust them then, and I don't trust him now."

"Come on, man. This guy's a Hungarian, not a German, he worked with Heisenberg, the government's probably given him the keys to the city and hired him to go through the atomic secrets at the U. of Chicago, the secrets too secret for the other Manhattan Project boys, the secrets the atomic scientists left behind under Stagg Field. You know what I'm saying? Now that they've finished up the A-bomb, this guy Zcink is probably working on the Z-bomb for Uncle Sam. He's as red, white, and blue as a Delaware Rooster."

Hank glanced at Marvin. "Delaware Rooster? What the hell's that?"

"I'm not sure. Maybe something the Pilgrims brought over in 1492? Anyway, what I know is that Zcink's got all of his bona-fides in order — you can bet on it. No Kraut, even a Hungarian Kraut raised on pure goulash, is gonna be given the secret of secrets unless he's one-hundred-ten-percent on the level."

Hank fished his lighter out of his pants pocket and lit his Chesterfield.

"Zcink? I don't know. There was something about him that seemed off…that Bela Lugosi charm. I don't know. I didn't like it."

"Jesus, Hank. You're working too hard. You're like that detective this morning in Washington Park. Give it a rest. Professor Zcink's okay. Pretty soon you'll be looking at me and thinking I look good for the Suitcase Charlie murders."

Hank cracked the window an inch and blew the cigarette smoke out of the corner of his mouth. The wind streamed it into the afternoon's gray wetness. Hank turned to Marvin. He wanted to tell him he was probably right, but he didn't really feel it and kept his mouth shut.

He took another drag and watched for the Roosevelt Road exit to Cook County Hospital.

CHAPTER 38

HANK AND MARVIN followed Miss Hathaway through the morgue. She moved past the bodies quickly in her long white lab coat, her high heels clicking on the gray-tiled floor. The two detectives didn't want to be there, and it was clear she didn't want to be there either.

Earlier, when they found her in her second-floor office, she was pulling on her raincoat, getting ready to go out for lunch. It was three o'clock by then, and she still hadn't eaten. Her face looked thinner, more drawn than when they met her a week ago.

Hank could tell that she remembered them, but she didn't seem very enthusiastic about talking to them or helping them out. Hunger would do that, he knew. Marvin laid on the charm double thick: He told her how important it was, told her lives were at stake — and since that was no more than the truth, he didn't have to fake the sincerity. Miss Hathaway sighed, and then she stuffed a packet of crackers from her top desk drawer into the pocket of her lab coat and marched out of the office.

Walking past the bodies in the morgue, Hank remembered a poem that Hazel had studied when she was taking courses at the junior college. It was by an American with a funny name, T. S. Eliot, Tough Shit Eliot. There was a line in it that always got him. Something about how Eliot didn't know that death had undone so many.

So many people undone. And what had they done to be undone? Fucked up somehow? Some had, some hadn't. It was like what the Polack Killer told them at the station house: Some people were just the wrong people in the wrong place at the wrong time. The school-boys Suitcase Charlie had killed were like that, Hank was sure. They were just kids, and kids didn't know enough to fuck up that bad.

Death does undo you.

Hank looked at the faces of the dead he was passing. They all looked the same. The flat, wide, long, short, round, oval, narrow faces — they all become the same face, finally. It was like that in the war. He remembered the time when he had just made Sergeant and his Second Lieutenant asked him to go down to the command post to identify bodies of some men from his company who had died in a firefight the night before. The soldiers, seven of them, were laid out in a row in front of some bushes. A dry, powdery snow had just started falling along the line of trees, and it was settling on the dead. Even after he brushed the snow off the faces with his hand, he'd still had a hell of a time pinning names to the faces of his buddies.

Miss Hathaway stopped before a door at the end of the morgue and turned around.

"We moved them here," she said before entering, "all four of the children. The three boys from last week, and the girl who was found this morning in Washington Park."

Hank and Marvin followed her into the room. It was small and bitter cold, and twin rows of fluorescent ceiling lights made it seem smaller and colder. It was empty except for the four dismembered bodies laid out, uncovered, on metal carts against the walls. The carts were large, built for adults, and the children on them looked even smaller than they really were.

The cold in the room cut into Hank, and he put his hat on.

In death, the three boys looked like brothers: the same blue tint to their skin, the same long, thinning faces, the same bodies chopped up by some crazy guy and reassembled like puzzle pieces by the pathologists. The dead girl, Hank thought, could have been their sister. In the hours and days to come, she would seem more that way as her body moved further and further away from what it had been.

Miss Hathaway walked up to the body of the young girl. "We know who she is. Her name's Cynthia Ferguson, Cindy. She was eleven years old, and she lived in the Brighton Park area with her parents. She disappeared two days ago along with another girl, Ursula Drewna, on Monday evening at around seven o'clock. She was on her way home from a store on the corner of Archer and Richmond. Her parents contacted the police, and they sent a squad car out looking for the girls. The police canvassed the neighborhood, but they didn't find anything."

"How did the girl die?" Marvin asked.

"Bled to death. She was dismembered after her blood was drained."

"Was she sexually assaulted?"

"It appears she was. I say 'appears' because at this point we can't be certain. We'll need to run some more tests. The body has received so much trauma because of the dismemberment that it's hard to be absolutely sure about anything, but the Chief Medical Examiner feels almost certain that she was."

Hank came closer to the cart Cynthia Ferguson lay on and bent his head down over the pieces of her right hand and arm, brought his eyes close to them. The fingers and thumb had been separated from the hand, and the hand was severed from the forearm at the wrist. The forearm was separated from the upper arm at the elbow, and the upper arm was detached at the shoulder. Eight clean cuts.

"What do you think the killer's using for this kind of cutting?" Hank asked. "Some kind of cutting machine, a slaughtering machine, something industrial like what they use up in the stockyards?"

"My guess? I don't think it's a machine. More likely, a professional cutting knife, sturdy and razor-sharp. Possibly the kind used in ritual slaughter."

"Ritual slaughter? Huh," Marvin said.

"Yes, like in the Jewish religion. You know, the Jewish faith requires that for meat to be kosher, an animal has to be slaughtered according to certain religious requirements. It's called *shechita*. The animal can't be stunned, it can't be inhumanely restrained, the killing has to be done with respect and compassion, and the person doing the killing, the ritual slaughterer, has to be pious. And the knife that's used to cut the animal's throat has to be so sharp that the animal feels as little pain as possible before unconsciousness and death."

"Wild, man."

Miss Hathaway looked at Marvin and shrugged. "Different people have different customs."

"My different people, I guess. I'm Jewish."

Miss Hathaway looked at him for a long moment and said, "Hmmm."

"Is that supposed to mean that I don't look Jewish?" Marvin asked.

Miss Hathaway didn't answer.

Hank looked back at the cart with Cynthia Ferguson's body. He looked more closely at her arm, at the place where the forearm was severed at the elbow. "So, you think the cutting here was done by hand with some kind of sharp, professional-grade knife?"

"That's what the forensic pathologists are saying."

"Where would someone get a knife like that?"

"They're not hard to find," Miss Hathaway said. "Almost any good cutlery store will sell you a blade that could do this. A good-quality butcher knife. Or a sword. A traditional Japanese samurai sword will cut cleanly through a three-inch hardwood table leg."

"That's a fact," Marvin said. "I saw some of that cutting in the Pacific when the Nips were running out of normal ways of killing us."

Hank moved to the foot of the cart. "Can we see the bottoms of her feet?"

"Of course, I was just about to point them out," Miss Hathaway said, and took a pair of rubber gloves out of her coat pocket. She pulled them over her hands and picked up one of the girl's feet and then another, showing the two detectives the sole of each foot. It was what Hank expected: On the girl's right foot, there were cuts there in the shape of an isosceles triangle with its tip pointing toward her toes, and on her left foot the triangle pointed toward her heel.

"So it looks like the same guy?"

"Yes, the suitcases, the way the body was dismembered, the triangles on the bottoms of the feet are all the same. And one more thing: flour. The body parts were brought into contact with wheat flour and water. The forensics people found slight traces of dough on Cynthia Ferguson's feet, near the cuts made to create the triangles. When they found the residues there, they went back to the other bodies and searched for flour, and they found some traces they hadn't noticed before."

"Crazy," Marvin said. "They think the kids were killed in a bakery?"

"Not necessarily. Just someplace where there's flour. Maybe a bakery, maybe a kitchen, maybe even a warehouse where flour is stored. The interesting thing is that although the flour had been in contact with water, the dough is plain and unleavened. No yeast at all, no egg, no oil or butter, no salt or sugar or baking soda either. Nothing that will make the dough rise or flavor it. It's like matzo dough."

"So what are the forensics guys saying?" Marvin asked. "Somebody is cutting up these kids and making them into some kind of Jew pie?"

Miss Hathaway gave Marvin the kind of look that said *where are you from and who raised you?* She was still holding the girl's right foot in her gloved hands. The lighting in the room made it seem a light blue, almost like a sculpture carved out of ice. "The forensics people aren't drawing any conclusions."

"But you are," Hank said. "You're drawing a conclusion. You said the stuff was like matzo dough."

"Yes, unleavened and plain, with nothing else added. If you bake a loaf of bread out of dough like that, what you get is basically a brick. If you roll it out flat and bake it at high temperature, it produces something that's more like a cracker than a normal bread. In this case, they're not even sure this was really dough — the traces on their feet could just be flour mixed with the moisture in the area where they were dismembered. There's no evidence that the killer mixed the flour and the water intentionally to make a dough."

"Are any of the forensics people talking about ritual killings?"

"Dr. Crowder, one of the older members of the team, mentioned the possibility," Miss Hathaway said, placing the foot back at the end of Cynthia Ferguson's leg on the metal cart, "but nobody is looking at that angle very seriously. It's what your partner, Detective Bondarowicz, would call 'too weird'. Ritual murders? In Chicago, in 1956? Something for the gossip rags, for newspapers like *Hot Crime Confidential* or the *Police Gazette*."

Marvin said, "Yeah, that's what I'd say. But this killer is in a weird groove. Definitely weird."

Hank shook his head and said, "Yeah."

"But let me tell you something, Detectives. I don't think at all that it's ritual murder. I don't think any Jew, anywhere, at any time did these terrible things, but somehow what's happening here is connected to the Blood Libel and the *idea* of ritual murder."

Hank looked at the jigsaw puzzle of bones and frozen flesh on the cart in front of him.

"Why do you think the Jews aren't involved?"

"A couple of reasons, Detective. First, Blood Libel accusations have been brought against the Jews for hundreds of years, and yet there's never been any kind of convincing evidence that these things really happened. Never. In every case, the evidence shows that the Jews were being scapegoated by someone. Second, the Jewish religion expressly forbids blood sacrifice, and Jews aren't permitted to eat any food with blood in it."

"The timing's all wrong, anyway," Marvin added suddenly.

"What do you mean?" Hank asked.

"OK, look, Jews eat matzo for Passover. That happens in April, sometimes late March, and it's the only time that it's used in any kind of special ritual. And believe me, the stuff tastes like cardboard — by the time the holiday's over with, everyone's so sick of it that they don't want to see it or smell it or even hear someone say the word 'matzo' for another year. So what Jew's gonna bake matzo in May or June? Nobody would want the stuff for almost a year, and stale matzo is even worse crap than fresh matzo."

Hank looked up from Cynthia Ferguson's body and said, "So how come you still hear about this stuff? People just giving the Jews a hard time?"

"Yes, a hard time, and more than a hard time," Miss Hathaway answered.

There was a pause, and then Marvin turned to look at Miss Hathaway. "You said Cynthia here was with a friend — Ursula Something? — when she disappeared. What happened to the friend? She turn up anywhere?"

"Not that I've heard, so far."

No one said anything for a moment, and Hank slowly glanced around the small room — the metal carts pushed against the walls, the four bodies, the hundreds of pieces of bone and flesh brought together to make four dead children. Why only four, he wondered. Someone was missing. He turned again to Miss Hathaway.

"There are only four bodies here. What about the colored girl we found on Friday night?"

"There was nothing to link her with these bodies," Miss Hathaway said. "She was killed with a knife, but that was multiple stab wounds, not neat cuts and careful dismembering. These children here were not killed in a frenzy."

"Did they check the bottoms of her feet for triangles?"

"I'm sure they checked."

"Do you know for certain?"

"For certain, no, but it would only make sense. A child killed following the deaths of three others? Someone must have checked her feet."

"Hmmm," Marvin said, and shook his head.

"I think my partner is suggesting that you can't always rely on the forensics people to do the work the way it should be done. Do you know if they checked her body for traces of flour?"

"I'm certain they didn't do that. We checked the first three bodies only today, after Cynthia Ferguson's body was found and they noticed the flour traces."

"Maybe we can do it now, get the colored girl's body checked for flour?" Hank said.

"I'm afraid not. The body was incinerated Monday morning."

Marvin looked at Miss Hathaway and said, "Smoke 'em if you got 'em."

CHAPTER 39

HANK KNOCKED AGAIN on the front door of the dirty gray house.

It was the one Professor Zcink mentioned, where he said he had dropped off Pascal Stoop.

"I'm telling you," Marvin said, "this is bullshit. That Zcink may be a Nazi A-Bomb whiz but he doesn't know shit from shinola when it comes to Suitcase Charlie."

Hank shrugged and knocked louder. This stop was his idea. There was something about the Professor that he didn't like. He wasn't sure what, but there was something bothering him about Zcink, and Hank was hoping that tracking down Good Samaritan Stoop would help get him a little closer to it.

"Come on, Hank. I'm starving here. Let's go get something to eat."

Hank was about to knock one last time when he heard a noise inside. He turned to Marvin and gave him a look.

A light came on in the front room and the door opened. A middle-aged, light-skinned colored lady smiled at the detectives. "May I help you gentlemen?"

"Yes, ma'am," Hank said, showing her his badge. "We're Detectives Purcell and Bondarowicz, and we're doing a routine follow-up regarding some trouble here in the Humboldt Park area. We're looking for Mr. Pascal Stoop. We were told he lives here."

"Of course, officers, please come in."

"That's not necessary, ma'am," Marvin said. "We only have a few questions for him. We can ask them out here."

"Officer," she said, "I would prefer if you came in. I wouldn't like the impression having two white gentlemen standing at my door would make with my neighbors. They already have too much to worry about, with a colored woman living so close to them. So please do come in."

Hank nodded and led Marvin into the front room.

"Ma'am, you do know Mr. Stoop?" Marvin asked as he took out his memo pad.

"Of course, I do, sir. He's my nephew. He lives right here with me, upstairs. I think he's taking a nap." She looked toward the ceiling and said, "I'll go up and ask him to come down and talk with you gentlemen."

"That won't be necessary," Hank said. "It's easier if we just go upstairs."

The woman looked worried for the first time, and after a pause she said, "I understand. My nephew's room is up the stairs, the first room to the left. Pascal is a good boy. He goes to Roosevelt University."

At the top of the stairs, Hank stopped at the first door. Some Billie Holiday was coming through it — the plain-talking truth of "God Bless the Child". Hank looked at Marvin and Marvin nodded.

Hank knocked and said, "Pascal Stoop?"

Standing in the hallway, Hank could hear the arm lifting off the turntable and Billie being cut off in mid-phrase: "Momma may have…."

The door opened and a tall, dark-skinned young man stood there.

Marvin moved toward him. "We're the cops, Pascal. Sit down on the bed."

Hank saw fear push across Pascal Stoop's face. He didn't move, and Marvin raised his hands, stepped closer, and shoved Pascal back, hard. He tumbled onto the bed and barely missed smacking his head against the wall.

"We're the police, Pascal," Marvin, "and you're not listening. Now listen."

Pascal didn't say anything. The fear in his face was beginning to look more like terror.

Hank stepped into the middle of the room. "We're not here for trouble of any kind. You didn't do anything wrong, and nobody is looking to arrest you or punish you for anything. We've just got a couple of quick questions for you. That's all."

Pascal still didn't say anything. His body was pressed into the bed, and he didn't even try to sit up.

"First, did you help a tall white man, around 40 years old, when his Plymouth broke down near Roosevelt Road and California, one week ago?"

Pascal finally spoke. "Yes, sir, but what's the crime in that?"

"No crime at all," Hank said. "This man gave us your name as his alibi. So you're helping him out again."

Pascal eased forward on the bed. "I'd be happy to help him. He was a kind man. Gave me a ride home. Not every white man in this town would let me ride with him, even after I helped him get the car going."

"Great. That's just the way he told it. About what time was this?"

"Early evening. Maybe seven. I was heading home, hitchhiking after class — a Tuesday and Thursday biology class that gets out around six most nights."

Hank looked down at the kid on the bed. That wasn't right. "A Tuesday and Thursday class?"

The fear started coming back to Pascal's face. "Yes, sir."

"And what night was that, when you helped this man?"

"Tuesday."

"Tuesday? You sure?"

"Yes, class always goes a little longer on Tuesday, and it was around 6:10 when we finally got out."

"Not a Wednesday?"

"No, sir, I don't go to school on Wednesday. That's my work day at the string factory on Belden."

"Thanks, Pascal," Hank said. "That's all we needed to know."

Chapter 40

HANK LOOKED AT the doorbell and knew he didn't have to ring it. He was home, and this was his doorbell. For a moment, he wondered about all the doorbells he'd had to ring in his ten years in the Chicago Police Department. A thousand? Ten thousand? Maybe not that many, but it felt like more. But at least he didn't have to ring this one. He had a key, and he knew what he would find inside. His wife Hazel would be busy cleaning up after dinner, and his daughter Margaret was probably off in her room doing her homework or reading a book. He unlocked his door and walked in.

He had hoped to get home in time for dinner, but it didn't work out that way. Driving to interview Pascal Stoop after visiting the morgue, and then driving back to the station, took a long time in the rain and late afternoon traffic, and it was a good thing: Lieutenant O'Herlihy was gone by the time they got back and filled out the day's paperwork. Hank knew that Marvin didn't want to have to tell the Lieutenant why they hadn't stuck to their assignment in the schools like they were supposed to, and Hank wasn't in any hurry to have that discussion either. They would be hearing from O'Herlihy soon enough. A little after seven, Hank closed up his log books and gave Marvin a ride home as usual.

So it was a little after eight when Hank opened the door to the closet off the living room and hung his hat and jacket up. They were mostly dry by then. He took his holster off too. When he first got married, he used to walk around the house with his shoulder holster on, but since Margaret was born, Hazel preferred him to leave it on the high shelf in the front closet. She didn't like him packing heat around the house, and he was okay with that. It made sense.

He stopped by the door to Margaret's room, leaned his head into it, and listened. There wasn't a sound. She was probably reading. She was like Hazel in that way, more than she was like him. He'd hated to read when he was a kid. He always wanted to be outside, running around or playing ball or riding his bike. The idea of sitting in his room and looking at words on a page for hours and trying to make some kind of real sense out of those words struck him as too much work. But his kid loved to read. It was a wonder.

He eased the door back a little and looked in. Margaret was lying on her stomach on the bed, her head in her hands. In front of her was a big volume the size of a phonebook. He watched her for a long moment and then said, "Hi, darling, whatcha reading?"

She didn't look up. "*Swiss Family Robinson.*"

"What's it about?"

"Sssssh, I'm getting to the good part!"

Margaret said that without raising her eyes, and Hank answered, "Okay, I'll go track down your mommy," and he walked to the kitchen at the back of the bungalow.

Hazel must have heard him, because she was drying her hands on a towel when he walked into the kitchen. He gave her a kiss and put his arms around her waist. She hugged him back, and they stood like that for a minute or two, just letting the day melt away.

He ate at the small Formica-topped table in the kitchen. Hazel had kept a dish warm for him in the oven. It was one of his favorite meals — a couple of breaded pork chops and some mashed potatoes and green beans — but he was tired and didn't have much of an appetite. It was only Wednesday, but it had already been a long week.

Hazel sat across from him, drinking a glass of red wine and watching him eat. When he put his knife and fork down on the plate, she said, "You're not going to finish the other pork chop?"

Hank shrugged and sipped his beer. "Maybe I'll have it cold later, before bed. But right now I think I'm done."

Hazel put her wine glass down. "I heard about the girl they found on the South Side, in Washington Park."

"Yeah, Marvin and I went down there. O'Herlihy had us doing some chicken-shit stuff in the schools to keep us out of his hair, but we drove down there anyway. I'm sure he's not going to be happy when he finds out."

"You want to talk about it?"

"Sure, let's go out on the back porch so I can smoke."

"You know you can smoke in here. It's okay."

"No, I promised Margaret I wouldn't smoke, and I'm still smoking but at least I'll keep it out of the house. Besides, I want to get some air. I've been indoors or sitting in the car too much today."

"Okay," Hazel said, and went to the kitchen counter. She picked up her pack of Luckies and followed him out onto the covered back porch.

When she got there, he was standing at the porch railing, exhaling smoke into the rain. It was dark already, and the lights in the bungalows across the alley seemed soft in the heavy rain that had been falling for hours and didn't look like it intended to stop any time soon. Hazel lit her cigarette from his and stood next to him.

"You know," he said, pointing with his cigarette into the darkness along the back fence, "we forgot to take those stupid tomato cages in last fall when we brought in the last of those green tomatoes."

"Yes, we did forget."

"Now it's time to plant the tomatoes again."

"Well, no, it's not, really."

"What do you mean?"

"We're late. We should have done it two or three weeks ago."

"Jeez," he said, and then he didn't say anything for a minute.

Hank looked into the rain and listened to it hitting against the roof of the garage next door. It had been raining hard like that most of the day and most of the night before. He thought of Suitcase Charlie dragging his suitcase with the girl's body across a couple hundred feet of Washington Park. The rain might have made it hard for people to see him do that, or maybe he did it late in the night or very early in the morning. There wasn't much traffic down on Grand Boulevard after midnight and before dawn, maybe just a few buses and taxis.

"So what are you thinking?" Hazel asked.

"What am I thinking? I'm thinking about why nobody sees this guy dragging around these big, heavy suitcases. Nobody sees it! Here he is, dragging a hundred or so pounds of dead girl, and nobody notices."

"You know, Hank, people just don't see what they don't see. It's raining, or even if it's not, it's probably dark, and you're tired, and you just want to get home. You don't want to be looking around, you just want to be home. Especially now when you've got a crazy killer on the loose. If you're walking, you're walking fast so you can get home. People are nervous, and nervous people don't see much."

"You should have been a cop, Hazel. You're right. People don't see much when they're nervous, and most people aren't such great observers even when everything's going fine for them. You know what O'Herlihy had us doing? He had us going around to the schools and trying to make the teachers and kids less nervous. Reassure them that things were okay, on the mend, the Chicago Police Department was on duty and alert and armed for bear. That's what he had us doing, and we skipped out on it. We shouldn't have. We both thought it was just a chicken-shit make-work job, and I still thought so 'til now. We should have kept doing the visits. We would have been doing some good, at least."

Hazel sat down on the old metal kitchen chair she and Hank had put out on the porch. "So what did you do instead?"

"What did we do? We talked to a nervous cop in Washington Park where that girl was found. Marvin got into an argument with him. It was stupid — Marvin was trying to rile him, the way he always does with people. Then we paid a visit to a guy down in Hyde Park, a professor at the University of Chicago. He was somebody Mr. Fisch mentioned, and we figured we would check him out. He wasn't nervous, not like Fisch. In fact, this professor was downright calm, pleasant. Even gave us some brandy to fight off the rain and cold, told us about how he got to America after the war."

"Was he a refugee?"

"No. If you can believe it, he's a Nazi scientist — or rather, a former Nazi scientist. One of the boys who worked on the Nazi A-bomb. Now he's helping our side with some secret Bomb stuff."

"You're joking."

"A charming guy, too. Hungarian. Marvin liked him, especially after he gave us each a couple of healthy shots of brandy. But there was something I didn't like about him. He sounded like Bela Lugosi in *Dracula*, if you can believe that." Suddenly, Hank stopped talking and threw his arm across the lower half of his face like he was hiding it with a cape. After a pause, he said in a thick fake-Hungarian accent, "Good eeevening, the moon is full, and I want to drink some...blood."

Hazel smiled and shrugged. "So he sounds like Bela Lugosi. That's no reason to be off on him."

"No, it wasn't the accent. I guess it had something to do with the nervousness I mentioned a moment ago. This guy wasn't nervous, and he should have been. We pretty much broke into his apartment, but he didn't really object strongly or question us much about it. And having a couple of detectives in your house asking you questions is supposed to make you nervous, no matter how innocent you are."

"You broke into his apartment?"

"Well, I guess we did, sort of, but the door was open, and he didn't mind much. Like I said, he was charming. He gave us the warm welcome, passed out drinks, told us the story of his life. Strange."

"You're too nervous, Hank. A guy's charming, and you figure he's some kind of master criminal? You need a couple days off, a short vacation."

"That's what Marvin says."

"I can't believe he and I agree on anything."

"Yeah.... There was something weird about the professor's pictures too. These photographs he had all over his walls."

"Like what?"

"They were photos of rubble. He took them in Berlin toward the end of the war. Shots of churches blown apart, altars smashed into dust, statues messed up. It was the statues that really got to me. Arms and legs and heads scattered around. I looked at those photos and

I immediately thought about the first boy, the boy I saw chopped up into pieces in the suitcase on Washtenaw Avenue. Why put so much gloom on your walls? Crazy."

Hank stopped talking again and looked at Hazel. She was holding her cigarette to her lips and drawing in a stream of smoke. The tip glowed redder. Behind him he could hear the rain falling. He felt cold suddenly. A chill. It didn't feel like it was almost summer. It felt like late autumn, like winter coming on.

Hazel put her cigarette out in the ashtray and said, "It's been a day."

"Yeah," he said. Turning around, he flicked his cigarette into the darkness. The glowing tip was a streak of red for a moment, and then it was nothing. "They incinerated the colored girl who died. The one Marvin and I found in Bronzeville. Nobody came to claim her, so they cremated her and dumped the ashes somewhere."

"Oh, Hank," Hazel said, and put her hand on his shoulder.

From inside, Margaret was shouting, "Mom, Dad, where are you two?"

CHAPTER 41

HANK WAS SLEEPING, dreaming about standing on the corner of a busy street, waiting for the bus.

As soon as he was awake, he tried to remember the dream, remember what street it was, but he wasn't able to. All that he could remember was standing there waiting for a bus. Usually he could remember every single stupid detail in his dreams, but this time he couldn't. He couldn't even remember where he was supposed to be going in the dream, just that he was waiting for a bus. What he did remember about the dream was that when the bus finally came, it pulled up just in front of where he was standing, and the door opened. He was about to climb aboard when a skinny old guy started slowly down the stairs of the bus.

It was a dumb dream, a boring dream, and he was waiting for something exciting to happen in it when Hazel shook his shoulder and said, "Wake up Hank, wake up. It's the phone. A woman wants to talk to you. She sounds drunk."

Groggy, he climbed out of bed and took the phone from Hazel. On the other end, a woman was saying something that he couldn't understand. He opened his eyes and ran his right hand through his hair and down his face. It was dark, but her voice was getting clearer.

"Hank, this is Stephanie Lee, and I'm drunk, so listen carefully. Marvin is here with me, your partner, at my place, and he is fucked up, blitzed, but he wants to talk to you, tell you something. It's important. Are you there, Hank?"

Hank looked at the alarm clock on Hazel's dresser. Now he knew who it was. Stephanie Lee, Steph, Marvin's lady friend when he needed one in a hurry. Hank tried to get his eyes to focus on the time. It was a little after one AM.

"Hank, are you listening?"

"Sure, yeah, Stephanie, put him on."

"He may not be able to say what he wants to say. He's drunk and he's been smoking a lot of weed tonight. He's really zonked, stoned out of his head."

"That's okay, put him on."

She did, but Hank didn't hear anything at first, just a low rumble from far away. Then he heard his partner's voice.

"Well, well," Marvin said in a voice that sounded softer and higher than his voice ever was. Then he said, "Well, well," again, and then he said nothing.

Hank was tired, and he had listened to too many of these one-in-the-morning dark-night-of-the-soul calls from his partner. "Marvin, it's your nickel, and you're keeping me awake. What do you want?"

"I'm getting to...don't rush." There was another long pause, and then the sound of something hard dropping near the phone Marvin was holding, and then another pause, and then Stephanie was back.

"Hank, it's me. Marvin's too gone, Hank, so here's the story. Are you listening? Joey Roses' mother works at the diner on Western and Armitage, across from the Oak Theatre. You know the Oak? Where they have the burlesque shows?"

"Yeah, I know it. What about Joey?"

"He's there. Marvin wants you to get him."

"Jesus. Joey'll be gone by the time I get there. Marvin can't get him himself?"

"Hank, Marvin is putting on his shoes, but he's drunk. He's never going to get them on in time to catch Joey. I know what Joey looks like, and he was just coming into the diner when I was leaving, maybe five minutes ago. He was wearing a long leather coat. Hank, honey, I'm sure you can make it."

Chapter 42

HANK SAT IN the unmarked Ford Mainline outside the Oak Theatre Diner. The rain was still falling steadily, coming down in big, loud, splashy drops. Streams spilled over the windshield, and with his motor turned off and his wipers not working, it almost felt like he was underwater, like he was a fish in a dark world of fish.

But the diner across the sidewalk was lit up like a neon highway, and Hank could see inside just fine. There was a long counter that ran the length of the place, from the front door to the toilet in the back, and there were only two people he could see there.

Behind the counter, a heavyset middle-aged woman in a white apron was standing and talking to a man sitting hunched at the counter. The man had his back to Hank, but Hank figured this was the guy Stephanie Lee spotted as Joey Roses. He was sitting there wearing a long leather coat, just like she said. Hank couldn't see what Joey was doing, but he was probably eating something off a plate. Once in a while, his head would go down and bob up, go down and bob up, and sometimes it would stop. That was probably when Joey was listening especially hard to what his mother, the heavy woman in the apron, was saying. He was being a good boy, a good son, eating what Mama gave him and paying attention to what she said.

It had taken Hank thirty minutes to get here on the wet streets, racing through red lights, swinging around stopped Chicago Transit

Authority buses and slow-moving jalopies, and all the while he figured he'd be late and Joey Roses, if it was really him, would be gone, disappeared like just another fish into the dark rain, but that's not what happened.

Joey was still in the Oak Theatre Diner, and Hank was just waiting, staring at him through the flood rolling over the city.

He had hoped that Marvin would have been able to get his shoes on and get down here. His girlfriend Steph didn't live that far from here, just a block away in fact, down the street in a third-floor walk-up on McLean Avenue. But it looked like Marvin was too drunk and stoned to make it down here.

Hank knew Joey, knew the kind of problem he might be if Hank tried to take him alone, even if this time it was Hank surprising Joey instead of Joey ambushing Hank from a closet. Sure, Joey was a little guy, but he was tough the way a guy raised by a crazy father was tough. Joey was always ready for any kind of mayhem. He was the kind of guy who wouldn't hesitate to go for your eyes with his teeth or stab at your privates with a Bowie knife. He had no sense of humor.

Hank stared at the diner through the falling rain and wished Marvin was with him in the Ford getting ready to take on Joey Roses. Marvin was a good guy in a fight.

Looking at Joey's back, Hank knew he had to time his move just right. If he moved too soon and went for Joey when he was sitting in the diner, his mother behind the counter would warn him and Joey would be streaking out the back before Hank was through the front door. If he waited until Joey left the diner, Hank didn't know if he could get out of the car quick enough to grab him before Joey was gone, disappeared into the rain. But that seemed like the only way to play it.

So he waited.

Hank looked at his watch. It was 2:54. If Stephanie Lee saw Joey getting into the diner at around one in the morning, that meant it was almost two hours that the guy had been eating and chewing the fat with his mother. He was taking his time. Maybe having dessert, some apple pie with raisins. Maybe just waiting for the rain to break. Hank glanced up at the night sky. Fat chance of that happening. Nothing but dark clouds and a world of heavy, quick-falling raindrops.

A wall of water suddenly smashed against the driver's side of Hank's Ford, and he jerked his head left toward Western Avenue. A trolley bus was speeding past rushing to get through the intersection before the light changed. It must have hit a puddle in a pothole.

Hank looked back at the diner. A man without an umbrella or a hat was opening the door and walking in — a shortish guy in some kind of dark suit, maybe a black one. He had a newspaper under his left arm, and he had no shoes or socks on. That was weird. Hank could see it plainly in the light from the diner — this fool was walking around without shoes in the greatest rainstorm since Noah and his three sons, Shemp, Moe, and Larry.

And then Hank realized he knew the fool. It was Marvin.

Hank saw the woman behind the counter glance up when the door opened, and then he saw Joey turn on his stool and eyeball the guy walking into the diner. What Joey saw must have seemed okay, just another busted-down wet guy without shoes on coming into a diner in the middle of the night to get out of the rain. Joey slowly swiveled his counter stool back and looked up at his mother. She was lighting a cigarette with a long kitchen match and yammering about something, maybe offering him another piece of pie, the cherry this time instead of the apple.

Hank pushed out of his car fast and ran through the rain toward the diner. He could see shoeless Marvin acting like a customer, picking a menu up off the counter and walking right past Rosetti. Marvin took a seat at the counter three stools past Joey Roses and put his newspaper down on the Formica. He opened the menu then and started checking out his dining options.

That's when Hank rushed up the last couple of steps to the door and pushed it open.

And that's when WGN's Friday Night Wrestling came live to the Oak Theatre Diner on a Thursday, hours before sun-up.

Joey's mother saw Hank first, and she gave out a long "Nooooo!" as she started to climb over the countertop. Joey Roses turned to see what the fuss was and why she was scampering over the gray Formica, and that's when he spotted Hank driving straight toward him. Throwing her big body over the counter, Mama Rosetti leapt for Hank and slammed herself against his right shoulder with another bleating "Nooooo!"

As she smashed into him, he jerked his body backward.

Her weight and Hank's jerk did what the detective hoped they would: she went sailing over his shoulder, back toward the plate-glass window that said Oak Theatre Diner in big black curling letters. Toward it and through it. She sailed through the splintering glass with a crash, screeching for her son, her baby boy.

Joey's eyes and mouth went big then, and he shouted, "Mom!" and put his two hands on the countertop like he was going to push himself away from it, lunge for Hank, and defend his mother, when out of nowhere a six-pound hammer came arcing down from Joey's left side and smashed into his left hand.

"Ohhhhh, mother fucker!" Joey Roses screamed and wrenched his body backwards, but he couldn't free himself from the hammerhead that Marvin was pressing down on with all his weight.

Lying on the floor, shaking little pieces of glass off his face and out of his hair, Hank could see that Joey's wasn't going anywhere. It was like Joey's body was nailed to the counter by that six-pound-plus-Marvin hammer. He couldn't shake his hand free. Desperate and crying "Oh, oh, oh," Rosetti reached for his busted-up left hand with his good right one, but he couldn't get it loose no matter how hard he tried. It was rooted there sure as a maple tree, buried under the hammer from nowhere that Marvin was pressing down on.

That's when Joey must have realized that he wasn't going to get anywhere trying to pull his hand free, so he leapt at Marvin instead and grabbed for his throat with his one good hand.

Hank couldn't get up in time to stop Joey Roses, but he reached from the floor for Joey's right foot and managed a hold that sent him crashing, his head bouncing between two stools on its way down to the gray tile.

Down to the hard gray tile, and out.

CHAPTER 43

HANK AND MARVIN dragged Joey Roses through the door of Shakespeare Station. His wrists were bound in handcuffs and his busted-up left hand was wrapped in a bloody towel from the diner, but he still struggled, trying to get his good hand on Hank and trying to get his teeth on Marvin's face or neck. The detectives shoved him toward the front desk.

"Jesus," Ackerman, the desk sergeant, said, jumping up from his chair. "He's a disaster. I heard on the two-way you guys was bringing him in."

"Yeah, we pulled him in," Hank said. "He was making a mess of the diner by the Oak Theatre. Him and his mother were busting the place up."

"He must've been doing it with his head — look at the bits of glass sticking out of his hair. And his hand. Jesus, and where's his mom now?"

"I don't know. She was gone by the time we got him out of the diner into the car. She must have dragged herself away."

Joey started struggling again, trying to butt his head against Hank and Marvin. "You're lying," he shouted. "My mother didn't run away. She wouldn't do that. You killed her, fucked her and killed her."

"He's a little upset," Marvin said.

"Fucked her and killed her! Fucked her and killed her! Fucked her and killed her!"

"We'll take him to one of the holding cells downstairs and fill out the paperwork when we get back."

"Good idea," Ackerman said. "Keeping him out here screaming like that isn't going to do anybody any good."

Hank hooked his arm under Rosetti's right shoulder and was pulling him away from the counter toward the staircase when he glanced up and saw Lieutenant O'Herlihy walking down the stairs toward them.

"Stop right there, Purcell," the Lieutenant said. "If that's Joey Roses, I don't want him in here."

"He was busting up a diner by the Oak Theatre, Lieutenant."

"Yeah," Marvin added, "him and his mother both."

O'Herlihy looked at Joey Roses. The punk was smiling.

The Lieutenant didn't smile back, and he turned back to Hank. "I don't want him here, and you know the reason."

Hank looked at his Lieutenant. Yeah, he knew the reason. Joey was probably involved in the killing of the colored girl somehow, or at least had to know something about it, and O'Herlihy didn't want to hear anything about that murder. It wasn't his job to know about what happened on the South Side.

Hank shook his head and pulled his arm loose from Rosetti, and Joey Roses made a quick grab for Hank's head. Hank jerked his head back, losing his hat, and sent a fist into Joey's stomach. Joey fell to his knees with a loud "ooomff".

"Pick him up, Bondarowicz," the Lieutenant said, staring at Hank. "I want you and your partner to take Rosetti down to one of the colored stations on the South Side. Drop him off at District 10, or maybe the one over on Fillmore. Yeah, that's better — take him to District 25. You got that?"

Hank stared at O'Herlihy and didn't say anything for a long moment. Then he nodded and said, "Yeah, I got it."

"Good."

Hank turned to help his partner Marvin pick Joey Roses up off the floor.

"Hold on, Purcell. I'm not done with you yet. You let Ackerman help Bondarowicz get Rosetti back into the car. I want to talk to you."

Lieutenant O'Herlihy turned and started walking up the stairs with Hank following. Reaching the half-landing between the first and second floors, O'Herlihy stopped and waited for Hank. When Hank was standing next to him, the Lieutenant took a step closer.

"You know what I'm going to say because I said it to you before, Purcell. You're pursuing your own case here. You're not doing the city's work. You know what the city's work is? To make people here feel like they are living in a city that works, where things — the right things — get done the right way. They don't want to hear about stuff that makes them feel like the city doesn't work. They don't want to know about Joey Roses, and they definitely don't want to know about the dead colored girl he's tied into. Stuff like that makes them think the city doesn't work, and when they start thinking that way, they start getting anxious and fearful, and nobody wants to feel that way. When they do, they start making noise about it, and that noise gets to the politicians, and the politicians get to us."

"You got no argument with me, Lieutenant. Like the new mayor says, Chicago's 'the city that works', and I know about the way the city works. But like I said before, Joey's also hooked in with these Suitcase Charlie killings. I feel it."

"And I don't. Drop it. Hear me? Just drop it, or you'll be walking a beat by the Russian Baths on Division. You and your cowboy buddy Bondarowicz. Do you hear me?" The Lieutenant looked at Purcell.

Hank didn't say anything. He just stared at O'Herlily.

"And another thing. We got some complaints from downtown about you putting the squeeze on some professor yesterday morning. A Professor Zcink. Breaking into his place and giving him the fish-eye. I don't know what you were doing down there, but whatever it was, it wasn't what you were supposed to be doing. I sent you out to scout the schools around Humboldt Park and calm things down, and you end up way down in Hyde Park playing some kind of bullshit with a college professor."

"We were following a lead, a good one."

"That's not what I told you to do. There's only one way this department's going to work, and it's my way. You don't like it? Start your own police force, or go private dick. Then you can play Mike Hammer all day long without anybody telling you different. 'Til then, you do what I say, and I'm telling you to leave off this professor, leave off the South Side, and leave off trying to crack this Suitcase Charlie case on your own. You got that, Purcell?"

Hank didn't say anything right away. He looked at O'Herlihy and felt something building up in him that he didn't like. He wanted to tell O'Herlihy to back off, get the fuck out of his face, but he knew he couldn't. Saying that would be the end of everything.

So Hank said, "I got that, Lieutenant."

"Now take this punk Joey Roses down to District 25 Station. Oh, and tell your partner to find himself some shoes."

"Yeah, I got that too, Lieutenant."

"Really, Purcell, your partner's a bum, and you're getting to be just like him. Breaking into somebody's apartment, this guy Zcink, a professor for Chrissake. And what's next? You and Bondarowicz will make quite a pair minding the drunks and the junkies down by the Russian Baths."

Hank looked at O'Herlihy and didn't say anything, didn't nod his head, didn't shrug.

O'Herlihy shook his head and said, "Jesus," and then he turned around and climbed the stairs to the next landing. Hank watched him take the left to his Shakespeare Station office.

The anger in Hank's gut was a quick fire. He wanted to bust something up, slap somebody. He wanted to put the fire out, but he couldn't. He just started walking down the stairs. He had heard it before, about their duty to the city, what the responsibilities of the cops were to law and order and the possibility of living in a world without fear.

Hank picked up the hat that he'd dropped when he was dodging Joey Roses, and walked toward the door to the street.

He wondered about a city where some people had a right to live without fear and others didn't. He thought about President Roosevelt and what that old cripple in his wheelchair had said about fear. He said that we had nothing to fear but fear itself. Well, he was wrong. There was plenty to fear. Plenty.

As sure as the turning of the earth.

CHAPTER 44

THE RAIN HAD finally stopped, and the night sky above the city was dark blue and clear. It looked to Hank like a still, endless ocean. With Shakespeare Station and Humboldt Park behind him, he was driving south on California Avenue and looking for stars.

He wanted to see a million of them flickering like lightning bugs in August, but he couldn't. The city's lights spread into the sky, washing out all but the brightest stars. Hank could see a few of them together, not in a straight line like Orion's belt — Draco? Scorpius? — and what he thought might be part of the constellation Virgo, but that was pretty much it.

Just Virgo and one of the other two. The sweet goddess of the harvest and a monster — either the dragon or the scorpion. Maybe not the best omen, Hank thought.

Behind him, Joey Roses was quiet in the back seat. He had been that way since Hank had climbed into the car, and Hank was surprised. It wasn't like Joey. He liked to talk, give his opinions, tell you what was bothering him: the weather, his bones, the White Sox, his busted-up hand. Especially after the kind of beating he and his mom took. Hank wondered if Marvin had knocked Joey on the head, just for insurance, before pushing him into the back seat.

Hank turned to Marvin. He was bent over, tying on one of the rubber-soled sneakers he took off Joey Roses' feet.

"Did you sap Joey?"

"I figured Joey's shoes would fit me OK," Marvin said.

"Did you hit him with a sap?"

"Huh? Sap him? Do you really want to know?"

"No, not especially."

"Okay," Marvin said as he finished tying the laces and sat up straight.

"You know," Hank started, "O'Herlihy told me he was getting heat from the big chiefs downtown about our snooping around. I guess Professor Zcink didn't like our visit as much as he seemed to at the time."

"Imagine that. What kind of world is it where even professors have clout? I don't know where my surprise begins or ends. Does this mean we owe somebody an apology? Where would we even start?"

"You could probably start with Lieutenant O'Herlihy. He wasn't happy with you barefooting around his station."

"What did you tell him?"

"I don't think I told him anything about that. I was too busy trying to figure out what to tell him about how come we broke in on Zcink and why we dragged Joey here down to Shakespeare Station."

"Thanks for standing up for a brother officer."

"Forget about it," Hank said as they approached Chicago Avenue. "It was my pleasure."

"And where's my pleasure?" Joey suddenly asked from the back seat. "You dicks talk about your pleasure, but you ain't got no time for the common man and his pleasures."

"Say, Joey," Marvin said, "you sound as drunk as I am."

"Yeah?" Joey came back. "Did you hear the one about the guy who walked into the bar with his two-legged dog?"

"No, I didn't," Marvin chuckled, "but I'm all ears."

"Well, I'll tell you then. That pooch, he was a real pisser."

Hank looked in the rear-view mirror. Joey was grinning like a jack-in-the-box.

Marvin turned around and looked at Joey. Like Hank, Marvin seemed to be waiting for the punch line, but there wasn't one. Instead, Joey spat at him, and the crap from his mouth hit the detective's lips.

Marvin didn't stop to clean it off. He whammed the side of his fist into Joey's right eye.

In the mirror, Hank saw Joey's head whip back.

But that snap didn't save him.

Marvin said, "Fuck," and whammed Joey again, this time slamming the flat of his fist into Joey's nose. Hank heard the wet, muddy sound of breaking cartilage as he slowed for a red light on Chicago Avenue. Joey's scream came right after. Hank was glad the windows were rolled up so that the two old women in babushkas waiting at the bus stop across the street couldn't hear the screaming.

Hank waited for the light to change so he could make the right onto Chicago.

"Joey," Marvin said, wiping the spit off his face with his handkerchief, "you don't know when to stop. You got a problem with self-containment, humor management. You're always wise-cracking. That ain't gonna make you any friends in the Chicago Police Department."

For a while, Hank waited for Joey to say something, but he didn't say anything, didn't reply. He was leaning against the door, as far from Marvin's fists as he could get, and pressing his cuffed hands to his face. It looked like he was praying in the back seat, but Hank knew that wasn't likely. Joey wasn't the kind of street punk to go soft for Jesus, even under arrest with his nose broken.

The light blinked to green, and Hank eased the Ford forward.

"Now, Joey," Marvin said as he turned to face the back seat again, "we're gonna talk about the colored girl we found you with a couple days ago. Our Lieutenant, a real cracker from Crackersville, doesn't think it's any big deal; but my partner Detective Purcell here is an Eagle Scout of the first order, and he wants to get to the bottom of every fucking crime committed in Chicago. It doesn't matter if it's on the North Side or the South Side. No sparrow falls here without him making a beef about it and taking names. He's a regular Saint Francis of Assisi."

"That's me," Hank said, and looked into the rear-view mirror. He saw Joey Roses pressed harder into the corner. His head was tilted back and his mouth was open wide, a big, black hole in the middle of his face. Hank could hear the whimpering coming out of that hole. Joey was hurt.

"So start talking, Mr. Roses. You don't have a lot of time," Marvin said, and then he didn't say anything for a long moment.

Hank listened to Joey breathing. His deep gasps were full of blood and phlegm, mucus and smashed cartilage. If the punk was thinking about anything, he was thinking about how much pain he was in, that and the blood flowing down the back of his throat and blinding his eyes and covering the hands pressed across his face.

"Pull over to the side, Hank," Marvin said. "I want to get in back with our friend for a short visit."

"I'm not pulling over, Marvin. Do it from where you're sitting."

All Marvin said was "Pussy" as he pulled his sap out of his coat pocket and smashed it across Joey's fingers and the back of his hands. The punk gave out a moan; and then Marvin thumped him again, and Joey gave out another, louder moan.

"The wrong one, she was the wrong one," Joey blurted out. "He didn't want her. We fucked up. The wrong one."

Marvin reached back, grabbed Joey by his throat, and jerked him forward away from the door he was pressed against. "What're you talking about?"

"Please — the wrong one. He didn't want her."

"Who?"

"Dracula."

"Dracula was the wrong one?"

"No, he said she was the wrong one."

"Who?"

"She was the wrong one. Wrong color."

Marvin pushed Joey back and released his hold on his throat. "Hank, pull over. This isn't making any sense. I want to get in the back."

Hank knew Joey was about to give them something, so he said, "Okay," and eased the Ford Mainline to the curb just east of Sacramento Boulevard. Before the car stopped rolling, Marvin threw the door open and started climbing into the back. Joey lunged for the door, trying to make a break, but Marvin had been a cop for a long time and he was ready. He brought his knee up fast, caught Joey in the chest, and then pushed him back with a kick from his own sneaker.

Hank stopped looking into the back seat and checked out the neighborhood.

The corner of Sacramento and Chicago Avenue was quiet. Hank didn't see anybody around, nobody waiting for a bus or walking his dog, but Hank wasn't surprised. This was one of the secret places in the city, a place where most of the time, summer or winter, rain or shine, you wouldn't see a guy standing around reading a paper or a gal buffing her nails, especially at night. Heavy industrial railroad yards lay to the south, factories and some old wood-frame houses to the north. Not much going on here in terms of the human comedy.

Hank looked back in the rear-view mirror. He could see Marvin. His partner lit a cigarette and gave it to Joey.

Maybe Marvin Bondarowicz was calling a truce with Joey Roses, or maybe he was getting ready to give Joey a blindfold and a bullet to the head to go along with the cigarette.

Hank turned around so he could watch.

Joey took a drag and coughed. He hacked up something and spit it on the back of his hand.

Marvin struck a match and lit a cigarette for himself.

"Before we start the formal part of this interrogation, Mr. Rosetti, I'd like you to answer me one question that my partner, Detective Purcell, and I have been arguing about. Would you do me that favor, Joey?"

Joey lifted his head and put the cigarette in his mouth and sucked in the smoke. The glow from the ember gave Hank just enough light so he could see Joey's face. His head was quivering, and a deep inverted V sat just below the ridge of his nose. The blood was drying black, and his face was a mess. Dark red threads were running from his swollen nose, drifting down over his lips and across his chin.

"A couple nights ago, you remember?" Marvin said. "I shot at you in Humboldt Park, and I was wondering if I hit you."

Joey didn't answer. He bent forward and coughed. It sounded like he was trying to bring something up that was stuck deep in his lungs and wasn't going to break loose no matter how much he poked at it. He coughed some more, and his head bobbed up and down as he did.

"Hmm," Marvin said. "Well, if you won't answer that, let me ask you what you were thinking when you cut me with your knife? Thirty-seven fucking stitches, eight per inch."

"Marvin, just give him a break," Hank said. "Let's stick to what we need to know."

"You're getting too serious for this line of work, Hank. With you, it's always business, business, business."

"Just ask him the question before he dies on us."

"Okay, okay," Marvin said, and pushed Joey hard, back into the seat. Hank could see there wasn't much fight left in the greaseball. Rosetti's body slumped back, and Marvin started in again. "Now let me see if I got this straight. You killed the wrong one?"

Joey's hand was shaking as he brought the cigarette to his lips. "I'll tell you, but you got to promise you won't take me to District 25. The nigger cops know me there. They'll kill me."

"Sure, Joey, I promise," Marvin said, "and my friend Hank the Eagle Scout, he promises you too. So tell me what you mean. You killed the wrong one?"

"No, we snatched the wrong one."

"But you didn't kill her?"

"Right. Nick killed her because he didn't want the girl we got him. He didn't want a nigger."

"Nick didn't want her?" Hank asked.

"No, Dracula, like I said."

"Dracula didn't want her? Who the fuck is Dracula?"

"Yeah, like in them old movies. He talks like Dracula."

"Baloney," Marvin said, and slapped Joey Roses. His head jerked back and slammed against the side window.

Joey covered his head with his arms. "Jesus, please, it's true," he said. "Don't hit me. I swear it. He sounds like Dracula. When he saw the nigger girl in the bedroom, he was cool. He walked up to her chained there to the radiator, and he said, 'She just won't do.' Just like that, and he turned around and walked out." Joey Roses started coughing again, a long string of short, shallow coughs that almost sounded like a soft laugh, ha-ha, ha-ha. His head was bobbing with each cough. He wasn't laughing.

Marvin handed him a handkerchief, and Joey pressed it over his mouth and coughed some more.

"So who killed her?" Marvin asked.

"Nick, the nigger who runs the gang. You saw him at the flat. When Dracula walked out, Nick ran into the kitchen and grabbed a knife. Came back and stabbed her. Like a crazy man. Stabbed her maybe a hundred times."

"Thirty-two times, the forensics guys say, not a hundred," Hank said.

"Fuck thirty-two. Dead is dead."

"What else do you know about this Dracula guy?" Marvin asked.

"Nothing. Nick, he set it up. He made all the arrangements. He's the one who screwed up. He couldn't find a white chick in time, so he grabbed that nigger girl. He figured it wouldn't matter."

"And he was wrong," Hank said.

Joey nodded and coughed again.

"Did Dracula tell Nick what he wanted the girl for?"

"Nick didn't tell me nothing. I figured the guy wanted to fuck her. Or drink her blood, or maybe both," Joey said, and started laughing.

It wasn't real laughter.

CHAPTER 45

THE CREAMY ORANGE sun was starting to come up over the city when Hank pulled the Ford to the curb in front of the old colored station on the corner of Fillmore and Pulaski Road.

When he killed the engine, Hank looked at Joey Roses in the back seat. Hank didn't know what kind of beef the colored cops had with Rosetti, and he didn't much care. Joey was a bum, a thief, and probably a killer. If he hadn't killed the colored girl in the apartment on Washington Boulevard a couple nights ago, he had probably done it to somebody else. Fucked them and killed them, or killed them and fucked them. He was bad.

As Marvin opened the back door and reached in for him, Joey started writhing and flailing his handcuffed hands. He was screaming over and over, "You lied to me, you fucking lied to me."

He was right about that. Hank and Marvin had lied to him, broken the promise they made back on Sacramento not to bring him to this station and its colored cops. But that was okay. Hank didn't care, and he knew Marvin cared even less.

Hank on one side and his partner on the other, the two detectives jerked Joey Roses toward the station's heavy wooden door. Joey fought back. His shoeless feet scrambled for some purchase on the sidewalk in front of the station, anything to stop him from being dragged through the door into the station. His legs were like rubber whips, kicking out and grabbing for something to keep him from being carried further. "Mother-fuckers lied to me!"

As they got to the entrance, Joey grabbed the doorknob with his bloody manacled hands. Growling like a mad dog, he bared his teeth and swung his head toward Marvin's face. He tried to get his teeth into the detective's cheek and tear it off. Marvin wrenched his face away from Joey's mouth and pulled his arm hard to break his grip on the doorknob, and he did break it — but that sent Joey rocketing into Marvin, and they both went crashing back onto the sidewalk in front of the station.

In a second, Joey was on top of Marvin and chopping at his face with his cuffed wrists, battering at it with the chromium steel rings.

"Jesus, Jesus," Marvin shouted, and Hank jerked his service revolver out of his shoulder holster and hammered its wood-gripped butt against Rosetti's head, slamming it just above his ear six or seven times until Joey's eyes finally rolled back into his head and the fight left him quiet as a sleeping kitten.

A colored cop, a sergeant, pulled the station house door open and stepped out into the morning sunlight. There were three other colored cops behind him. One of them was laughing and fanning his face with a *Chicago Tribune*.

The sergeant stopped and looked down at the three figures scattered in front of him and shook his head slowly.

"You boys sure know how to make an entrance," he said. After a moment he added, "You look like maybe you could use a hand there." He clapped his hands softly three times.

Hank looked at him and recognized the joke. He smiled, nodded, and said, "Thanks, Sergeant, but I think we can handle this part." He rolled Joey Roses off his partner and onto the sidewalk, spread-eagled and sunny-side-up. Then Hank reached down and helped his partner up. Marvin seemed shaky, and blood seeped down from a line of cuts on his forehead where Joey's cuffs had dug into his face.

"Can you stand on your own?" Hank asked.

"What do you think?"

"Okay, just asking," Hank said, and turned to the colored sergeant. "Say, can you help me drag this punk into the station?"

"I don't mean to be disrespectful, gentlemen," the sergeant said and smiled. "But can you tell me why it is that you are dragging this white monkey-assed desperado into my nice, clean, quiet little colored police station?"

"I'm Detective Hank Purcell, and this is my partner Detective Bondarowicz. We had orders from our Lieutenant to escort our prisoner to this station, but apparently the prisoner didn't want to come down here."

"Well, Detectives, I sure am glad to know that. It's not every day we get a white man coming down to this station, and seeing three of you all together trying to get through my door at the same time drove us all into a state of considerable confusion."

Hank nodded and smiled. "I can understand that, Sergeant. It's been a hell of a night."

"Well, morning's here now, so why don't you two detectives let my patrolmen here help bring your rather disreputable charge into my station, and we will see what is up with him."

"That's fine with us," Hank said and turned to Joey Roses. Rosetti's eyes were still closed, but the right side of his face was twitching and his lips were moving a little. He looked like maybe he was trying to say something. Hank knelt down and put his ear close to Rosetti's lips and listened for a moment.

"What did he say?" Marvin asked.

"He said he wants us to tell his mom where he is and that he'll be okay."

Marvin stepped toward Joey Roses and stood looking down at him for a moment. Then he drew back his foot and kicked him in the ribs.

"Listen, punk, the next time I see your momma, I'll put a bullet through her head."

The colored sergeant laughed. "You white boys from the North Side sure are mean, talking about a man's mother like that. Yes sir, real mean. Mind if we help you with Joey Roses here?"

"No, we don't mind a bit," Hank said.

One of the colored patrolmen bent down and hoisted Joey up by his arms. The two other cops grabbed a leg each, and they carried him into the station while the Sergeant held the door open.

"Now, what did you say he did?" the sergeant asked Hank.

Picking Marvin's hat off the sidewalk, Hank handed it to his partner and turned to the colored cop. He spoke slowly, "Lieutenant O'Herlihy sent us down here with this guy because he figures he's somehow involved with the killing of that girl who was stabbed over on Washington Boulevard last Friday."

The colored sergeant shook his head. "Yeah, I heard about the killing. Stabbed thirty-some times. Some bad motherfuckers killed her, like they were happy to do it."

"That's for certain," Hank said. "Joey says he didn't have anything to do with it, but his gang boss Nick did. I don't know about that. Joey's not a guy you can always count on to tell the truth."

Marvin swayed a bit and pressed a handkerchief to the cuts on his forehead. "You fellows just keep talking. I'm going in to get some bandages on this thing."

"Well, Detective, you've come to the right place," the colored sergeant said. "We got all kinds of bandages. Let me show you where we keep them."

He pulled open the door and held it for Marvin. Hank took his partner's arm and steadied him as they walked in.

"You know, Detectives," the Sergeant said, "there seems to be a lot of killing going on for so early in the summer. The Washington Boulevard stabbing, plus those five white children getting chopped up."

"Five?" Hank said. "I thought it was four."

"No sir, I believe that there are five of those suitcase children now. They found another one just this morning. She was a friend of the other girl, named Ursula Drewna. They found her down by Washington Park, same as the last one. That makes five."

"Five?" Hank asked again.

"That's right. Five in just over a week. No offense, but I bet you my pension that it's a white man doing this killing. Colored man? He kills out of some strong feeling. Hatred or rage or love gone bad…but a white man? He kills out of some crazy idea that's stuck in his brain and eating up his insides like a termite. That's what this killing feels like. A crazy termite idea busting up a white man's head."

CHAPTER 46

HALF ASLEEP, HANK was driving again, moving the black unmarked Ford Mainline slowly east through the morning traffic on Pershing Road. There was a lot of it, and he didn't like it.

Hank wanted to be out of the car and knocking on Zcink's door, not groping like some mud turtle through this slow-poking mess. Every kind of old Packard and beat-to-shit Hudson was hell-bent for slowness on the streets at this hour. Cars Hank hadn't seen on the North Side since he was a kid at the start of the Great Depression were alive and clunking along toward the lake ahead of him or the prairie behind him, way west of town.

He remembered something he once heard about the Indians, how they would ride a horse until it was almost dead and then they would get another couple hundred miles out of it. The colored people were the same way with their busted-fender DeSotos and Model T's that should have been scrap metal a dozen years ago but were still chugging and clanking around him. A couple of minutes ago, he even passed an old horse-drawn farm wagon hauling a sloppy mountain of moldy mattresses and rusty box springs.

When he saw that, he almost woke Marvin up to tell him to get an eyeful of what might be the last horse and wagon in the whole city of Chicago, but he didn't. Marvin was sound asleep, bunched against the door on the passenger side. It had been a bad week for his partner. He was a regular Fearless Fosdick, that comic strip character in the *Chicago Tribune* who was always getting punched, stabbed, shot, and generally busted up, but still kept going strong. Yeah, Marvin was sort of like that.

Hank turned his head for a moment and saw his partner's face. The wide bandage he had picked up at the colored station on Fillmore covered his eyebrows and most of his forehead, and blood was still seeping through the cotton — not much, but enough so Hank could see a thin, red stain of it moving down Marvin's cheek and toward his jaw line.

Just then, Marvin's eyes popped wide open, and he shouted, "What the fuck?"

"You're awake?"

"Of course I'm awake, you slimy bastard. You woke me up."

"Me? I didn't say anything, didn't do anything. I was just looking at the bandage that sergeant at the Fillmore station put on you."

"Says you, Superman. You looked at me with your x-ray vision, and the fucking heat woke me up."

Hank shook his head. "You're nuts, but at least you're awake. That's something. Here's the traffic report. It's almost 8 AM and we're on Pershing Road coming up to Western."

"Yeah, I can see McKinley Park up ahead. Is that where the body of the new kid turned up?"

"No, it was in Washington Park, near where they found the other girl."

"So it's a girl again this time."

"Yeah," Hank said, and looked to the left at McKinley Park.

It was like all the other big parks in Chicago. Humboldt, Washington, Garfield, Lincoln, you name them. They were all bordered by heavy, thick rings of tall bushes. He knew what the point of that was: If you were in the park, you wanted to have the feeling that you were somehow adrift, let loose from the city and its crime and filth. The guy who designed the parks and landscaped them wanted you to feel like you were in some kind of Eden, a paradise where it was just you and God and, if you were lucky, some little Eve.

And Satan? Well, the guy who built the parks probably felt that the ring of bushes would keep him out.

He was dead wrong. That park designer was nothing but a fool in floppy shoes and shit pants.

"Hey, Hank, wake up, man; pay attention to the road. You're driving as slow as these rag-headed grannies in their colored jalopies."

"Sorry."

"Now, explain it to me so a white man can understand it," Marvin said as he pulled a cigarette from his pack of Luckies. "What are we doing? I thought the Lieutenant told us to stay clear of all this Suitcase Charlie stuff."

"That's right. He did, and we are. We're not going to Washington Park. We're going to see Professor Zcink again. I got a hunch."

"Your hunches are terrible," Marvin said, tamping the cigarette on the back of his hand. "What's this one tell you?"

"It tells me to take another look at Professor Zcink."

"Because Joey Roses said that the guy who was mixed up with the killing of the colored girl sounded like Count Dracula?"

The stoplight ahead at South Damen Avenue clicked from yellow to red, and Hank eased down on the brake, took the transmission out of gear, and slowly came to a stop.

"Yeah, that's part of it. Zcink sounds like Dracula, and the guy Joey talked about sounds like Dracula."

"Is there some other part that's maybe a little more convincing to professionals like us, highly qualified, experienced detectives for the world-famous Chicago Police Department?"

"No, that's pretty much it. That, and the fact that he worked for the Krauts on their A-bomb. If he and the other Nazis had their way, all of us forgotten 'Bastards of Bastogne' would have been fried as crisp as those radiated sons of Nippon you see in the newsreels from Hiroshima and Nagasaki."

"This whole thing makes less sense the more you talk, my friend. Maybe you should just can it for a while, Hank. I mean, you haven't even started to think about these kids Zcink is supposed to be chopping up, and the Jewish symbols on their feet, and the way their bodies have been drained of blood and dipped in flour that might be matzo dough. What do you do with all of that?"

The light turned green, and Hank pressed down hard on the gas and popped the clutch. The Ford's big 272-inch Y-block shoved the two cops back into their seats. From here to Ashland Avenue, Pershing was two lanes in each direction, and Hank figured he could make up some time.

"Wow, man, we're rocket-propelled and ready for takeoff!" Marvin laughed until he started coughing; and then after a couple moments, he added, "But you still can't get around my question, Hank. How do you link Zcink up with all this ritual murder stuff? I've seen his nose, and I can tell you that he doesn't look even a little Jewish."

Driving down the street at fifty miles per hour, Hank turned to Marvin and said, "That's the easy part. I'm not saying Zcink is Jewish. Like Miss Hathaway said down at the morgue, no Jew would pull all this stuff with the blood and the symbols. No Jew would mix the blood of Christian kids with matzo dough and eat the matzos for

Passover. And even you pointed out that June isn't matzo-making time. That's all just bullshit meant to make people think the Jews are doing it."

"What about Zcink complaining to the police brass about us, getting them warning us to stay away from him? That takes a lot of clout, and I don't think most people who chop up school kids do it because of how much clout they have."

Hank shrugged and said, "Al Capone had clout."

Marvin didn't say anything for a block or so while Hank weaved in and out of the lines of old, battered cars. Then finally Marvin shook his head and said, "Hank, everybody says that I'm the nutcase in this partnership. I'm supposed to be the cowboy with the loose marbles, while you're supposed to be the guy with the smarts and the savvy and all the self-control. You're Sherlock Holmes to my King Kong — but really, it's not like that at all. You, my friend, truly are one gone and deeply agitated daddy-o. A complete nut job."

"Marvin, I'm telling you, I got a feeling."

"And Hank, my friend, let me tell you, your feeling is nuts, but you're my partner so I'm backing you on this anyway. Like they say: all the way."

"Thanks, Marvin," Hank said and smiled at his partner. "I wish I could say the same for you."

"Now you tell me!"

CHAPTER 47

IT WAS NINE in the morning, and already the sun was a big yellow heat blister over Lake Michigan.

It was hot again too, and Hank knew it was going to get hotter. When he and Marvin pulled up in front of Professor Zcink's brownstone on South Dorchester, Hank could feel the sweat building up and thickening on the back of his neck. It reminded him of that night when the first boy was found in the suitcase by the convent. It was the same kind of heat, rousing itself in the morning and getting ready for some serious misery by noon.

Looking at Zcink's place through the side window of the black Ford, Hank said to Marvin, "You better wait in the car. You don't want to scare the professor with your bandages and blood."

Marvin turned to his partner. "If this guy's the monster you say he is, a few drops of my blood ain't going to scare him a lick. It'll hop him up. He'll want it like a raging dope-fiend wants his smack. I'll probably have to pistol-whip him just to keep him off my lily-white neck, he'll be so hot for my Jew red blood cells."

"Seriously, man," Hank said after a couple seconds, "you up for this? You've been taking a beating these last few days. Nobody would fault you. You could lay low here in the car."

"While you do what? Go up there and cuff this guy and bring him in yourself? I don't see it. Whatever happens, you're going to need backup, and I'm the only one who'll give it to you. Anybody else would tell you that you're being a complete idiot on this case. But not me. I'm going in with you. And that's serious. I just want to know one thing, Hank: Have you figured out yet what we're gonna do once we get in there with Zcink?"

"No, not yet."

"I didn't think so, but that's okay. I'll bet you'll figure it out once you get in there and he comes at you with his cleaver or his samurai sword."

"Napoleon's Famous Two-Part Battle Plan again. It worked last time, more or less."

Hank tried the door to Zcink's apartment. It was locked this time. He turned around. Marvin was right behind him, a big, ugly smile spread across his face and his hand resting inside his sport coat on the grip of his .45.

"Say, Hank," Marvin whispered, "if you hear some kind of scary music or a coffin lid creaking open in there, you shoot first and ask questions later, okay?"

Hank didn't say anything. He just nodded and put his finger on the white doorbell. But he didn't press it yet.

Marvin had said he was ready, but Hank didn't know if he himself was. What was he going to do once he saw Professor Zcink? Beat a confession out of him with Marvin's sap? Force him to let them search the basement for knives and a chopping block? Would Zcink just crumple in front of him and Marvin and admit to anything they wanted?

None of that seemed likely, so finally Hank pressed the doorbell.

It made the same soft, tinny tinkle as before, like a kid somewhere rattling a teaspoon around an empty can. But this time Hank didn't have to ring the bell twice. He heard footsteps moving across the living room floor, then a hand on the doorknob and a key turning in the lock on the other side of the door.

He took a step back and reached into his jacket, his fingers moving slowly and quietly for the wood grips of his .38.

CHAPTER 48

WITH A SLIGHT creaking sound, the door pulled back. Hank could see the hot morning light filtering into the living room on the other side of the door, and he waited for Zcink's voice or his face, but that's not what he found on the other side of the door.

A tall, heavy-set, middle-aged guy in a blue business suit and tie stood in the doorway. He was bald and smiling, with a pencil mustache. For a second, Hank had the crazy idea that maybe this guy was Zcink's old boss and hero, the German atomic scientist Werner Heisenberg.

"Can I help you, gentlemen?" the big man asked.

Hank took a quiet breath and eased his pistol back into his shoulder holster. The guy wasn't a Kraut or a Hungarian. He was an American. His accent was East Coast, probably Harvard or at least Boston College. Hank let his fingers slide back to rest on the top button of his sports coat.

"Yes, sir," Hank said. "I'm Detective Purcell, and this is my partner, Detective Bondarowicz. We're with the Chicago Police Department. We were hoping to see Professor Zcink here."

"Please come in," Harvard said, pulling the door open wide so they could pass. "You're the pair we heard about."

"Who's you?" Marvin said, following Hank into the living room.

"We're the FBI. I'm Senior Special Agent Simmons."

The place was empty now, except for a wooden card table and four folding chairs arranged around it. The paintings and the photographs Hank had looked at last time were gone. The room's light-blue carpet was rolled up and pushed against the wall. A couple of brown leather pullman cases were set next to the carpet.

"The Federal BI?" Marvin said, walking over to the table and putting his fedora on it.

"Yes, we heard you and your partner have been harassing Professor Zcink."

"We're involved in a criminal investigation. We're investigating, not harassing. Harassing isn't part of our job."

"That's not the way we heard it," the agent said, and then after a pause he asked Marvin, "What happened to your head?"

Hank looked at Marvin's bandaged forehead. Blood was still seeping.

Marvin glanced up at his bandage and touched it. His fingers came away bloodied. He rubbed his fingertips together and looked at Agent Simmons.

"This is blood," Marvin said. "One Joseph Rosetti, a.k.a. Joey Roses, harassed me a little this morning — he tried to get inside my head using his handcuffs for a can-opener. A colored cop over on Fillmore Street fixed me up. You like the job he did?"

"I've got nothing against our colored brothers, but can you get a refund?"

"You got a sense of humor."

"Yes, I do."

"They teach you that at Yale?"

"Not Yale. Harvard."

"The rich get rich, and the poor get babies."

"I guess so. It's the way of the world, my friend," Simmons said and smiled. "Now, tell me, what can I do for you gentlemen today?"

Marvin put his hand on his heart and grinned back at the FBI agent. "What can you do for us? I'm no good at explaining. My partner's the one who's good at that. I'm here for comic relief. Tell the man what he can do for us, Hank."

Hank had walked over to take a look at the suitcases while Marvin and Simmons were talking. He turned to face them when he heard his name.

"Be happy to," he said as he stepped away from the pieces of luggage and took off his hat. "I'm going to give it to you straight, Mr. Simmons. We think Zcink's connected somehow with these Suitcase Charlie killings. We've been…"

"What are you talking about?" Agent Simmons broke in. "Professor Zcink connected to the killing of those three boys and the little girl? Not likely."

"Two little girls. They found the other missing girl this morning in Washington Park," Hank said. "That's about a mile from here."

Simmons looked at Hank. His face didn't show anything much, but clearly the Senior Special Agent wasn't buying it. It was time for Hank to start stretching the truth.

"Listen. These two suitcases here," Hank began again, pointing at the pullmans, "are exact duplicates for the three suitcases found in the Humboldt Park area and the first one the police found in Washington Park. I can tell because of the grain of the leather, the shape and size of the case, and — most importantly — the lock. This kind of lock is unusual, very rare in fact, made only in two regions of Hungary. One of these regions, Nzesyetzpho, is where Zcink comes from. How many of these suitcases are here in the whole

United States? Maybe ten altogether. And four of them — probably five, now — are accounted for. They had five dead children in them, three little boys and two little girls. Bled to death, chopped up, sacrificed. Those suitcases are down at the Crime Detection Lab right now, being examined for fingerprints or anything else that will further link these crimes to Professor Zcink. Two more of these suitcases are in this room, right here next to this blue rug. I'd stake my reputation on the fact that the one that was found in Washington Park this morning when they came across that second dead girl was the same kind, and came over here along with all the others."

Agent Simmons turned his head and looked at the two suitcases near the wall. He didn't say anything for a moment; then he sat down at the card table and faced Hank again. "You're telling me that the investigators at the Crime Detection Laboratory are looking at these suitcases?"

"That's right."

"What that tells me is that you Chicago cops don't have anything on our Professor. If you had something real, you wouldn't be standing here diddling me with these Charlie Chan 'facts' about rare locks and suitcases from someplace not even God's ever heard of. Instead, you'd be yanking my lapels and shouting, screaming at me that we have got to get this son-of-a-bitch right away before he kills another child."

"We do have to get this son-of-a-bitch right away before he kills another child."

"No, I'm not buying it," Simmons said. "You've got nothing that ties Professor Zcink in any real way to these killings, except for a couple of suitcases."

Marvin sat down across from Simmons, picked up his hat, and placed it on his bandaged head.

Hank walked over to the suitcases. "Did you take a look at them? Look inside?"

"No, I haven't. I'm guessing they're locked, and Professor Zcink's got the key."

Hank put his hand on the grip of the nearer suitcase. He didn't know what was in it, but he had a good idea how much a suitcase like this filled with clothes should weigh — about forty pounds, give or take. One with a dead child should weigh in at twice that, maybe a little more, eighty or eight-five pounds. He tightened his hand on the grip, braced himself, and tried to lift the suitcase.

There was no child in it.

He did the same with the other suitcase. It weighed what a twenty-five-inch pullman full of socks and ties, shirts and pants, underwear and toothbrushes should weigh.

"Happy?" Simmons asked.

"No, not yet."

"I'm afraid you'll have to live with a little unhappiness, Detective. I think you're dreaming stuff up about Professor Zcink. He's an okay guy. Like you, like me, he's working for the government, trying to keep people here safe."

"I don't think so. I think he's connected to these killings."

"You've got nothing to support that. Why don't you and your partner just walk out of this apartment, and that'll be that? I know you're trying to do your job, but there's no way Professor Zcink is tied in with this. The Bureau keeps a pretty tight watch on him. Guy like that, the job he does, the hours? There's no way he can be doing to kids what you say he's doing."

Hank looked at Agent Simmons sitting at the card table and knew the man was wrong, but also knew that he couldn't prove it so it would stick, so it would lead to a courtroom downtown and the electric chair over at Cook County Jail.

"Yeah, we'll walk out of this apartment," Hank said. "Just tell us where Zcink is."

"I can't do that."

"And what's going on here? Why no furniture? Is Zcink leaving? Moving?"

"I can't tell you that either."

"Listen," Hank said, "I'll make you a deal. We let you walk out of this place with your face in one piece, in exchange for information about where Zcink is and thirty minutes to get to him. Like you said, we're all working for the same thing here, to make the place safe for everyone, children included, and we have to talk to him again, try to eliminate him as a suspect."

"That's a threat," Simmons said, still sitting calmly at the card table. "Are you going to carry it out?"

"Not me, but my partner, Marvin Bondarowicz here, is."

Simmons turned to Marvin, sitting across the card table from him. The bandage had come loose, and Marvin was trying to reset it over the cuts Joey Roses had made with his handcuffs. The FBI agent started laughing and then abruptly stopped. "Don't make me laugh. I outweigh your partner by a good hundred pounds."

"That's okay. He's crazy and tenacious. If you think his forehead looks bad, you should see what Joey Roses looked like after their little discussion this morning."

"Tenacious?" Agent Simmons laughed again. "You must have been with me at Harvard. Where'd you learn a word like that?"

"The nuns taught me. They were pretty tenacious, too."

Simmons started to laugh harder, his stomach rising and falling, his head shaking up and down, his laughter filling the empty room. After a few moments, the laughing tapered off into chuckling. "You know, Detective Purcell, you're a stitch."

"He's not the only one," Marvin said. "I've got thirty-seven of them at the moment. And I am the tenacious one, in fact — if I have to do what my partner said I'd do, I'll do it."

"I like you two fellows," Simmons said as he took a blue memo pad out of his breast pocket. "You're not too bright, but you are game, and I'm going to do you both a favor even if you didn't go to Harvard, or even Yale. Professor Zcink's giving a lecture at ten o'clock this morning at the Museum of Science and Industry, something about the connection between the Manhattan Project experiments done here at the University of Chicago and the ones at Los Alamos, New Mexico. It's 9:25 right now, and I've got some notes to make in my memo pad here about the trip the Professor is taking to Los Alamos this afternoon. It'll take me about half an hour to finish up with my notes, and then I'm going to go to the museum and collect the Professor for his trip."

Hank walked over to Simmons and shook his hand. "Thanks. I'll remember this."

"I'd prefer you didn't. It might come back to haunt me."

"You're probably right. Don't worry, then. I'm a great forgetter."

"Me too," Marvin said. "And by the way, I got a blue memo pad just like yours. Very nice."

"Thanks," Simmons said. "Let me just say one last thing before you boys show yourselves out. The Bureau always has its field agents work in pairs. My partner, Buddy Rodgers, is with Professor Zcink right now, making sure nobody bothers him. I'm the cute and cuddly agent. Special Agent Rodgers is the tenacious one, so you fellows be careful now."

On the way downstairs, Marvin turned to Hank. "Not bad for an Eagle Scout. What was all that crap about Hungarian suitcases?" he asked quietly.

"The first one, the one on Washtenaw and Evergreen, really was from Hungary, and something about the lock on it really was special — O'Herlihy told me that the lab boys got all excited about it."

"And the others?"

"The two from Humboldt Park were American-made. The rest, who knows? I may have stretched the facts just a little to try to convince our FBI friend up there," Hank admitted.

"And your little geography lesson? Nzeshitsfoo or whatever crazy-assed place the suitcase came from?"

"You think you're the only one who can bullshit a Harvard man?"

CHAPTER 49

WITH ONLY A FEW minutes to go before the start of Zcink's lecture, Hank pulled the Ford up in front of the Museum of Science and Industry and parked. Marvin looked up from the army-issued Colt .45 he was holding in his two hands and turned to his partner.

"Got any idea how we're going to find Zcink in this place?"

Hank's eyes scanned the white façade of the enormous building with its rows of giant columns and concrete statues of the maidens of science and said, "Some."

The museum was pretty much the biggest structure south of the loop, bigger than the Civic Opera House, bigger than the Art Institute, bigger than Union Station. Maybe bigger than all three of them put together.

Hank knew it wouldn't be easy. Built alongside Lake Michigan, the Museum stood about four or five stories high and took up about a dozen acres, he figured, and those acres weren't easy to navigate. The place had three floors of public exhibits, and those tens of thousands of exhibits were scattered across a labyrinth of rooms that housed antique cars, railroad engines, doll houses that had belonged to silent-movie stars, giant plastic throbbing hearts, cafeterias, toy trains, and even an actual, full-scale, one-of-a-kind German submarine, the U-505, captured during World War II. All told, the place probably took up a quarter-million square feet of floor space.

Hank pushed open the car door and stepped out. "I guess first we'll have to find the information desk."

Marvin clicked and snapped the barrel one more time and slipped the pistol into his shoulder holster. "You got any idea where it is?"

"Inside, I guess. Should be near the entrance. Come on."

Swinging open the tall glass doors leading into the museum, Hank walked into a space the size of one of those European cathedrals they keep building and then knocking down whenever they get into a war.

Looking up, he saw full-size airplanes hung from the domed ceiling. Way off in the back, there was an elevator for a coal-mine exhibit, next to what looked like an oil derrick. A set of model trains took up a space the size of one of those ranch houses they were building west of Harlem Avenue, and in between and under all of these exhibits, people came and went or just stood around.

Right in front of Hank, a few dozen school children clustered around three nuns in their black-and-white habits. Other school groups were there too. The kids were excited and antsy, looking around, staring at everything, barely even pretending to listen to their teachers. They wanted to be off and running around the museum, looking at everything all at once.

Seeing the students, Hank remembered that teachers liked to bring kids here as a treat just before summer vacation. That would explain why there were so many kids today.

Marvin pointed to the information booth about fifteen feet in front of them, and Hank started toward it.

"We're with the Chicago Police," Hank said to the woman behind the desk, "and we need to find Professor Zcink as quick as possible. We understand he's giving a lecture here this morning."

"Yes, of course," she said, and opened a three-ring binder. She ran her finger down the first page and then onto the second. She stopped a couple of lines from the bottom. "Here he is. Professor Zcink. He's downstairs on the ground level in one of the medium-sized lecture areas, the one you enter through the Hall of Electricity. Do you officers need a map?"

"No thanks, Miss," Hank answered as he turned and started walking quickly to the staircase that led to the lower level.

"You know where you're going?" Marvin asked as they rushed down the stairs. "This place doesn't look the way it did when I came here as a kid with my older brother."

"Yeah, come on," Hank said. "I've been here recently with Hazel and Margaret."

When Hank and Marvin got to them, the double doors leading into the lecture hall had already been pulled closed, and it was clear to Hank that the lecture had started. He checked his watch. It was 10:10.

Marvin took his hat off and, just to make sure, pressed his ear to one of the wooden doors. It was thick, but he could hear a voice.

"Yeah, this must be the place, Hank. It sounds like Herr Professor is on the other side of this door doing his best Dracula imitation."

"What are we waiting for?"

"Relax, chum, we got some time. That FBI agent, Simmons, ain't gonna be looking up from his little blue memo pad for a while yet. If he said he'd give us a thirty-minute head start, I bet he gives us an hour. What we got to worry about is his partner, Billy Rodgers."

"That's Buddy, not Billy. And worrying about him now would be kind of pointless, since we haven't been worrying or thinking much about how any of this is going to play out. We don't know if Rodgers is in there; and if he is, we don't know what he looks like. Maybe he's wearing a blue suit like Simmons, but there will probably be a lot of guys in there wearing blue suits."

"Okay, and do we have a plan, Sherlock?"

CHAPTER 50

"A PLAN?" HANK SAID, and then he didn't say anything. He was tired and growing more tired. He remembered that he had barely gotten to sleep last night when Stephanie Lee called him about Joey Roses at the Oak Theatre Diner. A long hard night, a long hard day yesterday, and today wasn't shaping up any shorter or easier.

He looked around the room that ended at this double wooden door. There were all kinds of electrical gizmos scattered around the Hall of Electricity. Giant light bulbs, bicycles hooked up to more light bulbs, and generators powered by hand cranks and levers. School boys and girls manipulated all kinds of knobs and levers and pedals. The kids cranked and pulled and pushed and lifted and dropped, trying to light up something or get it to squeak or buzz.

It was all supposed to inspire the kids to think big thoughts, have bright ideas, super-bright ones, in fact, but it didn't do much for him. Hank didn't have a plan, except for the Famous Two-Part one.

"Come on," he said, and pushed open one of the doors.

The lights in the lecture hall were dim, but Hank could see well enough in the half-light. The hall had about two hundred seats divided down the middle by an aisle, and just about every seat was occupied. From where Hank stood, it looked like the audience was mainly made up of school kids. About half a dozen nuns and a handful of other adults were scattered here and there. Most likely,

Hank figured, they were teachers or parents there to keep the kids out of trouble.

He didn't see anyone who looked like he could be the FBI agent that Simmons had mentioned, Buddy Rodgers.

Hank glanced up at the raised stage. A man in a brown suit stood at a podium: Professor Zcink with a microphone in his right hand and a wooden pointer in his left. He was directing the students' attention to the lower-left-hand corner of a black-and-white photograph projected on a screen behind him. The picture — old, grainy and faded — was of a football stadium. Hank could make out the goal posts and the yard lines.

"Here is where it happened," Zcink said, pressing his pointer hard against the screen, "in an abandoned handball court under the west grandstands of Alonzo Stagg Stadium at the University of Chicago, less than a mile from where you sit today: the first artificial, self-sustaining nuclear chain reaction in an experimental nuclear reactor."

He paused for a second, and a hand swept up in the middle of the block of seats to the right of the stage.

"Yes?" Zcink said, raising his microphone.

A man stood up. "Professor, you said we could ask questions, and I've got one. Did the scientists at the time know how dangerous this experiment was?"

"Thank you, sir, for your question. The answer is 'yes and no.' The scientists, gathered there under the leadership of the Italian physicist Enrico Fermi, did not know exactly what would happen when the reaction took place. Today, we all know what the Atomic Bomb can do. We have read about mushroom clouds and seen photographs; but at that time, scientists theorized that there would ultimately be some kind of an explosion and that it would be significant, but they felt — *almost* unanimously — that they could successfully control a nuclear reaction like the one in the experiment."

Listening to Zcink answering the question, Hank stepped away from the closed doors and walked forward slowly down the central aisle. He stopped about fifteen feet from the stage and raised his hand when Zcink finished speaking.

"I've got a question too, Professor."

"Yes, please," Zcink said as he raised the hand with the microphone above his eyes and tried to make out who was speaking.

"I guess I came in late, so maybe I missed what you said, but could you tell us something about how the Nazis would have used the Bomb if they had finished it first?"

"Ah, now I recognize the gentleman speaking, my friend from the Chicago Police. Good day, Detective. Your question, of course, is a political and military question rather than one purely dealing with science; but some say that science can never be totally pure, so I'll be happy to address it. You ask what the Germans would have done with the Bomb?"

Zcink paused. Hank watched him move away from the screen and toward the lectern. He leaned his pointer against the lectern, picked up a glass of water, drank some, and replaced the glass. Then, putting his right hand on the lectern, he bent his head. It looked to Hank like he was searching for something.

Hank heard a soft click from the stage, and the Stagg Stadium picture behind the professor was suddenly replaced by one of a mushroom cloud rising into the sky. The photograph was clearly taken from an airplane, maybe the Air Corps plane that dropped the Bomb on Hiroshima, the Enola Gay.

The cloud projected on the screen looked thin and elongated. It seemed to be slowly twisting outward, expanding as it rose skyward and toward the plane.

"The Germans.... Well, as I suggested, I am not a military strategist. I'm a scientist, a man concerned with learning what needs to be learned about the nature of the world we live in."

Hank took a step toward the stage. "I understand that, Professor Zcink, but I would still like to hear your thoughts. Can you give us your best guess?"

"Yes, of course, we can all guess, so what do I conjecture? Hmmm... I believe the Germans would have done what the Americans did with their Bomb. You used it to save the lives of your soldiers. It is estimated that the Allies would have suffered a million causalities invading Japan before forcing it to surrender. The Germans would have done something similar if they had achieved their Atomic Bomb."

Hank now knew what he wanted to do. He wanted to egg the Professor on. "So you see no difference between the Germans and the Americans?"

"A scientist must be impartial, so I must say that finally, judging things from my own experiences and observations, in terms of real difference there is nothing substantial between these former foes and present allies."

Hank took another step forward and paused. He glanced around. Some of the school children were listening to what he and Zcink were talking about, but most of them weren't. They were looking around, searching in their lunch bags, whispering to their friends, or playing with their fingers.

"What about the Nazi concentration camps? Auschwitz, Buchenwald, and all the rest? The way the Jews were treated? The extermination camps and the slave-labor camps?"

"Again, this is not science, but politics," Zcink said into his microphone. "The Americans had their camps, the Germans had theirs."

"You don't see a difference?"

"Perhaps a couple. One difference is that the Germans had more time to develop their camp system. As a result, the Jews perished in numbers greater than the Japanese in America."

"That's the only difference? The Japs started the war against us. But the Jews? The Jews didn't do anything. They just got caught up in the war the Nazis started."

"Detective, I'm afraid you are mistaken. Speaking only of facts, it has been well documented: The Jews started the war." Professor Zcink said it calmly and quickly, apparently without thought, as if he had said it a thousand times before.

"What did you say?"

Zcink paused and stared at Hank for a second. Then Zcink said, "That there is no difference."

"No, that's not what you said. You said that the Jews started the war."

"No, I believe you are mistaken."

Throughout the hall, the whispering and fidgeting was getting louder. The teachers who had been trying to make sense of the back-and-forth between Hank and the Professor turned to their students and started giving them the cold stare and the almost inaudible "Shush!" Some of the more unruly schoolboys were starting to get impatient, becoming what Hank knew the nuns in their habits and wimples would call "rambunctious".

One of the boys, a thin boy in a blue baseball cap, suddenly stood up, lifted his fist way above his head, and drove it down, punching the boy sitting next to him in the neck.

The boy screamed.

Zcink turned to the screaming boy and said, "Enough of that! Stop it immediately."

The screaming boy ignored him, or maybe didn't hear him. Instead, he kicked out at the boy who had punched him, and then he jumped up. Throwing his arms around the thin boy's neck, he dragged him to the floor of the lecture hall. Now both boys, rolling around near the stage, were screaming and yelling. Others were standing up to see the fight, and they were starting to shout too.

Zcink quickly stepped closer to the edge of the stage and looked down at the two boys tumbling and grabbing at each other.

"I insist!" he shouted into the microphone, and the microphone made a long, electrical "*aaaaeeeeeeeaaaa*" sound. Zcink took the microphone away from his lips, slapped its head, and tried again. "This is a lecture hall." *Aaaaeeeeeeeaaaa!* "Stop it, this fighting!" *Aaaaeeeeeeeaaaa!*

A nun sitting at the end of the second row stood up and started quickly toward the two boys. She was holding tight to the long rosary at her side. A second nun from the row behind her rushed forward too.

From the back of the room, Hank heard another voice. It was Marvin's, shouting down to Professor Zcink, "No, you said it. I heard you plain as soda water. You said that the Jews started the war."

Zcink looked up from the boys scrambling beneath him and, speaking into the microphone, said to Marvin, "And what if I did? Instead of arguing with me, you should be stopping this fighting. That's what's wrong with this country. Lack of discipline. Children fighting, police officers ignoring their duty, nuns scuttling about being useless. It was like this before the war, and it came from the

Jews, their motion pictures and actors, their comedians and singers, their communist politics." *Aaaaeeeeeeeaaaa!*

Hank watched the nun with the dangling rosary grab the thin boy by his hair and yank him off his screaming victim. The other nun pulled that kid off the floor and started pushing him toward the corner of the lecture hall. But before she could get him there, he spun loose from her and ran back toward the thin boy. The rosary nun, holding the thin boy with one arm, tried to fend off the other one, but he socked her in the face.

And then there was silence as if a large stone had fallen from the sky and landed squarely on everyone in the lecture hall.

The nun who had been hit took a step back away from the boys. They had stopped struggling, even though she didn't say anything. She just shook her head and stared at the boys. Hank could tell they knew it was all over for them. One of the boys just stood there looking at his shoes; the other kept shaking his head as he stared at the nun. She pointed to the two chairs that the boys had been sitting in before they started fighting, and she stared at them until they sat down. Then she started back to her seat.

Hank turned back to Zcink.

The Professor lifted his microphone up to his mouth again and began talking into it when another *"Aaaaeeeeeaaaaa"* erupted from the speakers. But it didn't matter, because Hank could hear Professor Zcink even without the microphone. He was smiling.

"This is a farce, and exactly what I was talking about," Zcink said as he put the microphone on the lectern and walked into the shadows at the back of the stage.

Hank watched him open a door, walk into a lighted corridor, and pull the door shut behind him.

Marvin joined Hank, and they both ran up the stairs to the stage and the exit at the back.

"I'm going after him," Hank said.

"I'm with you."

"No, you're not. You wait for the other FBI agent, Rodgers. I don't know where he is, but if he's going to come looking for Zcink, it'll probably be through this door. You keep him here. I don't want him interfering with me and Zcink."

"I'm giving him five minutes, but if he ain't here by then, I'm leaving and coming to find you."

"Right," Hank said, and ran out the door to find Professor Zcink.

CHAPTER 51

HANK FOUND HIMSELF in a wide, empty corridor without any kind of exhibits, and he didn't know where he was.

There were posters on the walls for tourist attractions in Chicago, but that was all there was to see here. To his left, the corridor ran for about fifteen yards and opened onto one of the exhibit halls. Hank saw a sign near the end of the corridor just before the turn that read "Hall of Electricity." To his right, the corridor seemed to run for about twenty-five yards and then opened into something else — maybe another corridor, maybe another exhibit hall. He couldn't tell which way the Professor had gone, but he knew what he would have done if he were trying to get away from a lecture gone bad or a cop harassing and heckling him.

Hank turned toward the right, away from the place he knew, the Hall of Electricity. The professor had a minute's lead on him, but Hank figured that a guy running away from a cop is usually going to be moving slower than the cop chasing him. He wasn't sure why that was, but it was a fact — maybe because the guy running away usually stops to look back, and the cop only has to look forward.

Hank started moving faster as he got to the end of the first corridor and turned a corner into a second, shorter one. This one was also decorated with framed posters of some of Chicago's tourist sites:

Riverview Park, Lincoln Park Zoo, Adler's Planetarium. Chicago looked like a swell place to visit.

Hank didn't see any sign of Zcink, but he kept moving anyway. Like Marvin's father used to say, "Don't stop 'til you get to the top."

The second corridor opened up into a big exhibit hall. Rows of antique cars filled the room, and Hank ran past Studebakers and Duesenbergs, Packards and Cords, all clean and gleaming under the bright lights. At the end of the hall, Hank stopped to look around. Now he had a problem.

The antique-car room opened into a small alcove with some restrooms, and this in turn opened onto a large exhibit hall that appeared to have three paths leading out of it in three different directions. There were a few people walking purposefully through the hall. The ones going to his right were heading to a cafeteria; Hank could smell the stale, dry odor of baked potatoes and over-fried chicken. The people going to the left seemed to be heading back toward the wonders of the Hall of Electricity. And ahead of him was a large area devoted to "Ships and Sea Power".

While he tried to figure out where Zcink would be heading, he got a break.

He hoped.

Thirty or forty yards ahead of him, Hank saw a tall, thin guy walk out from behind a billboard that said "U-505" with a big blue arrow pointing in the direction he was hurrying. It looked like Zcink, or at least he was wearing the same sort of mustard-brown suit.

Hank knew where the German submarine was. It was just beyond the Sea Power hall, and he quickly ran on a diagonal to cut Zcink off. But the professor must have heard him coming, and moved surprisingly fast. When the detective got to the entrance of the submarine exhibit he was just in time to see Zcink hurry up the ramp to the entrance to the U-505 and disappear.

Hank followed him in.

CHAPTER 52

HANK HAD BEEN on the U-505 submarine before. September of 1954, right after its formal dedication, he had taken Hazel and Margaret to see the only German sub captured during the war. The endless lines snaked and looped through the different museum halls. It took Hank and his family more than two hours to get into the sub, and then it was so crowded and claustrophobic that — even though the hatches between most of the compartments had been cut away — he and the girls filed out without seeing much except a lot of battleship gray.

It wasn't like that this time.

Standing at the front of the submarine and looking down the long narrow interior, Hank could see that it was pretty much empty. Maybe it was just a quiet day today, or maybe it was because it was lunch time and most of the people in the museum were down in the cafeteria searching for something to eat that wouldn't give them ptomaine.

Hank started forward through the U-boat's long corridor. The ceiling was low and the passage through the sub was narrow, so he found himself moving slowly, with his head slightly bowed. He wasn't sure if Professoer Zcink was still in the submarine, but if he was, there wasn't going to be much of a problem finding him.

There wasn't anywhere in the sub to hide. The only doors left were the two hatches that had been left intact. So Hank walked head down and eyes forward, past the torpedo room with its long, thin, shark-like killing machines, past the sailors' mess, and past the conning tower. He searched until just beyond the mid-point of the submarine. That's when he came across a faded green curtain spread across a doorway that ran parallel to the central walkway.

Hank looked at the wooden sign next to the curtained doorway. Its black gothic lettering said "Captain's Cabin". Without pausing, he pulled back the curtain.

The room was small, and Professor Zcink was sitting on a narrow bed next to a desk. His legs were crossed at the knees, and he held a Beretta pistol loosely in his right hand.

"Come in, Detective Purcell, and please sit down. I don't want to say I was expecting you; that would be too much like something from one of your bad gangster movies. But as you can see by my pistol, I was. I saw you, probably about the same time you saw me, in the corridor as you were hurrying toward me. But do sit down here, across from me."

Zcink pointed with his pistol to a small metal-gray chair that stood to the left of the green curtain Hank had pulled back, and the detective sat down.

"You don't seem worried, Professor."

"Why should I be worried?"

"You killed five children, and I can prove it."

"An interesting allegation, but I don't think you can prove it. That is just some of your American cowboy bravado. Besides, it's a crime that doesn't make any sense. I am a nuclear scientist, a physicist. Why would I kill five children that I don't even know?"

"You want to implicate the Jews."

"Oh, yes, I read about that in the paper this morning, the *Sun-Times*, all that mumbo-jumbo about bones sprinkled with matzo dough and Stars of David carved in the soles of the poor victims. But why would I try to implicate the Jews in these killings? Why, I even study English with a Jewish tutor, the amiable Mr. Fisch, who would be more than happy to write me a sterling letter of recommendation. It doesn't make any sense, Detective, that's what people would say. The police, the lawyers, the judges, the newspapermen — all of them. And besides, where's my motive?"

"Your motive? That's easy, Zcink. You're an un-rehabilitated Nazi. You hate Jews and you want other people to hate Jews."

"Everything you say is true, Detective Purcell. I do want people to hate the Jew as much as I do, and the fact that the crimes look like Jewish ritual murders might convince some people that they should hate the Jews also. And maybe it is working. Some of the papers are starting to suggest such a link. The reporter in the *Sun-Times* sees the crime this way; in fact, he's demanding that the police look at the Peterson and Schuessler killings too, for signs of matzo and Jewish stars cut on the soles of their feet. That's smart of him."

"You did those, too?"

"Come now, Detective, do you expect me to confess? No one will tie me to the Peterson and Schuessler killings, and why would they? I'm working for your Uncle Sam, unlocking the secrets of the atom so that we can keep the forces of Communism and anarchy at bay. The Nazis? Nobody even remembers them."

Hank had to keep him talking. He knew somebody would show up pretty fast. The submarine was a popular exhibit.

"What about the little girl by St. Fidelis School, the one you gave the sketch of the Star of David to? You don't think she can recognize you?"

Zcink shrugged. "How seriously will one stupid little Polish girl be taken?"

"I don't get it," Hank said, leaning back, away from Zcink and his pistol. "What gives you the right to kill these kids?"

"The right? There is no right, just a duty, a responsibility that all right-thinking Aryan people should accept. The Jews are exactly what Hitler said, vermin, an Asiatic plague."

"I still don't get it."

"Well, that much is obvious. It's like Jesus Christ: You either have him in your heart or you don't. You work with a Jew, your partner, Detective Bondarowicz, and yet you don't see what he's like. Why you can't see the threat in him is something I can't explain to you. Sometimes I think the human mind is like the atom — in the end, it's something only a rare few of us can truly understand."

Hank looked down at the pistol in Zcink's hand. He held it loosely in his long fingers, and the cyanide-blue barrel was pointed down. There were only about four feet between him and the Professor. If he lunged for him, Hank was almost sure he could slap the pistol to the side and take Zcink down.

He was about to make his move when he heard footsteps on the wooden planking that ran the length of the inner corridor of the submarine. Someone was coming.

Zcink heard it too, and said to Hank, "Ah, at last, the two FBI agents, my escort, are coming to take me to Los Alamos so I can discuss the discoveries I've made with my esteemed colleagues there.

I'm looking forward to the trip and to the dry air in New Mexico. Summers here in Chicago are far too humid."

Zcink turned his head to the corridor then and said calmly, "Agent Simmons, Agent Rodgers, I'm over here in the captain's cabin. Please hurry."

Hank looked at the curtain by the doorway and heard the footsteps coming faster, and then a few seconds later, he heard a voice.

"Sorry, Professor, it's just me, Detective Bondarowicz, and I'll be right there. Just you wait."

Zcink suddenly turned to Hank, and Hank slammed his right fist into the professor's face. Hank didn't think he'd hit him that hard, but Zcink's head jerked back and smashed against the gray metal wall of the submarine. The Professor gave a loud "ooff", his eyes rolled back in his head, and his body slumped forward and began sliding down the bunk. With his left hand, Hank scooped the Beretta out of Zcink's hand before the Professor collapsed to the floor of the cabin.

A hand pulled the green curtain back, and Marvin stood there looking in.

"What gives?"

"The Professor seems to have accidentally knocked himself out," Hank said.

"Amazing. What're we gonna do with him?"

"That depends on how much time we have. Where are Simmons and Rodgers?"

"I ran into Rodgers and told him the Professor wanted to meet them on the second floor, overlooking the toy train exhibit. He told me he and Simmons were supposed to meet with the Professor down here at the sub, but I explained that the Professor had changed his mind. I'm guessing the FBI guys are waiting for Zcink up there and watching the trains go 'round and 'round the track."

"That means we've got a little time. Grab an arm, and let's get him out of here."

"You know, Hank, we got nothing solid on him."

"That's right," Hank said. "We got nothing that will stand up in a court of law. Not even in Chicago. But he and I did have an interesting conversation before his unfortunate accident."

"So what are we gonna do with him?"

"We're going to frog-walk him out of here through the side exit just beyond the submarine, and then stick him in the trunk of the Ford. After that, we'll drive him to one of those forests near Lake Geneva or Lake Como just over the Wisconsin border, and we'll bury him there."

"But he ain't dead."

"It's possible that he may be by the time we bury him."

"Hmm," Marvin said. "That'll work."

"Yeah. Grab his arm, and let's get moving."

Chapter 53

EASING OFF THE narrow dirt road, Hank drove slowly toward a small clearing flanked by a brace of huge trees. He stopped finally near some smaller pines, turned off the engine, and switched off the car's headlights.

He put on his fedora and turned to his partner. Marvin was curled up asleep in the back seat, his hat pulled low over his eyes. Hank shrugged and looked out the window into the darkness.

There was no moon. No stars. No streetlights. No neon lights from a gas station or tavern nearby. No campfires. No flashlight beams. No troop of girl scouts twirling their silvery sparklers like semaphores.

The black and gray clouds above him didn't reflect any light either, nothing to shine down on him and the trees around him in this little clearing in the woods north of Lake Como. There was just darkness.

Hank stared into it.

He remembered another narrow path, another forest, another darkness.

It was January 11, 1945, or maybe it was January 12. It didn't matter, really. He remembered standing on a two-bit forest path in the Ardennes. The night trees around him were dark and frozen, barely moving in the cold air. Everywhere around him snow was falling, and a wind that wasn't much of a wind pushed the flakes around just a little. There was no moon then either, not a sliver, but from somewhere a little light shone, so Hank could see the flakes slowly turning in the wind. He felt the cold too, he always felt the cold. It found his hands and face no matter how hard he tried to shield them.

There was fear too. It moved through his body like an anaconda grown fat and slow on discarded rinds and terror.

He stood there in the dropping flakes and the slight wind from nowhere and the cold and the fear, and he looked down at the body in front of him. Sergeant Nowak was dead, his head split apart by some Kraut bullet, his brains spilled and scattered in the snow at Hank's feet. Nowak wasn't the only dead man there. Beyond some bushes, maybe five yards off, his friend Bill — the only other guy from Chicago — leaned dead against a tree trunk that a German 88 had cracked in half, and just beyond Bill there was Junior, the dead corporal from Arizona with hair so yellow they used to call him Mr. Sunshine. And just beyond that another dead G.I. and another dead G.I. and another.

Hank remembered standing in the near-complete darkness of the Ardennes and looking at the .45 Colt in his hands. It was loaded with a fresh clip, but it was useless. It hadn't kept his friends alive, hadn't stopped the Germans from doing what they wanted to do, hadn't stopped them from killing his buddies and moving forward past this forest clearing to the next clearing.

The Germans did it and moved on, leaving Hank there on the narrow path in the Ardennes. They didn't know he was alive. They must have figured he was like Bill and Junior and Sergeant Nowak and his other buddies, dead like the other guys the Krauts left behind them and like the guys ahead of them that the Krauts were going to turn into more dead guys....

Marvin began stirring in the back seat of the Ford. He pushed the brim of his hat up over his eyes and asked, "Where the fuck are we, Hank?"

Hank didn't say anything for a minute.

He kept staring into the darkness that was no longer the darkness of the Ardennes, staring into the pine trees and ash trees and spruce that surrounded the unmarked black police car. Nothing about this clearing was different from the way it was when he saw it before the war, before the Ardennes, back when he was a kid that one summer during the Depression when his dad got a job at a restaurant up on Route 50, the two-lane state road from Lake Geneva to Delavan. After finishing his chores with the chickens, Hank would ride a beat-up old bike out here to the woods along the northern shore of Lake Como, and sometimes he'd camp, spend the night in the woods, dreaming of pioneers in coonskin caps and buckskin jackets and pants.

He loved the darkness then, the brightness of the stars, the way they would light up the forest, feed his imagination and dreams of Indian braves trekking through the silence.

That was before the war, before the Ardennes and what happened there in the darkness.

Marvin took his .45 out of his shoulder holster then, checked the clip, and said, "Hank, don't get all dreamy on me, man. We're here to do a job, and it ain't gonna get any darker."

"Yeah," Hank said. He pushed open the door of the black Ford and stepped out.

The night was cool and dry, the ground soft. That would help. Hank liked that.

"Come on," he said, "let's open up the trunk and see how Zcink's doing."

"I don't think he's doing very well. Not a peep from him since we crossed the Wisconsin line an hour ago."

Hank took his revolver out of its holster, held it with both hands, and nodded toward Marvin. "Open the trunk."

Marvin nodded back, and after fumbling with the keys for a moment he unlocked the trunk. The lid slowly lifted, and a dim light came on.

Awake and lying on the floor of the trunk with his hands and feet tied, Zcink stared up at Hank and Marvin. Hank could see he was a mess. Zcink's face was dirty with some kind of grease smear across his left cheek, and his forehead still bled from where Marvin brained him with his .45, knocking him out again before they put him in the trunk. Hank had stuffed a rag into his mouth then and bound it there with a rope to keep him quiet for the trip up to Wisconsin, but it had gotten loose somehow.

Zcink didn't seem enraged, or frightened, or even nervous. He just stared at Hank like the detective was a waiter who had just done something stupid in a fancy restaurant.

"Time to get out, Zcink," Marvin said finally, and pulled the Professor out of the trunk until he was resting on the back bumper.

Zcink shook the blood out of his eyes and looked at Marvin first and then at Hank. "Now what, my friends?"

"Now we kill you," Hank said.

The Hungarian scientist worked up a smile and said, "That's ridiculous. You can't kill me. Not like that!"

Hank and Marvin didn't say anything. While Hank holstered his gun, Marvin took the shovel they'd bought out of the trunk. Then they grabbed Zcink by the arms and dragged him past some bushes to the edge of the clearing a little further from the dirt road.

Once there, they dropped him at the base of a pine tree, and Hank took his pistol out again.

Zcink pushed himself up onto his knees.

Hank expected him to start weeping or pleading then, but he didn't.

"Gentlemen, this is irrational," Zcink said. "You're going to kill me? Just like that? You're law-enforcement officers. You have a duty to the law. Where's your American justice? Where's your compassion? You talk about us Nazis, our cruelty, the millions of Jews we burned in the ovens, and yet you're ready to kill me without a trial, without anything. I don't believe it. Besides, you'll get caught and jailed for murdering me."

Marvin laughed. "I don't think so, Professor. Nobody saw us take you out of the museum. Everybody's gonna say you got away from Hank. We'll say we figured you went to join your FBI friends upstairs. It'll look like you gave us all the slip and escaped somewhere, out a side entrance — maybe you skipped all the way back to Europe. They'll all think you were just too smart for us stupid Chicago cops. Just like Suitcase Charlie — we never caught him, either."

"Ridiculous!"

"Fuck you," Marvin said, reaching for his .45. "I'm going to kill you now, and no shit from your mouth is gonna change that."

"Shut up," Hank said to Marvin.

Marvin looked at him. "What?"

"I'm doing it."

Marvin didn't say anything for a few seconds. He just looked at Hank.

"Can we flip a coin?"

"No, I'm doing it," Hank said, and walked up to where Zcink was kneeling. The detective didn't hesitate for a moment. He extended his arm, pointed the stubby barrel of his .38 at Zcink's forehead, and fired.

Zcink's head jerked back and exploded, and the scientist's body jerked itself backwards onto the carpet of pine needles.

Zcink was dead. The sound of the blast echoed through the trees for a moment.

Hank holstered his pistol.

"What the fuck, man? That was fast," Marvin said, looking at the ruined mask of Zcink's face.

"I didn't want to stand around talking about it like this was that *Petrified Forest* movie or *The Ox-Bow Incident*. I wanted it over."

"I guess," Marvin said, still looking at the mess of Zcink's face. "It sure is over."

"Let's bury him. Give me the shovel."

"Sure."

The Next Day: Friday, June 8

CHAPTER 54

BEFORE HE HAD closed the front door, Hank saw the ceiling light on in the kitchen. He'd hoped Hazel would be asleep by the time he got back from the woods north around Lake Como, but that wasn't the way it turned out. He unstrapped his shoulder holster and hung it up in the closet by the front door. Then he started toward the kitchen.

When he came in, Hazel looked up from the *Life* magazine she was reading. "Long night?" she asked.

"Yeah, real long."

"You know, sometimes you could call. That would be nice."

Hank didn't say anything. He walked over to the stove and felt the side of the glass percolator. It was still warm, and he took down a light-blue cup from the rack and poured himself some coffee.

"You're not going to say anything?" Hazel asked.

He didn't say anything.

He carried his cup over to the window at the back of the kitchen and looked out at the garden he and Hazel had cultivated last year. The tomato cages were empty, and they would probably stay empty until next year. It was too late to plant tomatoes or lettuce.

Finally he turned around. "What can I say, Hazel? It's been a long night, a long day, a hard week."

"You can't say more than that? You leave while I'm sleeping and you come back when I should be sleeping, and you can't tell me more than 'it's been a hard week'?"

"I'm sorry," Hank said. "It's this business, the Suitcase Charlie thing."

"I thought O'Herlihy told you to stay away from it."

"Yeah, he did."

"And you're still working it?" she said, shaking her head slowly.

"Yes, I am."

Hazel closed the magazine and laid it flat on the table. "Hank, this is what you get for working with Marvin Bondarowicz. O'Herlihy will demote both of you."

"Probably."

"You know Marvin's a cowboy, a maniac. The things you tell me about him…. I don't know why you stay with him."

"Marvin's not the problem. He's not really any crazier than half the guys on the force. It's this case. It's just insane, the way it's unwinding. You heard there was another body found?"

"Yes, a girl, another one, down by Washington Park."

"That's five kids chopped up in suitcases, Hazel," Hank said as he stood with his back to the window. "I just don't want there to be any more."

"I know, Hank. It's terrible what he's doing to these children."

Hank nodded and lifted his coffee cup to his lips. The coffee didn't seem as warm as it had at first, but he sipped some of it anyway.

Suddenly, a quiet cry came from the front of the house.

Hank looked up.

Hazel turned around.

"It's Margaret," she said.

Another cry sounded from their daughter's bedroom.

Hazel shook her head. "I'll go see," she said, and got up from the kitchen table and started down the dark hallway to Margaret's room. Hank watched her.

At Margaret's doorway, Hazel stopped and turned around for a moment. "Hank, I want to talk about this. Please, don't go anywhere."

Hank nodded and put his coffee cup on the counter. The kitchen was clean, everything in its place. He switched off the ceiling light and looked out the window to the backyard again. With the city lights bouncing off the clouds, he didn't need the light to see. The fences, the bushes, the garage — everything was clear and sharp and white and black.

He knew it was late, at least 3:30 or 4:00 in the morning, but he didn't know what time it was for certain. He had lost his wristwatch, his Bulova, someplace in Wisconsin, probably while they were burying the Professor. He didn't see it when they were cleaning up afterwards, so the watch was probably buried along with Zcink.

He thought back to the long drive back to Chicago from the Wisconsin woods. It seemed endless, and both of them were exhausted by the time they stopped at a roadhouse near Spring Grove and the Illinois border. In the middle of the dark prairie, the place seemed cheery. It still had its red and green Christmas-tree lights up, and Marvin sang a couple lines of "Rudolph, the Red-Nosed Reindeer" when they pulled into the parking lot. Marvin wanted to buy a pint of Jack Daniels, something sweet for the ride home.

Hank had a couple inches of that Jack, but it was mostly his partner's bottle. Marvin pulled it down pretty fast. It mellowed him out, and Hank was glad it did. Marvin stopped making up jokes about Zcink and burying the body in the shallow grave in the woods, stopped talking about "Zcink being in the sink" and putting a stake in Dracula's heart. Marvin stopped all that jokey bullshit after a couple of good long shots.

But after that, Hank and Marvin didn't talk much the rest of the way back. Marvin didn't usually like to talk much when he was drinking, and Hank didn't want to shoot the breeze either, not this time.

He knew what it was like to kill a man in combat.

Afterward you're hopped up, feeling the adrenaline, the magic of doing what everybody has always told you not to do, the rush of being the one walking away alive. You're happy it wasn't you, and you're grinning and slapping your buddy's back and talking fast and excited like you just got kissed for the first time, and you know that there will be more and better kisses, and that they'll never stop. Never.

But now Hank knew it wasn't always like that. This time it wasn't like that for a fact, and Hank didn't want to talk about it. Hazel said she wanted to talk, but he didn't want to. Not to his partner Marvin, and not to his wife Hazel. Not now. Hank was glad the Professor was dead, glad that he'd shot him and buried him in the woods on the other side of the Wisconsin-Illinois line.

But he didn't want to talk about it at all, and he stood with his back to the kitchen and looked out the window at the empty tomato cages in the backyard. Some were bent; others were leaning into the garage. He tried to remember what he was doing the weekend he should have planted the tomatoes, but he couldn't.

He hoped that Hazel would be in their daughter's bedroom for a long, long time, trying to soothe away the bad dreams that Margaret was having so she could ease her back to sleep.

THE END

AFTERWORD
Suitcase Charlie and Me

I STARTED WRITING *Suitcase Charlie* about sixty-three years ago when I was 7 years old, just a kid.

At that time, I was living in a working-class neighborhood on the near northwest side of Chicago, an area sometimes called Humboldt Park, sometimes called the Polish Triangle. A lot of my neighbors were Holocaust survivors, World War II refugees, and Displaced Persons. I grew up seeing people with Auschwitz tattoos on their wrists, sympathizing with Polish cavalry officers who still mourned their dead comrades and their beloved horses, and hearing the stories of women who had walked a thousand miles to escape the Russian Gulag. They were our moms and dads. Some of us kids had been born here in the States, but most of us had come over to America in the late '40s and early '50s on US troop ships when the government started letting us refugees in.

As kids, we knew a lot about fear. We learned about it from our parents. They had seen their mothers and fathers shot, their brothers and sisters put on trains and sent to concentration camps, their childhood friends left behind crying on the side of a road. Most of our parents didn't tell us about this stuff directly. How could they?

But we felt their fear anyway.

We overheard their stories late at night when they thought we were watching TV in a far-off room or sleeping in bed, and that's when they'd gather around the kitchen table and start remembering the past and all the things that made them fearful. My mom would tell about what happened to her mom and her sister and her sister's baby when the Germans came to their house in the woods — the rapes and the murders.

You could hear the fear in my mom's voice. She feared everything: the sky in the morning, a drink of water, a sparrow singing in a dream, me whistling some stupid little Mickey Mouse Club tune I picked up on TV. Sometimes when I was a kid, if I started to whistle she would ask me to stop because she was afraid — that kind of simple act of joy would bring the Devil into the house. Really.

My dad was the same way. If he walked into a room where my sister and I were watching some TV show about World War II — even something as innocuous as the sitcom *Hogan's Heroes* — and there were some German soldiers on the screen, his hands would clench up into fists, his face would redden in anger, and he would tell us to turn the show off immediately. He was normally the sweetest guy in the world, but his fear would turn him toward anger and he would start shouting about the terrible things the Germans did: the women he saw bayoneted, the friends he saw castrated and beaten to death, the men he saw frozen to death during a simple roll call.

This was what it was like at home for me and most of my friends. To escape our parents' fear, however, we didn't have to do much; we just had to go outside and be around other kids. With them, we could forget the war and our parents' fear. We'd laugh, play tag and hide-and-go-seek, climb on fences, play softball in the nearby park, go to the corner store for an ice cream cone or a chocolate soda — you name it. This was in the mid-'50s at the height of the baby boom, and there were millions of us kids outside living large and — as my dad liked to say — running around like wild goats.

In the streets with our friends, we didn't know a thing about fear, didn't have to think about it.

That is, until Suitcase Charlie showed up one day.

It happened in the fall of 1955, October, a Sunday afternoon.

Three young Chicago boys — 13-year old John Schuessler, his 11-year old brother Anton, and their 14-year old friend Bobby Peterson — went to downtown Chicago, the area called the Loop, to see a matinee showing of a Disney nature documentary called *The African Lion*. Today, parents of boys that age probably would take them to the Loop, but back then it was a different story. Their parents knew where they were going, and the Schuessler boys' mother had even picked out the film they would see and given the brothers the money to pay for their tickets. At the time, it wasn't at all unusual for kids to be doing this kind of roaming around on their own; we were "free-range kids" long before the term was even invented (or needed). Every one of my friends was a latch-key kid. Our parents figured that we could pretty much stay out of trouble no matter where we went; we'd take buses to museums, beaches, movies, swimming pools, amusement parks, all without any kind of parental guidance. There were times we'd even just walk a mile to a movie to save the 10 cents the bus ride would cost. We'd seldom do this alone, however. Kids had brothers and sisters and pals, so we'd do what the Schuessler brothers and their friend Bobby Peterson did.

We'd get on a bus, go downtown, see a movie, and hang out in the area afterward. There was plenty to do, and most of it didn't cost a penny: there were free museums, enormous department stories filled with toy departments where you could play for hours with all the toys your parents could never afford to buy you, libraries filled with books and civil war artifacts (real ones!), a Greyhound bus depot packed with arcade-style games, a dazzling lake front full of yachts and sailboats, comic book stores, dime stores where barkers would try to sell you incredible non-stick pans and sponges that would clean anything, and skyscrapers like the Prudential Building where you could ride non-stop, lickety-split elevators from the lobby to the 41st floor for free. And if you got tired of all that, you could always just stop and look at the wild people in the streets! It was easy for a bunch of unsupervised kids to spend an afternoon down in the Loop just goofing off and checking stuff out.

Just like the Schuessler Brothers and their friend Bobby Peterson did.

But the brothers and Bobby never made it home from the Loop that Sunday in October of 1955.

Two days later, their dead bodies were found in a shallow ditch just east of the Des Plaines River. The boys were bound up and naked. Their eyes were closed shut with adhesive tape. Bobby Peterson had been beaten, and the bodies of all three had been thrown out of a vehicle. The coroner pronounced the cause of death to be "asphyxiation by suffocation".

The city was thrown into a panic.

For the first time, we kids felt the kind of fear outside the house we had witnessed inside the house. It shook us up. Where before we'd hung out on the street corners and played games 'til late in the evening, now we fled inside when the first street lights came on. We also started spending more time indoors, at home or at the homes of our friends, even when it was sunny out; and we stopped doing as many things on our own out on the streets: fewer trips to the supermarket or the corner store or the two local movie theaters, the Crystal and the Vision. The street wasn't the safe place it once had been. Everything had changed.

Suddenly we were conscious of threat, of danger, of the type of terrible thing that could happen at any moment to shake us and our world up.

We started watching for the killer of the Schuessler Brothers and Bobby Peterson. We didn't know his name or what he looked like — nobody did — but we gave him a name and we had a sense of what he might look like. We called him Charlie, and for some reason we were sure he hauled around a suitcase, one that he carried dead children in. Just about every evening, as it started getting dark, some kid would look down the street toward the shadows at the end of the block, toward where the park was, and see something in those shadows. The kid would point at the darkness then and ask in a whisper: "Suitcase Charlie?"

We'd follow his gaze, and a few seconds later we'd be heading for home.

As fast as we could.

About the Author

Born in a refugee camp in Germany after World War II, John Guzlowski came to America with his family as a Displaced Person in 1951. His parents had been Polish slave laborers in Nazi Germany during the war. Growing up in "Murdertown" — the tough immigrant neighborhoods around Humboldt Park in Chicago — he met hardware-store clerks with Auschwitz tattoos on their wrists, Polish cavalry officers who still mourned their dead horses, and women who had walked from Siberia to Iran to escape the Russians. In much of his work, Guzlowski remembers and honors the experiences and ultimate strength of these voiceless survivors.

An acclaimed poet, Guzlowski is also a respected teacher, literary critic, and author of both fiction and nonfiction. His recent poetry collection *Echoes of Tattered Tongues* won the 2017 Montaigne Medal of the Eric Hoffer Awards as one of the most thought-provoking books of the year.

Guzlowski received his BA in English Literature from the University of Illinois, Chicago, and his MA and PhD in English from Purdue University. He is a Professor Emeritus of English Literature at Eastern Illinois University, and currently lives in Lynchburg, Virginia.

Acknowledgments

It has been said — even by writers who have faced down many a blank page — that writing is heaven.

Editing? Editing is hell.

But I've been lucky to have help with this season in hell.

Three great people have been with me during the editing of *Suitcase Charlie*. First, there was my wife, Linda Calendrillo, who read every draft of the novel and not only pointed out my incredibly frequent spelling errors; she also made plotting and character suggestions that made each draft better than the last.

Then there were Don Radlauer and Yael Shahar of Kasva Press. Like the best possible surgeons, they went over every comma, semi-colon, and period; and more importantly, they checked every fact in the novel, from what phase the moon was in on June 6, 1956 to whether Marvin's slang was all correct for the time. They even listened to all the songs, and Don became an expert on the geography of Chicago, a city he has never visited.

To all three, I owe my biggest ~~boqette~~ bouquet [DonR] of flowers.